B.M. 83·5
82
Bk
P.H.
LAMB'S CONDUIT PASSAGE
House
PRINCETON ST.
P.O.
School
FORD ROW
JOCKEY'S
Bdy.
RED LION STREET
RED LION COURT
GRAY'S INN PASSAGE
P.H.
L.B.
SANDLAND STREET
FEATHERSTONE BUILDINGS
HAND COURT
High Holborn House
P.H.
C.R.
81
77
L.B.
H I G H H O L B O R N
P.H.
80
79·2
P A R K
Pearl Assurance Buildings
W H E T S T O N E
NEWMAN'S ROW
F.W.
L.B.
INN FIELDS
Union

RANDOM
HOUSE
LARGE
PRINT

V2

ALSO BY ROBERT HARRIS
AVAILABLE FROM
RANDOM HOUSE LARGE PRINT

The Second Sleep
Munich

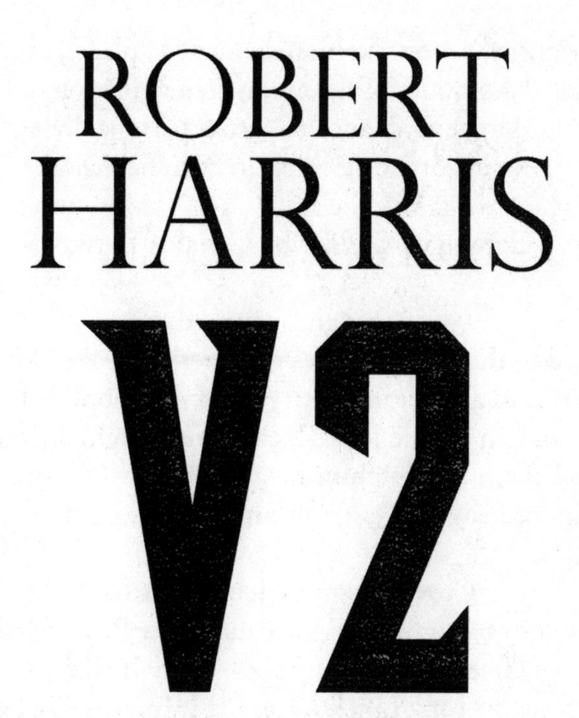

A novel of World War II

Published in the United States of America by Random House Large Print in association with Alfred A. Knopf, a division of Penguin Random House LLC, New York. Originally published in Great Britain by Hutchinson, an imprint of Cornerstone, a division of Penguin Random House Ltd., London, in 2020.

Cover design by Jenny Carrow
Cover images: (background) **Air Raid Near Piccadilly, London** by George Greenwell / Mirrorpix / Getty Images; V2 missile launching by Tony Linck / The LIFE Images Collection / Getty Images

Endpaper map: London Metropolitan Archives

The Library of Congress has established a Cataloging-in-Publication record for this title.

ISBN: 978-0-593-34235-0

www.penguinrandomhouse.com/large-print-format-books

FIRST LARGE PRINT EDITION

Printed in the United States of America

10 9 8 7 6 5 4 3 2 1

This Large Print edition published in accord with the standards of the N.A.V.H.

For Sonny Mehta
1942–2019

AUTHOR'S NOTE

This story takes place over five days at the end of November 1944. The framework is factual. The V2 strikes on London all occurred with the results and in the sequence described. The Germans fired the missiles from the woods around Scheveningen on the Dutch coast. A British counter-operation, including at its heart a team of WAAFs, was mounted in response. I have also tried to make the history of the rocket programme and the work of the photographic reconnaissance interpreters at RAF Medmenham as accurate as they reasonably can be in a work of fiction.

But this **is** a novel. Apart from such well-known historical figures as Wernher von Braun and SS-General Hans Kammler, my cast of characters and their particular adventures are all purely imaginary. For those readers who would like to know more about the history of the V2, I have added a list of sources in the acknowledgements at the end.

Robert Harris
July 2020

1

ON A SATURDAY MORNING IN late November 1944, in a railway shed in the Dutch seaside resort of Scheveningen, three ballistic missiles, each nearly fifteen metres long, lay in their steel cradles like cosseted patients in a private clinic, their inspection covers open, hooked up to monitors and tended by technicians in the shapeless grey denim overalls of the German army.

That winter – the war's sixth – was notoriously hard. The cold seemed to emanate from the concrete floor – to rise through the soles of even the heaviest boots and penetrate the flesh to the bone. One of the men stepped back from his workbench and stamped his feet to try to keep his blood flowing. He was the only one not in uniform. His pre-war dark blue suit with its row of pens in the breast pocket, along with his worn plaid tie, proclaimed him a civilian – a maths teacher, you might have said if you had been asked to guess his profession, or a young university lecturer in one of the sciences. Only if you noticed the oil beneath his bitten fingernails might you have thought: ah yes – an engineer.

He could hear the North Sea barely a hundred metres away, the continuous rolling crash of the waves somersaulting onto the beach, the cries of the gulls as they were flung around by the wind. His mind was filled with memories – too many memories, in truth; he was tempted to put on his ear defenders to shut them out. But that would have made him look even more conspicuous, and besides, he would only have had to take them off every five minutes, for he was constantly being asked questions about something or other – the propulsion unit or the pressurisation in the alcohol tank or the electrical wiring that switched the rocket from ground to internal power.

He went back to work.

It was just before half past ten that one of the big steel doors at the far end of the shed rattled back on its rollers and the soldiers nearest to it stiffened to attention. Colonel Walter Huber, commander of the artillery regiment, stepped inside amid a blast of cold rain. There was another man at his shoulder wearing a black leather greatcoat with the silver insignia of the SS on the lapel.

'Graf!' shouted the colonel.

Turn away, was Graf's immediate instinct. **Pick up your soldering iron, bend over your workbench, look busy.**

But there was no escaping Huber. His voice rang out as if he were on a parade ground. 'So this is where you're hiding! I have someone here who wishes to meet you.' His high leather boots creaked as he marched across the repair shop. 'This is Sturmscharführer Biwack of the National Socialist Leadership Office. Biwack,' he said, ushering the stranger forward, 'this is Dr Rudi Graf from the Army Research Centre at Peenemünde. He's our technical liaison officer.'

Biwack gave a Hitler salute to which Graf made a wary return. He had heard about these 'NSFOs' but had never actually met one – Nazi Party commissars, recently embedded in the military on the Führer's orders to kindle a fighting spirit. Real die-in-a-ditch fanatics. The worse things got, the more there were.

The SS man looked Graf up and down. He was about forty, not unfriendly. He even smiled. 'So you are one of the geniuses who are going to win us the war?'

'I doubt it.'

Huber said quickly, 'Graf knows all there is to know about the rocket. He can fill you in.' He turned to Graf. 'Sturmscharführer Biwack will be joining my staff. He has full security clearance. You can tell him everything.' He checked his watch. Graf could tell he was in a hurry to get away. He was an old-school Prussian, an artillery officer in the Great War – exactly the type who had come under suspicion after the army's attempt to assassinate Hitler.

The last thing he would want was a Nazi spy listening at his keyhole. 'One of Seidel's platoons is scheduled to launch in thirty minutes. Why don't you take him over to observe?' A quick nod of encouragement – 'Very good!' – and he was gone.

Biwack shrugged and made a face at Graf. **These old-timers, eh? What can you do?** He nodded at the workbench. 'So what's that you're working on?'

'A transformer, from the control unit. They don't much care for this cold weather.'

'Who does?' Biwack put his hands on his hips and surveyed the shed. His gaze came to rest on one of the rockets. **Vergeltungswaffe Zwei** was their official designation. Vengeance Weapon Two. The V2. 'My God, she's a beauty. I've heard all about them, of course, but I've never actually seen one. I'd very much like to watch this launch. Do you mind?'

'Of course not.' Graf retrieved his hat, scarf and raincoat from the row of pegs by the door.

Rain was gusting off the sea, funnelled down the side streets between the abandoned hotels. The pier had burned down the previous year. Its blackened iron spars protruded above the running white-capped waves like the masts of a shipwreck. The beach was sown with barbed wire and tank traps. Outside the railway station a few tattered tourist posters from before the war showed a pair of elegant women in striped bathing costumes and cloche hats tossing a ball to one another. The local population had been expelled. Nobody was about apart from soldiers, no vehicles could be seen except for army lorries and a couple of the tractors they used to move the rockets.

As they walked, Graf explained the set-up. The V2s arrived by rail from their factory in Germany, shipped under cover of darkness to avoid enemy aircraft. Twenty missiles per shipment, two or three shipments per week, all destined for the campaign against London. The same number were being fired at Antwerp, but they were launched from Germany. The SS had their own operation going in Hellendoorn. The batteries in The Hague were under orders to fire the rockets within five days of arrival.

'Why the rush?'

'Because the longer they are exposed to the wet and the cold, the more faults they develop.'

'There are a lot of faults?' Biwack was writing down Graf's answers in a notebook.

'Yes, many. Too many!'

'Why is that?'

'The technology is revolutionary, which means we're having to refine it all the time. We've already made more than sixty thousand modifications to the prototype.' He wanted to add that the real wonder wasn't that so many missiles misfired; it was that so many took off at all. But he decided against it. He didn't like the look of that notebook. 'Why are you writing so much down, may I ask? Are you making a report?'

'Not at all. I just want to be sure I understand. You have worked for a long time on rockets?'

'Sixteen years.'

'Sixteen years! Looking at you, it doesn't seem possible. How old are you now?'

'Thirty-two.'

'The same age as Professor von Braun. You were at the military proving ground at Kummersdorf together, I believe?'

Graf gave him a sideways glance. So he had been checking on von Braun as well as him. He felt a twinge of unease. 'That's right.'

Biwack laughed. 'You're all so young, you rocket fellows!'

They had left the built-up streets of the town and entered the forested suburbs. Scheveningen was ringed by woods and lakes. It must have been pretty before the war, Graf thought. Behind them a driver hammered on his horn, forcing them to scramble to the side of the road. Moments later, a transporter roared past carrying a V2 in its hydraulic cradle – the fins first, closest to the cab, then the long body and finally, protruding over the end of the trailer, the nose cone with its one-ton warhead. Camouflaged tankers followed close behind. Graf cupped his hands and shouted in Biwack's ear as each one passed: 'That's the methyl alcohol . . . the liquid oxygen . . . the hydrogen peroxide . . . It all comes in on the same trains as the missiles. We fuel at the launch site.'

After the last of the support vehicles had disappeared around the corner, the two men resumed their walk. Biwack said, 'You're not worried about enemy bombers?'

'Of course, night and day. Luckily they haven't found us yet.' Graf scanned the sky. According to the Wehrmacht's meteorologists, there was a weather front passing over northern Europe that weekend. The clouds were grey, heavy, oozing rain. The RAF would not be flying in this.

Further inside the treeline, they were halted by a checkpoint. A barrier lay across the road, a sentry post beside it. Graf glanced into the woods. A dog handler with a big Alsatian on a leash was moving through the dripping vegetation. The dog cocked its leg and stared at him. One of the SS guards shouldered his machine gun and held out his hand.

No matter how many times Graf attended a launch, it seemed to amuse the sentries to act as if they had never seen him before. He reached into his inside pocket for his wallet, opened it and pulled out his identity card. A small photograph slipped out with it and fluttered across the road. Before he could move, Biwack had stooped to retrieve it. He glanced at it and smiled. 'Is this your wife?'

'No.' Graf didn't like seeing it in the SS man's hands. 'She was my girlfriend.'

'Was?' Biwack put on the professionally sympathetic face of an undertaker. 'I'm sorry.' He handed it back. Carefully Graf returned it to his wallet. He could tell Biwack was expecting a fuller explanation, but he did not want to provide one. The barrier lifted.

The road with its ornamental street lamps stretched ahead, crowded on either side by trees, once a place for a stroll or a bicycle ride, now shrouded overhead by camouflage netting. At first it looked empty. But as they penetrated deeper, it became apparent that along the tracks running off to right and left, the woods concealed the main business of the regiment – tents for storage, tents for testing, scores of vehicles, a dozen missiles wrapped in tarpaulins and hidden beneath the trees. Shouts and the throb of generators and of engines revving carried on the damp air. Biwack had stopped asking questions and was striding ahead in his eagerness. The land to their left fell away. Through the branches a lake glinted, dull as pewter, with an island and an ornamental boathouse. As they rounded the sweep of a bend, Graf raised his hand to signal they should stop.

Two hundred metres further on, in the centre of the lane, hard to distinguish at first because of its ragged green-and-brown camouflage, a V2 stood erect on its launch table, solitary apart from a steel mast to which it was attached by an electrical cable. Nothing moved around it. A thin stream of vapour vented silently from above the liquid oxygen tank, condensing in the misty air like breath. It was as if they had come upon some huge and magnificent animal in the wild.

Biwack instinctively dropped his voice and said quietly, 'Can't we go closer?'

'This is as far as it's safe.' Graf pointed. 'Do you

see the support vehicles have withdrawn? That means the firing crew are already in their trenches.' From his raincoat pocket he pulled out his ear defenders. 'You should wear these.'

'What about you?'

'I'll be all right.'

Biwack waved them away. 'Then so shall I.'

A klaxon sounded. A startled game bird – it must be a real survivor, Graf thought, as the soldiers liked to shoot them to supplement their rations – struggled out of the undergrowth and took clumsy flight. Its hoarse panicked cry as it flapped noisily down the road echoed the note of the klaxon.

Graf said, 'She weighs four tons empty, twelve and a half fuelled. On ignition, the fuel is gravity-fed. That yields eight tons of thrust – still lighter than the rocket.'

A voice carried over a loudspeaker: 'Ten . . . nine . . . eight . . .'

Sparks, vivid as fireflies in the gloom, had begun cascading from the rocket's base. Suddenly they coalesced into a jet of bright orange flame. Leaves, branches, debris, dirt whipped into the air and flew across the clearing. Graf turned and shouted at Biwack, 'Now the turbo pump kicks in, thrust goes to twenty-five—'

'. . . three . . . two . . . one!'

His last few words were lost in a sharp-edged cracking roar. He clamped his hands to his ears. The umbilical cable fell away. A mixture of alcohol and liquid oxygen, forced by the turbo pump into the combustion chamber and burned at a rate of a ton every seven seconds, produced – so they claimed at Peenemünde – the loudest sound ever made by man on earth. His whole body seemed to tremble with the vibrations. Hot air buffeted his face. The surrounding trees were brilliant in the glare.

Like a sprinter poised on her starting block a split second after the pistol was fired, the V2 at first appeared stalled, then abruptly she shot straight upwards, riding a fifteen-metre jet of fire. A thunderous boom rolled from the sky across the wood. Graf craned his neck to follow her, counting in his head, praying she would not explode. One second . . . two seconds . . . three seconds . . . At exactly four seconds into the flight, a time switch was activated in one of the control compartments and the V2, already two thousand metres high, began to tilt towards an angle of forty-seven degrees. He always regretted the necessity for that manoeuvre. In his dreams, she rose vertically towards the stars. He had a last glimpse of her red exhaust before she vanished into the low cloud towards London.

He let his hands drop. The wood was quiet again. The only residue of the V2 was a distant drone, and very soon even that stopped. Then there was only birdsong and the patter of rain on the trees. The firing platoon had started to emerge from their trenches and were walking towards the firing table.

Two men wearing asbestos suits moved stiffly like deep-sea divers.

Slowly Biwack took his hands from his ears. His face was flushed, his eyes unnaturally bright. For the first time that morning, the National Socialist Leadership Officer seemed incapable of speech.

2

SIXTY-FIVE SECONDS AFTER TAKE-OFF, AT an altitude of twenty-three miles and a velocity of 2,500 miles per hour, an on-board accelerometer simultaneously cut off the fuel supply to the V2's engine and activated a switch that armed the warhead fuse. The unpowered rocket was now ballistic, following the same parabolic curve as a stone flung from a catapult. Its speed was still increasing. Its course was set on a compass bearing of 260 degrees west-south-west. Its aiming point was Charing Cross station, the notional dead centre of London; hitting anything within a five-mile radius of that would be considered on target.

At roughly the same moment, a twenty-four-year-old woman named Kay Caton-Walsh – her first name was Angelica, but everyone called her Kay, after Caton – emerged from the bathroom of a flat in Warwick Court, a quiet narrow street just off Chancery Lane in Holborn, about a mile from Charing Cross. She was wrapped in the short pink towel she had brought with her from the country and was carrying a sponge bag containing soap, toothbrush, toothpaste and her favourite perfume, Guerlain's L'Heure Bleue, which she had dabbed generously just beneath her ears and on the insides of her wrists.

She savoured the feel of the carpet beneath her bare feet – she couldn't remember the last time she had known that small luxury – and walked down the passage into the bedroom. A moustachioed man smoking a cigarette watched her from the bed through half-closed eyes. She put the sponge bag in her valise and let the towel drop.

'My God, what a vision!' The man smiled, eased himself further up on his pillow and threw back the eiderdown and blankets beside him. 'Come over here.'

For a moment she was tempted, until she remembered how rough his black stubble was before he shaved, and how he always tasted of tobacco and stale alcohol first thing in the morning. Besides, she preferred to anticipate her pleasure – sex, in her experience, being at least as much a matter of the mind as the body. They still had the afternoon to look forward to, and the evening, and the night, and perhaps – as it might be the last time for a while – the following morning. She returned his smile and shook her head – 'I need to find us some milk' – and as he flopped backwards in frustration, she retrieved her underwear from the carpet: peach-coloured, brand new, bought specially in anticipation of what the English, in their peculiar way, called 'a dirty week-end'. Why do we use that phrase? she wondered. What an odd lot we are. She glanced out of the window. Warwick Court, midway between Lincoln's Inn and Gray's Inn, was mostly full of lawyers' chambers – an odd place to live, it seemed to her. It was quiet on a Saturday morning. The rain had stopped. A weak winter sun was shining. She could hear the traffic in Chancery Lane. She remembered a grocery shop on the corner opposite. She would go there. She started to dress.

A hundred miles to the east, the V2 had reached its maximum altitude of fifty-eight miles – the edge of the earth's atmosphere – and was hurtling at a velocity of 3,500 miles per hour beneath a hemisphere of stars when gravity at last began to reclaim it. Its nose slowly tilted and it started to fall towards the North Sea. Despite the buffeting of cross-winds and air turbulence during re-entry, a pair of gyroscopes mounted on a platform immediately below the warhead detected any deviations in its course or trajectory and corrected them by sending electrical messages to the four rudders in its tail fins. Just as Kay was fastening the second of her stockings, it crossed the English coast three miles north of Southend-on-Sea, and as she pulled her dress over her head, it flashed above Basildon and Dagenham. At 11.12 a.m., four minutes and fifty-one seconds after launching, travelling at nearly three times the speed of sound, too fast to be seen by anyone on the ground, the rocket plunged onto Warwick Court.

An object moving at supersonic speed compresses the atmosphere. In the infinitesimal fraction of a second before the tip of the nose cone touched the roof of the Victorian mansion block, and before the four-ton projectile crashed through all five floors, Kay registered – beyond thought, and far beyond any capacity to articulate it – some change in the air pressure, some presentiment of threat. Then the two metal contacts of the missile's fuse, protected by a silica cap, were smashed together by the force of the impact, completing an electrical circuit that detonated a ton of amatol high explosive. The bedroom seemed to evaporate into darkness. She heard the noise of the explosion and the rending of steel and masonry as the fuselage and fragments of the nose cone descended floor by floor, a crash as parts of the plaster ceiling landed around her, and then an instant later the sonic boom of the sound barrier being broken followed by the rushing noise of the incoming rocket.

The shock wave lifted her off her feet and flung her against the bedroom wall. She lay on her side, more or less conscious, winded, but weirdly calm. She understood exactly what had hit them. So this is what it's like, she thought. The blast wave underground would be the problem now, if it had shaken the foundations sufficiently to bring the building down. The room was dark with dust. After a while, she became aware of a breeze and something flapping in the gloom beside her. She put out her hand and touched the carpet. She felt glass beneath her fingers and quickly withdrew them. The window had been blown in. The curtains were stirring. Somewhere outside, a woman was screaming. Every few seconds came the crash of falling masonry. She could smell the deadly sweet odour of gas.

'Mike?' There was no response. She tried again, louder. **'Mike?'**

She struggled to sit up. The room was in a kind of twilight. Particles of pulverised brick and plaster swirled in the pale grey shaft of light from the gaping window. Unfamiliar shapes – dressing table, chairs, pictures – were shadowed and askew. A jagged crack ran from floor to ceiling above the wooden bedhead. She took a deep breath to gather her strength, and sucked in dust. Coughing, she grabbed one of the curtains, hauled herself to her feet and stumbled through the debris towards the bed. A steel beam had come down and lay over the bottom part of the mattress. Large chunks of plaster, lath and horsehair were scattered across the eiderdown. She had to use both hands to throw them aside to uncover the shape of his upper body. His head was turned away from her. The eiderdown was drenched in something bright red that she thought at first was blood but when she touched it turned out to be brick dust.

'Mike?' She felt his neck for a pulse, and at once, as if he had been playing dumb, he turned to look at her, his face unnaturally white, his dark eyes wide. She kissed him, stroked his cheek. 'Are you hurt? Can you move?'

'I don't think so. Are you all right?'

'I'm fine. Can you try, darling? There's a gas leak. We ought to get out.'

She put her hands under his arm, gripped his hard muscled flesh and pulled. He twisted his shoulders back and forth in an effort to escape. His face contorted in pain. 'There's something on my legs.'

She went to the beam at the end of the bed and wrapped her arms around it. Each time she shifted it slightly, he groaned through clenched teeth. 'Leave it, for Christ's sake!'

'Sorry.' She felt helpless.

'Get out, Kay. Please. Just tell them there's gas.'

She could hear the edge of panic in his voice. He had told her once that his worst moment as a pilot wasn't combat; it was seeing a man burned alive in a plane crash after a botched landing – his legs had been trapped and they couldn't get close enough to pull him out: 'I wish to God I could have shot him.'

The clanging bell of a fire engine sounded nearby.

'I'll fetch help. But I'm not leaving, I promise.'

She pulled on her shoes and picked her way out of the bedroom and into the passage. The thick carpet was buried under plaster. The gas smell was worse here – the leak must be in the kitchen – and the floor seemed to be tilting. Daylight filtered through a crack that was as wide as her hand and ran all the way up to the ceiling. She unlocked the front door, turned the handle, pulled. At first it wouldn't open. She had to drag it free from its twisted frame, and then let out a cry as she found herself swaying on the edge of a twenty-foot drop. The second-floor landing and the exterior wall of the mansion block had gone. There was nothing between her and the shell of the tall building across the street, its windows gaping, its roof collapsed. In the road immediately beneath her feet, a landslide of rubble tumbled into the road – bricks, pipes, fragments of furniture, a child's doll. Smoke was rising from a dozen small fires.

A fire tender had pulled up, the crew unloading its ladders, unrolling hoses in the middle of what looked like the aftermath of a battle – bloodied, dust-covered victims lying full-length; others sitting dazed, heads bowed; civil defence workers in helmets moving among them; two bodies already set apart and shrouded; spectators gawping. Kay gripped the door frame, leaned out as far as she dared and shouted for help.

According to the records of the London County Council, six people were killed by what became known as 'the Warwick Court rocket' and another

292 were injured, most of them caught in Chancery Lane by flying debris. The dead included Vicki Fraser, a nurse aged thirty; Irene Berti, a nineteen-year-old secretary in a barrister's office; and Frank Burroughs, sixty-five, a heating engineer. The few photographs passed for publication by the censors show firemen's ladders stretching up into a wrecked building, the top floors of which have entirely collapsed, and a strange, short, gaunt man in his fifties, wearing a black overcoat and homburg, squeezing between the heaps of wreckage. He was a doctor who had happened to be passing and who volunteered to climb up into the unstable ruin, and he was the man who, after five minutes of her frantic appeals, came up the ladder and followed Kay and the rescue workers into the flat.

As they entered the bedroom, the doctor politely removed his hat as if he were making a routine house call, and asked quietly, in a Scottish accent, 'What's his name?'

'Mike,' she said. 'Mike Templeton.' And then she added, because she wanted them to treat him with respect, 'Air Commodore Templeton.'

The doctor went over to the bed. 'Right, sir, can you feel your legs?'

One of the firemen said, 'You should get out now, missus. We'll take it from here.'

'What about the gas?'

'We've shut off the main.'

'I'd rather stay.'

'No chance, sorry. You've done your bit.'

Another fireman took her by the arm. 'Come on, love. Don't argue. This place could collapse.'

Mike called out, 'It's fine, Kay. Do as they say.'

The doctor turned round. 'I'll see he's all right, Mrs Templeton.'

Mrs Templeton! She had forgotten that she wasn't supposed to be here.

'Of course. I'm sorry. I understand.'

She was halfway to the door when Mike called to her again. 'You'd better take your case.'

She had forgotten all about it. It was still on the ottoman at the foot of the bed, covered in dust and plaster, mute evidence of their infidelity. He must have been lying there worrying about it. She brushed off the debris, fastened the catches and followed the fireman out to the front door. He stepped onto the first rung of the ladder, took the valise and threw it down to someone below; then he descended another couple of rungs, held out his hands and beckoned her to follow. She had to shut her eyes as the ladder bent and swayed beneath their combined weight. His hands were hard around her waist. 'Come on, love, you can do it.' Slowly, pausing on each step, they descended. Just as they reached the bottom rung, she fainted.

She came round to find a nurse kneeling in front of her, holding her chin and dabbing iodine on her temple. She moaned and tried to pull away. The grip tightened slightly. 'It's all right, sweetheart. Keep still. Nearly done.' Something sharp was digging into her back, and when the nurse was finished and she was able to turn her head, she found she was propped up against the rear wheel of the fire engine. Two more ladders had been run up against the bombed-out building, and three men in steel helmets were standing in a row at the top, steadying a stretcher that was being lowered down to them by half a dozen firemen. The nurse followed her gaze. 'Is that one yours?'

'I think so.'

'Come on then.'

She held out her hand and pulled Kay to her feet. She put her arm round her shoulder as they stood at the foot of the ladder.

The stretcher came down slowly, the men shouting to one another to keep it steady. She recognised him by the curliness of his black hair. They had wrapped him in a blanket. As he reached the ground, he turned and saw her. His face was drawn with pain, but somehow he managed to pull his hand out from under the blanket and give her a weak thumbs-up. She took his hand in both of hers.

He said, 'Was it a V2?'

She nodded.

He smiled faintly. 'That's bloody funny.'

Kay turned to the nurse. 'Where are they taking him?'

'Barts. You can go with him if you want.'

'I'd like that.'

He pulled his hand away. His expression was suddenly remote, as if she were a stranger. He stared up at the sky. 'Better not,' he said.

3

THEY STOOD UNDER A DRIPPING fir tree, Graf smoking a cigarette, Biwack with his notebook open. Graf had wanted to return to Scheveningen straight after the launch, but Biwack had insisted on seeing how the regiment worked. They watched as half a dozen members of the firing crew cleared the launch site, rolling up the electrical cables and collapsing the mast. The firing platform itself was a round, squat, stout metal frame not much bigger than a coffee table, the same circumference as the V2, mounted on hydraulic legs, with a pyramid-shaped blast deflector in the centre.

'How heavy is that?'

'About a ton and a half.'

The crew dragged over a two-wheel trailer and manoeuvred it underneath the platform. They worked quickly, without talking much, to minimise the time they risked being exposed to enemy aircraft. Somewhere in the wood a tank engine cracked into life, coughing up pulses of dirty brown exhaust smoke, and slowly a half-track armoured car struggled up out of the ground.

'What's that?'

'The firing control vehicle. It's dug in during the launch.'

The half-track lumbered through the undergrowth towards them, and stopped with its engine idling while the firing platform was hitched to its tow plate. Then the men climbed up onto the mudguards and clung to the armoured shell. The engine revved and they moved off. Within a minute they had gone. Apart from the faint lingering smell of burned fuel and the odd scorch mark on the surrounding trees, there was nothing to show that a missile had ever been launched.

Biwack seemed as impressed by this as he had been by the rocket itself. 'That's all there is to it? My God, you really can fire this thing from anywhere!'

'Yes, as long as the ground is flat and firm enough. The corner of a parking lot or a school playground would do.' A year ago, Graf had never imagined they might be able to fire the rocket so easily. But then he hadn't thought they might be able to mass-manufacture the V2s in their thousands either. The appalling ingenuity of it all was a constant surprise.

'It must be wonderful for you,' said Biwack, 'to see something you have worked on since you were sixteen finally turned into a weapon to protect the Fatherland.'

It seemed such an oddly loaded remark that Graf darted a look at him, but Biwack's face was expressionless. 'Naturally.' He finished his cigarette, dropped it onto the forest floor and crushed it out with his shoe. 'Now we should get back.'

They had barely gone fifty metres along the road when they heard the rumble of the half-track returning, its engine whining as if in panic. It reversed around the curve at speed, without its clinging passengers, and braked hard. The side door was flung open and the sergeant in charge of the firing platoon – Schenk, a veteran from the Eastern Front, who had lost both ears to frostbite – stuck his head out. 'Dr Graf, there's an emergency at site seventy-three. Lieutenant Seidel wants you right away.'

He extended his hand to help Graf clamber aboard, but hesitated when he saw Biwack. Graf said, 'It's fine, he's with me.' Schenk hauled the SS man up and slammed the door after them.

Biwack said, 'Aren't you forgetting something, Sergeant?'

Schenk looked him up and down, puzzled and then amused. He slowly raised his arm. 'Heil Hitler.'

The half-track suddenly reversed off the road, then lurched forwards, knocking them off balance. Graf grabbed one of the two fixed swivel seats. Schenk caught the other. With a mocking display of courtesy, like a maître d' in a smart restaurant, he offered it to Biwack. They bounced over the undergrowth and rejoined the road.

The seats were arranged for the firing control officer and his second in command to observe the launch. Above the panel of instruments, through the narrow slits at the back of the half-track, the road receded behind them. Biwack was examining the dials and switches. He seemed to want another tutorial, but Graf's mind was too full of misgivings to answer any more questions. **There's an emergency.** How many times in the last month had he heard those words?

Jolting around in the stuffy compartment, he started to feel sick. He clung to the sides of the seat. After a couple of minutes, they slowed to pass a column of tankers parked at the side of the road. The soldiers stood sheltering under the trees with their hands in their pockets, forbidden to smoke so close to the fuel. The armoured car stopped and the sergeant opened the door. With relief, Graf jumped out into the cool wet air.

Lieutenant Seidel was waiting for him. There were three batteries in the regiment, each with three launching platoons of thirty-two men. Seidel commanded the second battery. He was about Graf's age, a fellow Berliner. Sometimes in the evenings, in the mess, if they weren't too exhausted, they played chess. They never talked politics. Seidel looked grim. 'We've got a fire in the control compartment.'

'A fire? You've shut off the power?'

'Completely. Come and look.'

They walked around to the front of the armoured car. Two hundred metres down the road, the rocket stood alone and unsupported, ready to launch. Seidel handed him a pair of binoculars. Graf trained them on the V2. Smoke was issuing silently from just beneath the warhead and was being whipped away by the wind.

'Is she fuelled?'

'Fully. That's why we've evacuated the site. Apparently they only noticed it a minute before launch.'

Graf lowered the field glasses. He stroked his chin and tugged at his nose with his thumb and forefinger. There was no alternative. 'I suppose I'd better take a look.'

'Are you sure?'

'I'm the one who built the damned thing.' He tried to make a joke of it. 'Frankly, it's not the thought of an explosion that scares me – it's climbing that damned Magirus ladder.' It was not far off the truth. He detested heights.

Seidel clapped him on the arm. 'Right, I need two volunteers.' He winked at Graf and glanced around. He pointed to a pair of soldiers standing nearby. 'You and you. Take the ladder over to the missile.'

They came to attention, faces suddenly grey. 'Yes, Lieutenant!'

Graf called after them, 'I'll need a pair of gloves, and tools for the compartment.' For the first time, he was aware of Biwack, listening to their conversation.

He turned back to Seidel. 'By the way, this is Sturmscharführer Biwack. He's joining the regiment as our new National Socialist Leadership Officer.'

Seidel laughed again, as if this were a continuation of their joke, but then Biwack clicked his heels and saluted – 'Heil Hitler!' – and his smile shrank. He returned the salute. 'And what exactly will your role be in the regiment, Sturmscharführer?'

'To raise morale. To remind the men what we're fighting for.'

Seidel's mouth turned down. He nodded. 'Useful.'

Graf had gone back to studying the rocket through the binoculars. Was it his imagination, or had the smoke got thicker? It wasn't the proximity of the heat to the warhead that worried him – until the fuses were armed, the amatol was no more dangerous than a one-ton lump of yellow clay. But the closeness of the fuel was a different matter. He had witnessed fuel tanks explode before. He had once seen three men blown to pieces directly in front of him. And that was by a small experimental tank, whereas the V2 contained eight and a half tons of alcohol and liquid oxygen. He tried to put the images out of his mind. 'We're wasting time,' he said. 'Tell them to hurry up with that ladder.'

He set off towards the rocket. There were footsteps behind him, and he turned to find Biwack catching him up. 'No, no,' he said, 'there's nothing you can do. You need to keep well back.'

'I'd prefer to come with you.' Biwack fell in beside

him. 'The lieutenant seems to believe I'm just some pen-pusher from the Brown House, whereas actually I fought in the East for two years. I am making a point to the men – you understand?'

'As you wish.' Graf lengthened his stride.

The V2 was a monster more than seven times his height, although at this moment it seemed even taller. As he walked, he took off his hat and squinted up at it. The transformer would be the problem, he was sure. At Peenemünde they had discovered that the rocket had a tendency to airburst at the end of its flight due to the heat of re-entry, so they had added a metal sleeve to protect the upper section. But somehow in the winter weather that seemed to increase condensation, which in turn shorted the electrics. You solved one problem and created another.

The ladder was on its way, towed on a trailer behind a small truck. The driver parked at the base of the rocket, jumped out and immediately began uncoupling it – the type of ladder that firemen used: three sections, extendable. The other soldier handed Graf a box of tools. Both men kept glancing anxiously at the smoke. Graf selected a couple of small wrenches, a screwdriver and a flashlight and stuffed them into his coat pockets.

The men ran the ladder up to a spot just below the smouldering control compartment, then set off on foot back towards their comrades – a dignified walk at first that quickly became a jog. Graf watched them go. Sensible fellows, he thought. He took off his hat, gave it to Biwack and pulled on a pair of asbestos gloves.

He put his foot on the first rung and began to climb. The bottom section, where the ladder was thickest, was firm enough, but as he ascended from one section to another, it became spindly and more rickety, and the wind grew stronger, whipping his overcoat around his legs. He kept his gaze fixed straight ahead, making sure he had his foot firmly planted on each rung before he took the next step. He passed the sections housing the engine compartment, the liquid oxygen tank, the alcohol tank. At the point where the fuselage began to taper to the nose cone, he reached control compartment number two.

Smoke was gushing out of the sides of the inspection hatch. He had to take off his right glove to hold the screwdriver and unfasten the hatch. When he pulled it open, there was a great billow of acrid fumes. He twisted his head away to avoid inhaling it, and the movement forced him to look off to the side. The road, the support vehicles, the distant soldiers watching him all slid into view, and his legs and arms seemed to lose their strength. He clung to the ladder until his nerves had recovered enough for him to be able to take one hand away and pull the glove back on.

He thrust his hands into the innards of the rocket, turning his head back and forth, coughing, his eyes smarting. It was just as well that he knew the layout of the control compartment blindfold, for that was effectively how he had to work, feeling his way down from the fuse box to the filter circuit to the main electrical distribution unit. He pulled a wrench from his pocket and ran it around until he found the pair of bolts holding the transformer in place, and after a couple of minutes he succeeded in unfastening them. He gripped the transformer in both hands and pulled it free. As he lifted it out of the compartment, he could feel the heat of the metal on his face. He called down a warning to Biwack, and then flung it as far away as he could.

The smoke inside the compartment immediately diminished. He switched on the flashlight and shone it around. Much of the thick rubber coating on the main cables had melted. The plywood casing that surrounded the compartment was charred. Otherwise there didn't appear to be any serious damage. He closed the compartment. Very slowly, taking care not to look down, he began his descent.

By the time he reached the ground, several dozen men had converged on the V2, on foot and in trucks – not just Seidel and the launch platoon, but Colonel Huber himself in the front seat of a staff car. Biwack was bending to examine the burned-out transformer. He tried to pick it up, but it was too hot to hold, even with his leather gloves, and he dropped it at once.

Seidel said, 'How badly damaged is she?'

Graf pulled off his gloves and squatted on his haunches to recover his breath. 'Not damaged at all that I can see, apart from the transformer.'

'What do you recommend?'

'Drain the fuel tanks. Send her back to the workshop to run some electrical tests.'

'We can't just fit a new transformer?'

'We could, but why take the risk?'

Biwack interrupted. 'I thought you said there was no damage?'

Graf pushed himself back to his feet. 'Probably not, but we can't be absolutely sure until the avionics have been tested.'

'How long does it take to drain the fuel?'

'A couple of hours.'

'So you'll lose half a day and London will have the afternoon off! Suppose you launch – what's the worst that can happen?'

'The missile could misfire,' replied Graf. He was starting to find it hard to hide his irritation – an hour in Scheveningen and already the NSFO was an expert! 'Or it could stray off target, in which case we'll have wasted a hundred thousand Reichsmarks.'

Huber came over to join them. 'So, gentlemen? What have we decided?'

Seidel said, 'Dr Graf recommends cancelling the launch. The Sturmscharführer seems to disagree.'

'Pay no attention to me,' said Biwack. He waved his notebook. 'I'm merely here to observe.'

Huber looked at the rocket, then at the blackened transformer, then at Graf, and finally he eyed Biwack's notebook. Graf could almost hear the machinery creaking in his brain. 'One must take risks in war,' he said at last. 'That is the essence of National Socialism.' He nodded to Seidel. 'Replace the component. Proceed with the launch.'

Graf turned away in disgust. He would have liked to smoke to settle his nerves. Instead he could only pace around the launch site, as he had done so often at Peenemünde while the final preparations were made.

A new transformer was fetched by motorcycle from the technical store and one of the NCOs in the launching platoon quickly climbed the ladder to fit it. The compartment was sealed, the ladder was collapsed and driven away, the electrical cables were reconnected. A klaxon sounded. The men took cover in their slit trenches. Seidel, Huber and Biwack, with Graf at the rear, made their way in single file through the undergrowth to the launch vehicle, buried almost up to its roof at the bottom of the slope leading down to its dugout.

It was cramped inside the armoured car once the door was closed, and cold – the roof hatch was still open. Over the loudspeaker, the radar station in The Hague confirmed there were no enemy aircraft within fifty kilometres. 'You are clear to launch.'

'What is the procedure here?'

Graf squeezed into a corner and left it to Seidel to continue Biwack's tutorial. 'There are five positions on the firing switch. We're now at position one . . .'

The sergeant controlling the launch stuck his head out of the roof hatch to observe the rocket. 'Begin the countdown.'

Ten . . . nine . . .

Position two closed the valves on the fuel tanks and pumped compressed air into the liquid oxygen tank.

Eight . . . seven . . . six . . .

Position three forced a mixture of peroxide and permanganate into the turbo prop to begin ignition. An igniter shaped like a swastika, spinning like a Catherine wheel, began throwing out a shower of sparks.

Five . . . four . . .

Position four released both main fuel tanks into the combustion chamber. A flickering roaring flame spread around the base of the rocket.

Three . . . two . . . one . . .

'Launch!' The sergeant ducked his head inside the cabin and pulled down the hatch.

Position five turned the turbo pump to full power, forcing fuel into the combustion chamber at high pressure. The armoured car shook. The noise seemed to start in one's solar plexus and radiate outwards. Small pieces of forest debris clattered onto the roof. Graf clamped his hands to his ears and prayed.

4

KAY WAS AT THAT MOMENT on the corner of Chancery Lane and Warwick Court, her suitcase in her hand, watching as the ambulance tried to make its way through the crowded street in the direction of Barts Hospital. It was seventy-six minutes since the rocket had struck. The area was clogged with survivors and spectators. The driver had to turn on his bell to clear a path. People looked over their shoulders, moved aside onto the pavement, pulled others out of the way then stepped back into the road again.

Finally the ambulance was swallowed from her view. The sound of the clanging bell faded. Even so, she did not move. Her mind seemed to be working at half speed. She could only make sense of one thing at a time.

Better not. Had he really meant that? Should she have insisted on going with him?

Midway over the North Sea, the missile was functioning perfectly, the twin gyroscopes – one controlling pitch, the other roll – turning at 30,000 revolutions per minute, holding the V2 steady on its flight path.

She realised she was cold, shivering in her dress without a coat. She looked about her for the first time, saw that virtually every shop window on Chancery Lane had been blown in – along with most of the glass in the higher storeys, and in the windows of the cars that were strewn at odd angles and abandoned in the road. The wide street, though packed, was oddly static, like the West End at night when the shows were ending and people stood around waiting for their friends to come out, discussing what they had just seen or what they should do next. There was a lot of blood – on faces, on clothes, in little patches on the pavement. An elderly couple were sitting on the kerb holding hands, their feet in the gutter. A small boy was clinging to an empty pram, crying. Shards of glass were everywhere, and bricks and lumps of masonry. She noticed an odd piece of thin flat metal at her feet and picked it up. It was still warm. She guessed it was a piece of the rocket, part of the fuselage casing perhaps, or a tail fin. She replaced it carefully. Someone said something to her, but by the time she managed to focus her attention, they had gone.

After a while, she began to walk in the same direction as the ambulance.

Barts Hospital was in the City of London – she knew that much. If she couldn't see Mike, she might at least stand outside on the pavement. She hadn't really thought it through.

A little over four miles to the south-east, in New Cross Road in Deptford, the Woolworths department store had received a consignment of saucepans – a scarce item in wartime Britain. Word had spread and a long queue of housewives had formed. This particular branch of Woolworths occupied a large building of four storeys. Saturday was its busiest day, lunchtime its busiest hour. A lot of the women had brought their children; many were at the confectionery counter. One young mother, with a two-month-old baby in her left arm, walking up New Cross Road on her way to the fabled saucepan bonanza, recalled forty years later 'a sudden airless quiet, which seemed to stop one's breath'.

When an object breaks the sound barrier and continues to travel at a velocity in excess of Mach 1 – 767 miles per hour – it carries the noise of its sonic boom with it, the way a speedboat pushes out waves from its prow in a constant wash. At 12.25 p.m. – she only knew the exact time because she saw it in the official report afterwards – Kay heard what sounded like a particularly noisy firework exploding in the sky, followed a few seconds later by a loud but distant bang, as if a heavy door had slammed. Then came the rush of the rocket. Everyone around her stopped and looked up.

The V2 hit Woolworths dead centre and ploughed through every floor before detonating to form a crater thirty feet deep. Most of the victims died instantly, either in Woolworths itself, or in the Co-operative store next door, or in the draper's across the street, or on the number 53 bus, where the corpses remained upright in their seats, their internal organs traumatised by the blast wave. One hundred and sixty people were killed.

Banfill, Brian John, aged 3; Banfill, Florence Ethel, 42 . . .

Brown, Ivy, 31; Brown, Joyce, 18 months; Brown, Sylvia Rosina, 12 . . .

Glover, Julia Elizabeth, 28; Glover, Michael Thomas, 1 month; Glover, Sheila, 7 . . .

In front of Kay, a thin smudgy column of brown smoke began to rise above the roofs.

There was a debate both during and after the war about which was the more frightening: the V1, the pilotless drone bomb, which you could see and hear, and which would only start to fall once its fuel ran out, potentially giving you time in the silence to try to find cover; or the V2, which struck without warning. Most said the V2. It preyed on one's nerves just as much as the V1 but offered not even a chance of escape. And it was also eerily futuristic – the harbinger of a new era, produced by an enemy who was supposed to be beaten. It made you wonder what else Hitler might have up his sleeve.

Kay contemplated the smear of smoke for a few more seconds, took a couple of steps backwards, then turned and began walking rapidly in the opposite direction, threading her way between the onlookers gawping at the sky, heedless of who she knocked into and the curses they shouted after her.

The distinctive double bangs had reverberated across London. The Saturday shoppers she passed had their heads down; their faces tense, their voices muted. When the V2s had first started landing in September, the authorities had put out a story that the huge blasts were caused by exploding gas mains. Nobody believed it. ('Have you heard about the Germans' new secret weapon – the flying gas main?') It was only in the last two weeks that Churchill had announced the truth in Parliament. A thin film of anxiety had settled over the city.

Kay hurried westwards, past Holborn station, Tottenham Court Road . . . There was a relief in the simple mechanical activity of putting one foot in front of the other. She knew a lot about the V2 – size, range, fuel, payload, launch sites; she had watched it grow before her eyes over the past eighteen months as a laboratory technician might watch cancerous cells multiply under a microscope. Her mental state was three parts panic to one part cool professional evaluation: if the Germans could land a pair of rockets on London in the space of little more than an hour, it suggested they might have increased their deployment and a whole new phase of the offensive was under way.

In Oxford Circus, a car backfired. She ducked instinctively, like everyone else. When they straightened, they exchanged rueful looks and resumed their separate journeys.

In the end, she walked nearly four miles, all the way to Paddington station. The next train to Marlow was in thirty minutes. She went into the ladies' and studied her face in the wide communal mirror. No wonder people had been looking at her oddly. She had white plaster in her auburn hair and on her face like a powdered Regency tart, streaks of soot on her cheeks, a smoke smut on her nose, a trickle of dried blood from the cut on her temple. Her dress was torn at the shoulder and filthy. A dirty weekend, she thought, and laughed out loud – it was exactly the sort of stupid joke that Mike would make – then gripped the edge of the sink and started to cry.

'Are you all right, dear?' A middle-aged woman in a headscarf at the next basin was looking at her in the mirror with concern.

'Yes, fine, sorry.' She turned on the tap, ducked and splashed her face with cold water, watched it turn black and swirl away, keeping her head down until she had recovered. She found an empty cubicle and locked the door, put her suitcase on the toilet seat, pulled her dress over her head and took out a pale blue shirt and black tie. Her fingers fumbled with the buttons. She did them up wrongly and had to start again. She tugged the heavy blue skirt over her hips and fastened it, shook out the matching blue jacket with its single braided band on the sleeves and tried to smooth away the creases. She buttoned it up and tightened the belt.

Back at the sink, hairgrips in her mouth, she put up her hair. Her fingers came away covered in dust. There was nothing she could do. Her cap would cover the worst of it. She applied the make-up she had bought for the weekend, as advertised by Merle Oberon in that month's **Vogue** ('Just a few seconds with Max Factor "Pan-Cake" and you're glamorous!'), dabbing it thickly over the cut. It stung like hell. She added some lipstick, adjusted her cap and tucked away a few stray hairs. She stuck out her chin and peered into the mirror, and a formidable woman who seemed a complete stranger – Section Officer A. V. Caton-Walsh of the Women's Auxiliary Air Force – stared back. Only her startled eyes, red-rimmed and raw, betrayed her. She picked up her case and went out onto the station concourse.

In the café, she took her usual seat, where she could keep an eye on the clock, cradling a cup of tea between her hands. She let her gaze wander over the crowds at the platform gates: the profusion of different uniforms – dark blue, light blue, khaki – a lot of Americans, their kitbags piled on a trolley, a party of noisy schoolchildren meeting their parents. High above their heads, the smoke-stained glass and wrought-iron roof was filled like an aviary with fluttering pigeons. Her eyes kept going back up to it. She pictured a missile crashing through it, then reproached herself. Absurd to imagine she could witness a third V2 in the same day. Nevertheless, she finished her tea and went in search of her train, and the needle whine of anxiety in the back of her mind was only quietened when her carriage began to pull out of Paddington, carrying her beyond the range of the V2.

The journey from London to Marlow took an hour – a pretty route along the Thames Valley, via Maidenhead, Cookham and Bourne End. She sat by the window and brooded on the green water meadows, the placid brown cows, the rivers and duck ponds and small grey stone churches. As part of her duties, she sometimes went to an RAF hangar in rural Oxfordshire to debrief pilots immediately on their return from reconnaissance missions over Germany. Young men, barely out of school, flirtatious, still in their flying jackets, dismissive of the dangers they had just faced – 'Piece of cake, ma'am' – with only the occasional shaking hand as they lit a cigarette to indicate their jauntiness was an act. Occasionally a plane failed to appear. The hours would pass, she would wait around, then it would be discreetly suggested she leave. She had often wondered whether she would have the courage to do what they did. Now she had her answer. For the first time in the war, she had faced death, and her instinct had been to get out of London as fast as possible.

Of course, she could excuse it. Mike's injuries did not seem life-threatening. He had told her not to come to the hospital. Without him she had nowhere to go and nothing to do. But that begged the question of what she had been doing in Warwick Court in the first place. To have an affair with a married man was bad enough. To make love with that married man in the bed he shared with his wife . . .

The flat is empty all weekend. We can take our time . . .

He had made it sound like nothing. But it had added an unnecessary extra layer of deceit, of cruelty really, whereas if they had simply gone to a hotel as they usually did, they would still be together. It was absurd to think it – she had long since lost her faith – but she couldn't help seeing the V2 as a punishment from God. The notion nagged at her, went round and round in her head.

At Bourne End, a trio of giggling young WAAFs came into her compartment – aircraftwomen, second class. They saluted when they saw the braid on her sleeves and went quiet. Their deference made her feel even more uncomfortable. She took down her suitcase from the overhead rack and went into the corridor. At the carriage door, she pulled down the window. The Thames flowed beside the track, high and wide from the recent rain, a pair of swans in the middle, motionless in the current.

She put her face into the wind and breathed in deeply until she could no longer taste the dust and coal gas.

At Marlow, she let the WAAFs leave first and

waited until the platform was empty before she made her way through the station to the lane. An army lorry was waiting. The aircraftwomen were in the back.

'Do you want a lift, ma'am?'

'No thanks, girls. I'll walk.'

Past the brick-and-flint cottages and into the broad Georgian high street: ivy-covered coaching inns and tea rooms, little shops with bow windows made of small-paned glass, timbered whitewashed houses, thatched roofs – the whole thing was absurdly picturesque, a Hollywood image of England, like a scene from **Mrs Miniver.** A football match was being played somewhere. She could hear a whistle, men shouting, a cheer. She left the town and walked along the Henley road, between fields and high hedges, occasionally glimpsing the river to her left. It was only after a mile or so that the war began to reassert itself. An anti-aircraft battery became visible in the woods. A squad of sweating, red-faced soldiers in PT kit ran past her. A camouflaged lorry emerged from a drive ahead. There was a guard post.

She showed her pass at the barrier.

'Do you want a ride to the house, ma'am?'

'I'm fine, Corporal, thanks. The walk will do me good.'

A lot of Britain's secret war was fought at the end of long, sweeping drives like this one, running through neglected parks, between overgrown rhododendrons and dripping elms, to hidden country houses where codes were broken, special operations planned, the conversations of captured Nazi generals bugged, spies interrogated, agents trained. Kay had walked this drive for the past two years – always with an unwanted memory of school – and at the end of it stood Danesfield House, a mock-Elizabethan mansion, built at the turn of the century, as sparkling white as the icing on a wedding cake, with crenellated walls, steep red roofs and tall red-brick chimneys. Its ornamental gardens ran down to the Thames. When she had first arrived, the grounds had provided a pleasant place to stroll between shifts. Now they were disfigured by dozens of long, low temporary wooden office blocks and ugly semicircular corrugated-steel Nissen huts that served as barracks, in one of which she lived with eleven other officers, four to a room.

She stood on the threshold of her hut for a moment and offered up a prayer that no one would be in, then braced her shoulders, opened the metal door and clumped in her heavy WAAF shoes along the wooden floor. Four doors led off to the right of the corridor – the toilet and shower room was closest to the entrance – with a coal-burning stove in the centre of the hut that had been allowed to go out. Her dormitory was at the far end. The shutters were closed, the room in darkness, the air permeated by a strong smell of Vicks VapoRub. It seemed to be empty, but then the blankets on the bed in the furthest corner stirred and the shape of a head turned to look at her.

'I thought you were in London for the weekend.'

Kay stepped over the threshold. It was too late to turn around. 'Change of plan.'

'Hold on.' A shadow moved. A clatter as the shutters were opened. Shirley Locke, an economics graduate from University College, London, who seemed to have had the same streaming cold for the past two years, only in the summer she called it hay fever, secured the shutters and clambered back into bed. She was wearing a flannelette nightdress with a pattern of pink roses buttoned up to her sharp chin. She put on her glasses and raised her hand to her mouth. 'My God, Kay, what have you done to your face?'

'Car accident.' It was the first lie that came into her mind. She had already decided not to mention the V2. The questions would have been endless.

'Oh no, you poor thing! Whose car was it?'

'Just a stupid taxi.' She opened her cupboard and put away her case. 'Had a blowout on the Embankment and hit a lamp post.'

'When did it happen?'

'This morning.'

'But why are you back? Couldn't your chap have looked after you?'

'Who said anything about a chap?' She made for the door. 'Sorry – got to dash. See you later.'

Shirley called after her, 'You do know you'll have

to tell us about him one day, don't you? Your mystery man?' And then, when Kay was halfway down the corridor, the nasal voice came again: 'You should get that cut looked at!'

Danesfield House had lost its gracious character. Renamed RAF Medmenham after the nearest village, it had acquired instead a stuffy bureaucratic smell, a compound of dust and pencil shavings, cardboard files and rubber bands, like the inside of a desk drawer rarely opened. The chandeliers had been taken down, the plasterwork boarded over, linoleum laid and printed signs put up everywhere. The ballroom, for example, had become 'Z Section/Central Interpretation Unit', and it was here that Kay headed that Saturday afternoon.

By this time it was after half past three. The winter light was fading. Beyond the terrace, a low sun glinted on the Thames. Inside the huge ballroom, twenty Phase Two interpreters, mostly female, seated at three rows of desks, had turned on their Anglepoise lamps and were bent over their work. The atmosphere was quiet, the air heavy with concentration, like an examination hall. From time to time someone crossed to the bookshelves and took down a box file or a manual, or stood in front of one of the charts that showed the enemy's equipment from every conceivable angle: armoured cars and self-propelled howitzers, fighters and bombers, submarines, warships, tanks. On a long trestle table, wire baskets were piled with black-and-white photographs, marked by sector: 'Ruhr', 'Saar', 'Baltic'. A WAAF sergeant sat behind it, filling out a record sheet.

Kay said, 'Anything in from Holland?'

The sergeant pointed to an empty basket. 'Weather's bad, ma'am. No coverage for forty-eight hours.'

Kay went out to the hall and started to climb the stairs. Phase One was 'current/operational' and was responsible for debriefing the pilots at RAF Benson as soon as they landed from their sorties. Phase Two, in the ballroom, analysed all the photographs taken over the past twenty-four hours that might be of immediate use on the battlefield. Everything longer-term was passed upstairs to Phase Three. This was where she worked, in what had once been the main bedroom suites and bathrooms. She walked along the corridor to the registry and asked for the past week's coverage of the Dutch coastal sector, from the Hook of Holland to Leiden. 'Actually, make that two weeks.'

While the duty clerk went off to fetch the file, she rested her elbows on the counter and leaned forward. She closed her eyes. She was starting to feel faint again. People passed by in the corridor behind her. A telephone rang briefly somewhere. A man sneezed twice. The sounds reached her oddly muffled, as if she were underwater. Behind her, a woman's voice said softly but precisely, 'Kay, dear, are you all right?'

She took a breath, forced her mouth into a smile and turned to confront the thin and serious face of

Dorothy Garrod – so slight a woman, barely more than five feet tall, it had proved impossible to find a uniform that did not look too large on her. She was in her early fifties, much older than the rest of them. Before the war, she had been Professor of Archaeology at Cambridge. Now her academic discipline was the photographic analysis of bomb-damaged German cities, to which she applied the same painstaking scholarship she had once devoted to the ruined settlements of the Palaeolithic era. Bomber Command might insist a target had been destroyed; she knew otherwise, and stood her ground. Air Marshal Harris was said to loathe her.

'A slight bump on the head, Dorothy, otherwise fine.' It was Professor Garrod, her supervisor at Newnham, who had recommended Kay for the Central Interpretation Unit in the first place. She still found it hard to call her by her Christian name.

'You're very pale. Are you sure you're not overdoing it?'

'I'm perfectly well, honestly.'

The clerk returned with her file. She signed for it, clutched it to her chest, smiled a quick goodbye and escaped from the registry.

She slipped into her usual place at a desk beside the window. The rest of her section were too absorbed to notice her arrival. She took off her cap, switched on her lamp and set out her equipment – a stereoscope viewer, a magnifier, mathematical tables, a slide rule – then opened the file.

The black-and-white photographs, flecked with wisps of cloud, showed a clear image of the long, straight, flat coast, the wide beach, the streets and buildings of The Hague and its suburbs, including Scheveningen to the north, and great sweeps of woodland interspersed with dunes and lakes. That the V2s were being launched from here was certain: it was the only German toehold left in Europe that was close enough to strike London, two hundred miles away. Patrolling Spitfire pilots had occasionally observed the rockets streaking through the sky above them. But where exactly were they coming from? That was the mystery.

Kay did not expect to solve it. They had been searching the area for weeks. But one never knew. Babs Babington-Smith had been asked if she could locate an object at Peenemünde that might be the Germans' prototype jet fighter, the Messerschmitt-262. She had spent weeks going back over the old coverage with a jeweller's Leitz magnifying glass until she discovered at the side of the airfield a cruciform less than a millimetre wide, which equated to a wingspan of twenty feet. Kay remembered the exact moment of discovery, Babs's quiet excitement: 'I say, Kay, come and take a look at this.'

And even if she did find something – so what? The launchers were mobile. They would almost certainly have been moved by now. But it was preferable to doing nothing; preferable to going back to the barracks and listening to Shirley Locke blowing her nose; preferable to lying on her bed and remembering that awful fraction of a second before the rocket hit, and afterwards Mike strapped to the stretcher saying **Better not.**

She laid two of the photographs side by side. One had been taken fractionally after the other, creating a sixty per cent overlap; when she placed her stereoscope on its folding stand above them, the two images magically fused to give her a three-dimensional image. Nevertheless, all she could see was a canopy of monochrome trees so tightly packed and tiny it was impossible to distinguish one from another. But that did not deter her. She would go on all night if she had to, as the sun sank over the Thames and the lights came on in the township of huts beyond the window, searching for what lay hidden in the forest.

5

IN SCHEVENINGEN, BY CANDLELIGHT, IN a corner of the mirrored dining room of the Hotel Schmitt – a large shabby-grand establishment that served as staff headquarters and officers' mess – Colonel Huber was hosting a small dinner to welcome Biwack to the regiment.

The guest of honour was seated to his right. To his left, also in the midnight-black uniform of the SS, was Obersturmbannführer Karlheinz Drexler, chief of security. He was equivalent in rank to Huber – bespectacled, balding, plump: an unlikely representative of the Master Race, Graf always thought. Facing them were the three lieutenants in command of the firing battalions: Seidel, the chess-playing Berliner; Klein, a taciturn and skilful engineer who had risen through the ranks; and Stock, who had a reputation for being highly strung and who relaxed in the evenings by reading westerns. At the end of the table sat Graf.

A couple of white-gloved orderlies served the food on the hotel's monogrammed pre-war china: a watery cabbage soup and the final, obscure remains of an ancient boar that had been shot in the forest by the SS guards the previous week. There was bread but no potatoes: the bulk of Germany's potato crop that year had been requisitioned to be distilled into alcohol for use as rocket fuel. Like pampered children, the V2s took food from the adults' plates.

Although Huber had produced two bottles of schnapps to celebrate the occasion and had told a couple of his risqué jokes, the atmosphere remained subdued.

The intimate patch of candlelight flickering in the tall mirrors emphasised the emptiness of the chilly dining room and the darkness of the surrounding tables.

Graf was only half listening to the conversations going on around him. Seidel was telling the other battalion commanders about the overheated transformer. Drexler was talking to Biwack about some action on the Eastern Front ('We had to burn down the village . . .'). What he really wanted to do was get drunk. He had finished his schnapps and was just eyeing the nearest bottle and wondering if it would be impolite to reach for it when Huber tapped his glass with his knife and stood.

'Gentlemen, as you know, a consignment of rockets is due to arrive at midnight, and therefore we need to finish early so that we can all get some rest in preparation. But before we disperse for the evening, I would like to welcome Sturmscharführer Biwack to the regiment. In the heat of battle, it's all too easy to forget the reason why we're fighting. The purpose of the National Socialist Leadership Officer in the German army is to remind us of our cause. I want you to make sure he has the chance to talk to all your men before the week is out.' He bowed slightly to Biwack. 'We are pleased to have you with us, Sturmscharführer.' Biwack smiled up at him and nodded. 'Today we launched six missiles,' continued Huber. 'An excellent tally! But let us make sure tomorrow is even better. I would like to set us a new objective.' He glanced around the table. 'Let us show our new comrade what we can do. Tomorrow we shall launch twelve!'

Twelve! Graf's eyes widened. He was conscious of a brief hesitation, then Drexler started pounding his fist on the table in approval. The artillerymen followed the SS man's lead without much enthusiasm.

'Good,' beamed Huber. He lifted his glass. 'Then I propose a toast.' As they all stood, Graf was able to take the opportunity to help himself to more schnapps. 'To victory!'

'To victory!'

They drank, then sat and banged the table again. Graf felt the liqueur burning the back of his throat, the warm rush of the alcohol hitting his system. He brought his fist down so hard they all turned to look at him.

'Twelve launches! Marvellous!'

Biwack studied him for a few moments. He said politely, 'Do you think twelve launches in a day is too ambitious, Dr Graf?'

'No, on the contrary – too modest! After all, what is the weight of bombs carried by a single Lancaster?'

Seidel said, 'Six tons.'

'So twelve launches carrying a one-ton warhead per missile are only equivalent in explosive power to a pair of Lancaster bombers. And how many bombers do those swine in the RAF send over to attack our cities in a night? A thousand! Twelve launches?' Graf thumped the table again. 'I say let's launch twelve hundred!'

Seidel laughed and looked down at his hands. Huber said, 'But a single V2 spreads as much terror as a hundred Lancasters, and strikes the earth with tremendous force – at three times the speed of sound. It inflicts far more damage over a wider area, and no air defence can stop it.'

'And besides all that,' said Drexler, who was polishing his spectacles with his napkin, 'it's the only means we have left of hitting London.' He put his glasses back on and surveyed the table.

There was a silence.

'Fascinating,' said Biwack. He had been following the exchanges like a spectator at a tennis match. He suddenly pushed back his chair and rose to his feet. 'Thank you for your welcome, Colonel.' He briefly touched his hand to Huber's shoulder. 'This is a social gathering, not the occasion for a political lecture, so let me just say that while I may have come here to inspire **your** faith, it is **my** faith in our ultimate victory that has been inspired by what I have witnessed today. How can we fail in our sacred task when our country is capable of such marvels of technology? Allow me to answer your toast with one of my own.' Unexpectedly, he swung towards Graf and gave him a gracious bow before lifting his glass. 'To the genius of our German scientists!'

Graf was uncertain whether or not he was supposed to stand. In the end, he did, and raised his empty glass with the rest.

'To our German scientists!'

When they had resumed their seats, Huber gestured to Graf. 'Doctor? Would you care to say a few words in reply?' **And make amends?** his tone implied.

Graf smiled and shook his head. 'I'm not a man for speeches.'

'There is no need for a speech,' said Biwack. 'Could you not tell us something of your work with Professor von Braun?'

'I would not know where to begin,' he said truthfully. How could one compress half a lifetime into a couple of after-dinner anecdotes? He suddenly wished von Braun were there. He would have had them mesmerised in a minute. There was no one he could not charm, not even Hitler. When he laughed, he would throw back that huge patrician head of his and stick out his broad chin in unfeigned delight, like a youthful FDR, and you were sure he must be the greatest fellow in the world. He was certainly the greatest salesman. But Graf was well aware he was no von Braun, and all he could say was, 'He is a brilliant engineer, I can tell you that much.'

There was a pause.

'Well then,' said Huber with a glare at Graf, 'I suppose we shall have to leave it at that. Goodnight, gentlemen.'

He caught up with Graf in the street outside as the engineer was walking back to his billet – grabbed him by the arm and pulled him into the shadow of the hotel. 'What the devil was that all about?'

'What?'

'Don't give me that! You know what I mean. You sounded like a complete defeatist in front of that Nazi shit. "Let's launch twelve hundred"! It reflects badly on us all.'

'It's not defeatism, Colonel, it's simply realism. We may have to lie to the public – I understand that. But what's the point of lying to ourselves?'

'The point? The point is to avoid being picked up by the Gestapo for treason!' Huber practically had him pushed up against the wall, so close Graf could smell the schnapps on his breath. 'You helped build the fucking thing. You lot rammed it down the army's throats! Take responsibility for it!'

The colonel held him trapped there a few more

seconds, then gave an exclamation of disgust and turned away. Straightening his tunic, he marched unsteadily back into the headquarters.

Graf stayed where he was, leaning against the wall. Huber was quite right, he thought. He, above all of them, had no business complaining. He should learn to keep his mouth shut. But a toast to victory? Really, it was laughable.

He realised to his regret that, despite his best efforts, he was more or less sober. He pushed himself back up onto his feet and walked around the corner. The clouds had lifted slightly; the weather front was passing. There was a hint of moonlight in the sky, softening the blackout. A couple of soldiers were lurching along the street towards him, doubtless on their way back from the Wehrmacht brothel, which was just nearby. This pair most definitely **were** drunk, and not on schnapps either, by the look of their glazed eyes, but on the methyl alcohol that fuelled the rockets. Although a purple dye was added to make it look unappealing and to give it a bitter taste, and although the barracks were covered in warning signs ('A one-shot glass will blind you! Several shots will kill you!'), the first thing every man assigned to the V2s learned was how to strain it three times through the carbon filter of his gas mask. You were left with a slightly off-colour drink that was 150 per cent proof. If you swallowed it quickly you would not throw up and Scheveningen in winter might suddenly seem not such a bad place after all. Graf stepped into the gutter to let the men stagger past.

He was billeted in a small hotel with a dozen sergeants and NCOs. He could hear them in the kitchen as he came into the dimly lit hall. He could also make out female laughter. It was forbidden to have relations with any of the local women in The Hague; even so, it was not uncommon for one or two to be smuggled past the guards, hidden beneath blankets in the motorcycle sidecars. He climbed the stairs to the third floor, stopping off at the lavatory on the landing to relieve himself, then unlocked his door, tossed his hat onto a chair and threw himself down on the bed. He didn't bother to turn on the light or close the curtains or even take off his coat. He simply lay there, listening to the incessant crash and roar of the sea on the other side of the promenade. After a while, he searched through his pockets for his cigarettes and lit one. He lifted the ashtray from the nightstand and balanced it on his chest.

He was thinking about von Braun. Biwack had seemed both well informed and remarkably curious about their friendship, as if he was trying to trick him into some disclosure. Perhaps he had seen his Gestapo file. That would make sense. It must be thick: never mind the reports of informers, his interrogation alone had lasted a week. No strong-arm stuff, no lights shone in his face, nothing like that – they had obviously been given orders that he was too valuable to be reduced to pulp. Just remorseless questions in a nondescript office in Stettin nine months ago, one session after another, sometimes at night, with plenty of time alone in his basement cell in between to work on his nerves.

When did you first make the acquaintance of Professor von Braun?

Well, that would depend on what you meant by 'acquaintance'. He had first **spoken** to him – he could be quite precise about this because he had a mind that always remembered such details – at the AVUS motor-racing circuit in Berlin on 23 May 1928, when they were both sixteen. He was sure of the date because it was the occasion when Fritz von Opel set a new land-speed record of 238 kilometres per hour in a car powered by twenty-four solid-fuel rockets. Wernher had stood out, even at that age, even in a crowd of three thousand.

Why?

Oh, his height, his good looks, his manner – a certain confidence in advance of his years. After the test run was over, they had both hung around von Opel, and his partner, the famous Austrian rocket pioneer Max Valier, and had even been allowed to take turns sitting in the driving seat of the five-metre-long monster car, the RAK-2. All four of them, including the two schoolboys, were members of the Verein für Raumschiffahrt, the Society for Space Travel. That was the dream, you see, even then. Rockets were the means, rather than the end. Not that he said that to the Gestapo.

He contemplated the ceiling and wondered what had happened to von Opel. He had heard a rumour he had fled to the United States when war broke out. Valier had been killed a couple of years after the speed record when a liquid-fuel rocket motor had blown up and a piece of shrapnel had severed his aorta.

As to when he had first become properly **acquainted** with von Braun, that would really have been the following year, and again he could be exact, because it was the premiere of Fritz Lang's movie **Frau im Mond – Woman in the Moon** – at the Ufa-Palast am Zoo cinema in Berlin on 15 October 1929. The Society for Space Travel had been hired by the studio to produce a working rocket for the occasion, which they had failed to do. But von Braun, whose family were rich and well connected, had managed to wangle Graf a ticket. He lent him a dinner jacket, so they could mingle with the VIPs. He even marched up and introduced them both to Lang. Graf would never forget how the great director had squinted at him through his monocle, as if this awkward schoolboy were himself a creature from the moon.

After that, they saw a lot of one another. Graf was an only child, the son of two teachers – one of English literature, the other of music – wonderful, kindly, somewhat elderly parents, neither of whom had the slightest interest in space travel or engineering, although they taught him English so that he could read the science fiction of H. G. Wells. Von Braun became his confidant. He would catch a tram and visit the von Brauns' mansion on the edge of the Tiergarten, where lemonade would be served by a butler. They wrote science fiction stories of their own about interplanetary travel and orbiting space stations. They raised money for the Society for Space Travel at a stall in the Wertheim department store. ('Ladies and gentlemen,' declared von Braun, 'the man is already alive who will one day walk on the moon!') They both enrolled at the Institute of Technology in Charlottenburg and studied theoretical physics, and they both did a six-month 'dirty hands' stint on the factory floor, von Braun at the Borsig locomotive works, and Graf at the Daimler-Benz factory in Marienfelde.

It was around this time that the society – an impecunious collection of amateurs and dreamers, plus one or two serious engineers, like Karl Riedel and Heini Grünow, both mechanics – persuaded the Berlin city authorities to let them use a stretch of waste ground out in the north of the city near Tegel, where there were a few big disused munitions bunkers left over from the Great War. They made a clubroom in the old guardhouse, brought in camp beds and a Primus stove so they could stay for days at a time, put up the publicity logo from **Frau im Mond** of a glamorous woman sitting on a crescent moon, and called their derelict swampy paradise the Raketenflugplatz, the 'Rocket Aerodrome'.

And in due course, thanks largely to Riedel, they did indeed build a rocket. They called her 'the Repulsor', after the spacecraft in one of the society's favourite science fiction novels, **Two Planets.** She was an ugly device, nothing like the shapely aerodynamic beauties they would eventually produce – 'Repulsive' would have been a better name. Her fuselage was a thin metal tube, three metres long and only ten centimetres wide, with the engine in an egg-shaped container in the nose and with a canister at the bottom containing a flare and a parachute. The innovation lay in the fuel configuration they came up with, which was the same as they eventually used in the V2: alcohol and liquid oxygen in separate tanks, one on top of the other, forced into the firing chamber by compressed nitrogen. It was a wonder they didn't blow themselves up. They would set the fuel running and start counting the seconds backwards from ten – a dramatic touch they borrowed from **Frau im Mond** – while one of them dashed out and touched a burning rag to the nozzle, then dived for cover. On a good day, 160 pounds of thrust would send the Repulsor shooting up to a height of a thousand metres and the parachute would bring her floating back to earth. There were plenty of bad days too, of course. The long metal broomstick often misfired, or headed off at tree height; one time they hit a police barracks.

Riedel might have been their senior engineer, and

Rudolf Nebel, an ex-pilot, their nominal leader, but it was von Braun even then who was the dominant personality: always smiling – they called him 'Sonny Boy' after the Al Jolson hit – a quick learner, good with his hands as well as his brain, intensely ambitious to be the first man in space. In the summer of 1932, his father, an aristocratic landowner, was appointed Minister of Agriculture in the von Papen government. Von Braun senior must have had a word over dinner with someone important in the defence ministry, because soon afterwards the society were invited to demonstrate their creation at the military proving ground at Kummersdorf. The test was a fiasco. The jet flame burned through a weld and the rocket crashed a few seconds after take-off. But the army officers loved von Braun, saw the potential in the twenty-year-old right away – he was one of those polite and lively young men who were always good with their elders – and a couple of months later he burst into the clubhouse at the Rocket Aerodrome to announce he had negotiated a deal. The army would fund their research. There was only one condition: they would have to continue their work in secrecy, behind the walls of Kummersdorf.

None of the others wanted to go. Nebel was a Nazi sympathiser and didn't like the conservative German army. Rolf Engel, another twenty-year-old, was a communist and wanted nothing to do with the military. Klaus Riedel was a utopian opposed to war. Graf's father had been gassed in the Great War and was a strong supporter of the League of Nations. Von Braun told them they were crazy to let such an opportunity slip. 'We haven't even worked out how to measure our test results – fuel consumption, combustion pressure, thrust. How can we make any progress until we have the equipment to do that? And how can we get the equipment except through the army?'

Your parents were communists, is that correct?

No, they were members of the Social Democratic Party.

One of the Gestapo men had rolled his eyes. Socialists, communists, pacifists – they were all the same to him.

The debate at the Rocket Aerodrome over what they should do turned nasty. Hard words were spoken. The upshot was that no one went to Kummersdorf apart from von Braun, who was now bound by the rules of military secrecy. That was the last time Graf spoke to him for the best part of two years.

A lot happened in those two years. Graf was in the centre of Berlin on the night when the Nazis' torchlit parade passed through the Brandenburg Gate to the Reich Chancellery to celebrate Hitler's arrival in power. The following month he saw the glow in the sky as the Reichstag burned down. When the regime made use of the ensuing panic to start harassing its opponents, his parents both lost their jobs. In the autumn, the Gestapo raided the Rocket Aerodrome, took everyone's fingerprints and made the members of the society sign an undertaking not to talk about their work to 'foreign powers' – a worthless promise as their experiments had dried up in any case for lack of money. By this time, Graf had left the Institute of Technology and was studying for his doctorate at the University of Berlin. Occasionally he would glimpse the tall figure of von Braun in a corridor or in the street nearby, and once when he was walking in the park near Alexanderplatz, he thought he might have seen him on horseback, but the rider was too far away for him to be sure, and besides, he was wearing SS uniform, so he dismissed the idea as impossible.

At any rate, it was not until the summer of 1934 that they met again – unfortunately this time he could not provide the gentlemen from the Gestapo with the exact date, though he remembered it was towards the end of the afternoon. He was sitting writing his doctoral thesis (**Some Practical Problems of the Liquid-Fuel Rocket**) in his grim one-room apartment in the Kreuzberg district of Berlin when he heard a car horn sounding in the road outside. The noise was so loud and went on so long that eventually he got up to see what was happening, and there was von Braun standing on the pavement, with his hand on the horn, staring up at the windows of the apartment block. There was nothing for it but to go down and tell him to shut up.

He was not in the least put out. 'Rudi! They said this was your building, but I didn't have your apartment number. Get in. I want to show you something.'

'Go away. I'm working.'

'Come on. You won't regret it.' The irresistible smile. The hand on his arm.

'No, it's impossible.'

Naturally, he went.

Von Braun in those days drove a tiny battered old two-seater Hanomag he had bought for a hundred marks and which looked like a motorised pram: open-topped and in several places open-bottomed as well. Graf could see the road skimming past between his feet as they hurtled south out of the city and into the countryside. It was too noisy to talk. He guessed where they were going. After half an hour, they swung off the road. Von Braun showed his pass to a guard, and they drove past the red-brick office block of the Kummersdorf army testing facility and across the flat heathland of the proving grounds to a collection of concrete buildings and wooden huts.

'Wernher—'

'Just hear me out.'

It was nothing much to look at from the outside. But inside, von Braun conducted him through what was to Graf a paradise: a dedicated design shop, workrooms, a darkroom, a control room full of measuring equipment, and last and best of all a concrete bunker, open to the sky, in the centre of which stood an A-frame three metres high built of heavy metal girders. From it hung a rocket motor on fixed brackets. Fuel pipes and electrical cables ran from its sides. A nozzle protruded from its base. Von Braun guided him to take shelter behind a low wall, then turned and gave the thumbs-up. A man in overalls – it was Heini Grünow, Graf realised, the mechanic from the Rocket Aerodrome – turned a pair of large wheels. A diaphanous white cloud appeared beneath the motor. Another man wearing goggles approached with a burning tin can of gasoline attached to the end of a long pole. Keeping his head averted, he extended it into the cloud.

A bluish-red pillar of fire – pure, defined, sublime – exploded from the base of the rocket motor. Lying in his darkened room in Scheveningen, Graf could still relive every one of the ten seconds during which it burned. The solid roar of the plume in that enclosed space; the vibrations as the motor struggled to free itself from its restraints; the heat on his face; the overwhelming sweet smell of burning fuel; the exhilarating sense of power, as if they had briefly tapped into the sun. When it was over, the bunker seemed plunged into night and the silence rang in his ears. He stayed immobile for half a minute, staring at the spent motor, until von Braun turned to him. No smile for once, but an utter and intense seriousness.

'Listen to me, Rudi,' he said. 'This is the absolute truth. The road to the moon runs through Kummersdorf.'

Graf signed a contract with the army that very afternoon: 'to assist, under the direction of Wa Prw 1/I, on the conception of, and conduct of experiments on, a liquid-fuel reaction-motor test stand at Main Battery West, Kummersdorf'. In return, he would be paid fourteen marks a day. Money he could give to his parents.

When they got back to Berlin, they went out for a drink to celebrate.

'Tell me, did I see you in SS uniform not so long ago, riding a horse?' He couldn't resist asking.

'Oh, that?' Von Braun waved his cocktail dismissively. 'I only joined the SS riding school at Halensee – not the SS itself. I've resigned now. It doesn't hurt to get to know these people. Besides, I like riding.'

He was to use exactly the same tone in 1937, when Graf had noticed a swastika badge in his lapel for the first time. 'You've joined the Party?'

'Technically. I'm number five million and something. Now, now, Rudi – don't give me that look! You won't get much support these days if you aren't prepared to show some commitment. I don't have to go to meetings or anything like that.'

And again in 1940, when they had entertained some bigwigs from the SS at Peenemünde, and he had turned up in the black uniform of an SS Untersturmführer – blond-haired, broad-shouldered, chin jutting, looking like an illustration from **Das Schwarze Korps.** 'It's purely an honorary rank. Himmler insisted. Don't worry – as soon as these fellows have left, it's going right back in the closet.'

A knock at the door of the hotel room. The voice of Sergeant Schenk: 'Dr Graf? It's after midnight.'

He had not realised it was so late. At some point he

must have fallen asleep. He sat up in bed and stared with regret at his burned-out cigarette. It would be the last he would be able to enjoy for some hours.

'Thanks. I'm coming.'

He picked up his torch from the nightstand, switched it on and shone it around the bedroom. Its thin light showed the sort of modest seaside accommodation he remembered from childhood holidays: an armchair, a chest of drawers, a tiny washbasin in the corner with a mirror above it, a wardrobe. Beside the wardrobe was a small roll-top desk and an old office chair that he had managed to scrounge soon after his arrival and where he sometimes sat and worked. He flicked the beam back to the wardrobe and let it travel up the centre of the doors to the suitcase lying on top. He hadn't looked at it for weeks.

He got off the bed and turned on the overhead light. He closed the curtains, dragged the chair next to the wardrobe, stepped up and took down the case. It was old, made of good-quality scuffed brown leather. Von Braun had given it to him just before he left Peenemünde. 'Do me a favour and look after this, will you?'

'What is it?'

'Insurance.'

He laid it on the bed, snapped open the catches and lifted the lid. Inside were a hundred or more small cardboard cartons, each containing a roll of 35 mm microfilm. They looked to be undisturbed.

He had occasionally wondered if he should find a better hiding place, but it had always seemed to him wiser simply to leave it where it was. He was sure no one would think of bothering with it. Even so, he plucked a strand of hair from the side of his head and carefully placed it in one of the catches before he closed it and put it back on top of the wardrobe. He turned off the light and descended the stairs.

Outside in the darkness, he could hear the whistle of the train approaching, the heavy clank of its wheels on the tracks as it crept slowly through the town at the end of its long journey from the rocket factory in central Germany. It took him less than two minutes to walk to the railway station, but the train beat him to it. He heard the exhalation of steam in the distance as the locomotive came to a stop.

The scene that greeted him had a certain surreal glamour, as if a movie star had arrived in town: hundreds of men waiting in the sidings under arc lights, breath billowing in the cold; a huge convoy of vehicles of all descriptions – transporters, tankers, bowsers, some with their engines already running – deployed alongside the flatbed trucks. The locomotive had halted so that the first of the missiles was directly positioned under the big crane that straddled the line. Already the technical troop were clambering over it, pulling away its tarpaulin, guiding the crane's steel cables into position. Once it was hoisted out of the way and swung over onto one of the transporters, the train would inch forward and the next missile would be lifted clear. The warheads were packed separately in big metal drums. Further down the train were the fuel tankers.

The soldiers had been trained to work quickly to get the rockets unloaded before daybreak, but tonight they seemed to be going through the procedure even faster than usual, and Graf guessed they must have been told that the regiment was under orders to conduct twelve launches by the end of the day. He could see Biwack standing with Huber. The colonel was gesturing, no doubt explaining what was happening.

Graf stood watching for a while. There would be nothing for him to do until the first missiles had been taken to the tents in the woods for technical checks. Their dream had come true, he thought, if not exactly as they had envisaged it. They had indeed created a Rocket Aerodrome.

He started to feel cold. That damned salt water again! It conducted the cold as effectively as it conducted electricity. He turned up the collar of his coat and moved towards the train.

6

AT 5.34 A.M., THE REGIMENT fired its first V2 of the day. Its orange flame rose like a sun in the wintry forest, setting light to the tops of some of the surrounding fir trees as it lifted into the darkness. The roar split the Sunday-morning silence over The Hague, bringing hundreds to their bedroom windows to see what was happening. The clouds over the sea glowed red for an instant then went black again.

Five minutes later, the missile struck Longbridge Road, a modern residential street in Ilford, Greater London, demolishing three houses. In the central house, number 411, which suffered a direct hit, Maud Branton and her daughter Iris, aged nineteen, were killed instantly; her husband Sidney was pulled out of the rubble but died later the same day in Barking Emergency Hospital. Next door, in number 413, Frederick and Ellen Brind were also killed outright; their twenty-month-old grandson, Victor, was taken to hospital but was pronounced dead on arrival. Also killed was one of the Brantons' neighbours on the other side, Charles Berman, aged thirty-nine. In all, eight died and another eight were seriously injured.

The second rocket, launched two and a half hours later at 8.02 a.m., veered almost a hundred miles off course and plunged harmlessly into the North Sea, close to the shingle strand of Orford Ness in Suffolk, where the explosion was observed by some startled early-morning fishermen casting their lines from the beach for mackerel.

What happened to the third missile remains a mystery. It took off perfectly at 10.26 a.m., but there is no record of an impact anywhere on the British mainland. Presumably it must have exploded in mid-air, perhaps during re-entry.

Twenty minutes later, at 10.46, the fourth missile was fired. It hit Orion Cottages in Rainham, Greater London, close to the River Thames. Two people were killed: Albert Bull, a thirty-nine-year-old fireman, who died in the blast, and his five-year-old son, Brian, who succumbed to his injuries later the same day at Oldchurch County Hospital. Thirty people were seriously hurt.

The day's fifth launch, at 11.20 a.m., landed on a modern detached house in Manor Road, Chigwell, killing Stanley Dearlove, aged forty. Six others were seriously injured.

The sixth rocket, fired at 12.50 p.m., struck 41 Gordon Avenue in Walthamstow, killing fifty-five-year-old Lilian Cornwell and seriously injuring another seventeen people.

Less than an hour later, missile number seven, launched at 1.39 p.m., scored a direct hit on All Saints' Church in East India Dock Road – remarkably, only two hundred yards from McCullum Road, Poplar, where a V2 had struck on Friday night, killing fourteen. It brought down the church's Georgian roof and the eastern side of the nave. Luckily, the main Sunday service was over. Even so, it killed four adults and one eleven-year-old boy, Aubrey Hing. Nineteen people were seriously injured.

Eleven minutes after that, an eighth missile plunged down on to Billericay in Essex, hitting some trees and exploding prematurely, seriously injuring two people.

Thirty-five miles away, in Danesfield House, Kay was at her desk beside the window on the first floor, her head bent over her stereoscopic magnifier. The two great skills of photographic interpretation were, first, the concentration to study the same area for months or even years, until one knew it is as well as one's own back garden; and second, the memory to spot the minute change that indicated enemy activity. If a lot of people walked across a field, for example, the trampled grass would show up lighter than the surrounding area. To what were their tracks leading? Was that odd shape a tank? A gun? The arrival of camouflage was a sure giveaway that something was going on. And it was surprisingly easy to spot, camouflage on the ground being mostly a matter of blending in **colours,** whereas in a monochrome image taken from an altitude of more than 20,000 feet it showed up as a difference in **tone.** But trees were an infallible camouflage – unchanging, impenetrable, a uniform dark grey blanket, even in winter, even if they were deciduous. There was simply nothing to see in the woods around The Hague. They mocked her hours of effort.

She lifted her head and rotated it to relieve the stiffness. Her eyes ached. Even so, she was in a better state than she had been the previous evening. She had slept deeply, without dreams, as if her mind had been determined to heal itself. She had barely been aware of Shirley's coughs and sneezes, or of Maud and Lavender, her two other roommates, coming in tipsy and giggling at nearly midnight, after a double date with a couple of pilots at the Hare and Hounds. And Sunday morning was the blissful high point when they took their bath. They were each allowed four inches of hot water a week, and they pooled their ration to ensure one full tub and followed a rota to determine who went first. Today it had been her turn to go last, but for once she didn't mind the greyish water and floating hair; it was luxury enough simply to wallow in the lukewarm depths and wash away the last of the dust. She wondered how Mike was doing. She thought she might call the hospital in a minute, not to try to speak to him, just to ask a nurse how he was. There could be no harm in that, could there?

She returned her eyes to the magnifier.

Hers was a strange sort of war, observing the panoramic struggle as if she were a god on Mount Olympus. She felt guilty at how absorbing she found it: more like an extension of Cambridge than proper military service. Her call-up papers had arrived in her pigeonhole at Newnham on her twenty-first birthday in the spring of 1941. The day after her final examination in June, she caught an early train from Cambridge with orders to report to an RAF base in Gloucester for basic training.

That had been an eye-opener for a convent girl from Dorset. Accents so thick – Geordie, Scouse, Glaswegian – and so studded with swear words she could barely understand what they were saying. The Nissen hut slept thirty, with a separate latrine and bathhouse. On her first night she heard shrieks of pain from one of the cubicles and tapped on the door politely: 'Are you all right?' 'No, I'm fucking well not all right, you posh cunt, I'm having a fucking baby!' It became a catchphrase for the rest of their training, as they drilled and marched and exercised, struggled with their ill-fitting uniforms and drew their meagre pay (one shilling and eight pence a day): 'Are you all right?' 'No, I'm having a fucking baby . . .'

At the end of two weeks, they were told where to report next. She was the only one assigned to RAF

Medmenham. She cried when she left the others. They had become her closest friends. The first person she saw when she arrived at Danesfield House was Dorothy Garrod: 'I put in a word for you, dear. You'll find the work quite stimulating. I believe I have now recruited the entire department of archaeology . . .'

She was promoted to aircraftwoman 1st class.

The following May – 1942 – the duty intelligence officer gave her a folder of photographs taken from a Spitfire 40,000 feet over the north German coast. 'Tell me something. You have a degree in history. Did the Romans ever get as far north as the Baltic?'

'Yes, it was where they got a lot of their amber. Why?'

'Would they have built any amphitheatres up there?'

'I shouldn't have thought so, no. Actually, certainly not.'

'Then what the devil are these?'

She studied the coverage of what appeared to be an island, with an airfield and a lot of construction under way. They certainly looked like amphitheatres – one huge elliptical embankment and three big circular earthworks in the woods very close to the sea. What could they be? Empty reservoirs, possibly? She checked the map reference to see where the photographs had originated. **Peenemünde, Usedom.** The name meant nothing to her. That had been the start of her relationship with the rockets.

'Kay! You're back from London? I heard you were in a car crash.'

Wing Commander Leslie Starr, her section leader, had come up quietly behind her and bent his head next to her ear. He ran his hands over her shoulders and squeezed the tops of her arms. 'The Wandering Starr', they called him. 'But you've got a cut . . .' He touched her temple. 'How are you feeling?'

She turned to look up at him and at the same time managed to twist herself free. 'More or less human now, thank you, sir.'

'Glad to hear it.' She couldn't have made her distaste more obvious if she'd slapped him in the face. He didn't seem put out. She supposed it must happen to him all the time. 'I gather the V2 launch site coverage is signed out to you?'

'Yes, sir. I had a day off. I thought I'd run over it again to see if we'd missed anything.'

'And have we?'

'I'm afraid not.'

'Damn.' He picked up one of the photographs and held it out at arm's length to examine it, frowning, chewing his lip. For the first time, she noticed that he looked unusually agitated. 'Stanmore's just been on to say they've tracked eight V2s so far today, five on target.'

Stanmore was shorthand for Bentley Priory, another stately home, this one on the northern edge of London, which served as the headquarters of RAF

Fighter Command. Its Filter Room monitored all incoming enemy aircraft.

'Eight? In one morning?'

'That's on top of the four yesterday, one of which hit Woolworths in Deptford and killed more than a hundred and fifty, mostly women and children.'

'Oh God.' She put her hand to her mouth. That must have been the blast she'd heard on Chancery Lane.

'Another hit Holborn. Plus there were five on Friday. I've been told to drop everything and go up for an emergency meeting at the Air Ministry right away.' He glanced at the photograph again, and then at her, weighing her up. 'You'd better come with me.'

'Yes, sir. What do you want me to do?'

'Sit there and look pretty.' He tossed the photograph back onto the desk. 'Meet me in the hall in ten minutes, okay?'

'Yes, sir.' The prospect of an hour or more in the back of a car with the Wandering Starr was not appealing. 'Sir,' she called after him. 'I'll need authorisation to take these out of the building.'

'I'll tell Registry.' He half turned to go, then turned back again. 'If you were in London yesterday, you must have heard them.'

She felt herself redden. 'I did, sir, yes.'

'Bloody Germans – never know when they're beaten.'

After he had gone, she gathered the photographs together and put them back in the file. Ten minutes didn't give her much time. She hurried out of the room and down the stairs, back to the hut to collect her greatcoat and put some make-up in her bag. By the time she reached the main hall, he was already waiting. She cast a wistful glance at the public telephone. No chance of ringing the hospital now.

Outside, he held the car's rear door open for her.

'Do you mind if I sit in the front, sir? I don't want to be sick all over you.'

Before he could object, she slid in next to the driver. The car crunched over the gravel and pulled away down the long drive. After tapping his foot irritably for half a minute, Starr grunted and opened his briefcase. When they turned onto the Henley road, Kay wrapped herself in her greatcoat, closed her eyes and pretended to doze.

She had never been to the Air Ministry before. Usually the top brass came down to Medmenham for briefings. That was how she had met Mike, eighteen months ago. By then, the intelligence people had begun to receive reports that the Germans were testing some kind of long-distance weapon capable of striking England, and the amphitheatres at Peenemünde had assumed a more sinister significance. Fresh reconnaissance flights were ordered, and the new photographs were a shock. She remembered the day they came in. A huge complex, practically a small town, was under construction, with its own power station and a harbour to bring in coal. Later, on a fan-shaped stretch of open foreshore, they observed what they described carefully in their report as 'a thick vertical column about forty feet high'.

Air Commodore Templeton was one of half a dozen senior figures who travelled to the Phase Three section to see it for themselves. He pulled up a chair and sat next to her, not all flirtatious and creepy like Starr and one or two of the others; just serious, focused, intelligent, asking a lot of questions. She was acutely aware of his physical presence, a kind of compact power. When someone told her he had been a hero in the Battle of Britain, she wasn't surprised. He was said to be the youngest commodore in the RAF.

In June 1943, on the Whit Bank Holiday Monday, Churchill himself came to take a look at what they were now sure was a rocket. He was driven over from Chequers with Mrs Churchill. Their daughter, Sarah, a glamorous red-headed actress, worked in Phase Two. Kay was struck by how small and pink he was, with a complexion like one of the sugar mice she used to buy as a child, and how when he bent forward to look through her viewfinder, he smelled not of cigars but of eau de cologne. Mike was one of the officers in the Prime Minister's entourage. After the Churchills had driven off back to Chequers late in the afternoon, he hung around and rather shyly asked if she fancied a drink in the pub: 'It is a holiday, after all.'

So many pubs after that! The Hare and Hounds. The Dog and Badger. The Old Bell in Hurley. The White Hart at Nettlebed. The Compleat Angler hotel on the Thames at Marlow, where they had stayed in bed the entire weekend and taken their meals in their room in case they were recognised by someone from Medmenham, the swans swimming back and forth directly in front of their window with a newly hatched flotilla of eight fluffy grey cygnets. 'They mate for life,' she told him, as he lay with his head in her lap, 'and sing just before they die.' 'You're such a romantic.' 'Well, one of us has to be.'

He was ten years older than she was, had joined the RAF long before the war, a professional airman. Would he leave his wife? He always said he would. He said they had only married on the spur of the moment in the summer of 1940 when it seemed that every day might be their last. Now she worked all week in intelligence at Bletchley, doing something so secret she wouldn't tell even him what it was. 'We hardly knew one another . . .' 'We've grown apart . . .' 'This bloody war . . .'

The memories drifted through her mind with such a strange and lazy intensity that she didn't really notice where they were until an hour had passed and they were in the centre of London, driving down Southampton Row towards the corner of Chancery Lane. She sat up with a start of recognition. The road was still cordoned off.

Starr turned his head to look. 'That must be where the Holborn rocket landed. Christ, it only just missed the ministry . . .'

She'd had no idea how close Mike's flat was to his office. Five hundred yards further on, the massive grey-stone edifice of Adastral House occupied the entire eastern corner of Aldwych. Damaged by a flying bomb in the summer, it looked grimy and battered, like a government building that had survived a siege by a revolutionary mob, its entrance protected by a rampart of sandbags and guarded by soldiers, its high windows criss-crossed by tape, an array of wireless antennae rising from its roof.

Starr leaned forward. 'Don't speak unless I tell you to, all right?'

'Yes, sir.'

Inside, the ministry on a Sunday afternoon was quiet. Starr went over to talk to the airman at the reception desk. Kay looked around the gloomy marble hall. In the centre was a display of propaganda posters: Lancasters, picked out by searchlights, bombing a city. **The Attack Begins in the Factory. The big raids on Germany continue. British war plants share with the RAF credit for these giant operations.** She heard a noise and glanced over her shoulder. A WAAF had come in and was holding the heavy door open for a man on crutches, his right leg in plaster, a bandage around his head. It took her a moment to recognise him. She jerked her gaze back to the posters in shock. **Never was so much owed by so many to so few.**

'Good afternoon, sir.' Starr's voice.

'Hello, Les.' Mike's reply sounded hollow in the deserted stone mausoleum of the reception.

'You look as though you've been in the wars, sir.'

'Bit of a close one. Nothing serious.'

'Nothing serious?' The woman's voice cut in: clipped, confident, exasperated. 'It's a miracle he's still alive, sir. Our flat's completely destroyed.'

Kay could hear her own pulse, her blood rushing in her ears.

'My God, sir, when was this?'

'Yesterday morning.'

'Not the V2 on Holborn?'

'That's the bastard.'

'Are you here for the meeting?'

'Of course I'm here for the bloody meeting. It's my show. I'm chairing it.'

'If you don't mind my saying, sir – shouldn't you be in hospital?'

The woman's voice again: 'That's what I told him, Wing Commander, but he discharged himself.'

'Well, he's the boss, I suppose. I've brought along one of our interpreters, sir, if it's all right with you. Section Officer! Come and say hello to the air commodore.'

Kay made an effort to compose her face, then turned, and walked the few paces to where they were standing. She saluted. 'Sir.'

Not a flicker of recognition on his gaunt white face. He nodded, smiled vaguely then peered at her as if he were trying to place her. For a moment she wondered if he might be concussed. He said, 'Haven't we met at Medmenham?'

'Yes, sir.'

'This is my wife, Mary. Mary, this is . . . ?' He cocked his head enquiringly. Was it really necessary to introduce her? She felt unnerved – humiliated even – that he should force her to play along. Besides, the act was all a bit too obvious. She sensed his wife had noticed it as well: in her suspicious glance could be read a whole volume of their marital history.

'Kay Caton-Walsh, sir.'

'Hello.' Mary Templeton put out her hand.

Kay took it. 'Pleased to meet you.' Looking at her was like facing a mirror: the same uniform, the same rank, the same thick auburn hair pinned up under the same cap, the same height and trim figure, the same age, more or less.

Starr said, 'I take it you weren't in the flat at the time, Mrs Templeton?'

'No,' she replied. She was still staring at Kay. 'Luckily for me, I was supposed to be on duty in the Midlands all weekend.' And now she was looking directly at the cut on Kay's forehead. 'But here's the oddest thing: I noticed at the hospital that I'm listed on the casualty sheet as "walking wounded". Apparently I was treated at the scene for a head injury.'

It was Starr who broke the silence. 'They must have confused you with someone else. Same thing happened to an aunt of mine.'

Mary Templeton's smile was bright and brittle. 'Yes, in the chaos, I suppose it must be easy to get wives muddled up.'

There was another pause. The air commodore said smoothly, 'Les, why don't you and the section officer go on up? I'll follow at my own speed. Second-floor conference room, next to my office.'

Kay was conscious of the click of her heels on the patterned marble floor, of the other woman's eyes drilling into her back. For some reason she had always pictured her as older. Clearly he had a type. **How many more of us are there?** She felt as if her knees would give way. When she reached the staircase, she had to grab onto the handrail to make sure she didn't fall. She hauled herself up after Starr, who was striding ahead, taking the stairs two at a time. On the second-floor landing, he didn't stop to wait for her.

Halfway along the corridor, a door was open. She could hear men's voices. He paused on the threshold and gave her a look. 'A car accident? Really?'

'What do you mean, sir?'

'Oh dear.' He sighed and shook his head. 'You're not the first and I'm afraid you won't be the last.' He put his hand around her waist and steered her into the room. 'Ladies first.'

Everything was a blur to her now. A large wood-panelled room with a carpet and a fireplace at one end. Half a dozen airmen in uniform around a table, most of them smoking, faces turning to stare as she came in. A large map of south-east England and the Low Countries mounted on an easel beside the fireplace, Greater London dotted with red pins. She took a seat in the corner, as far away from the rest as she could, and placed the file of photographs in front of her. Everyone knew Starr. There was a lot of 'Hello, Les', 'How are you, old chap?' and handshakes as he went round the table. He didn't introduce her. After a couple of minutes, the tap of crutches could be heard getting louder along the passage, and Air Commodore Templeton swung himself into the room, followed by a young flight lieutenant carrying a folder. Everyone stood.

'Thank you. Sit.' He handed the crutches to his aide, took the folder, and lowered himself, wincing with the effort, into his chair at the head of the table. 'And before we go any further: yes, I was caught by the rocket round the corner yesterday morning; no, I'm not badly hurt; and yes, this has suddenly got bloody personal.'

There was a release of nervous laughter.

'So,' he opened the folder, 'the Secretary of State has been telephoned this afternoon by the Prime Minister and the Home Secretary, and he has in turn telephoned me to ask me to give him something he can tell the Cabinet tomorrow in the light of the increase in V2 activity over the past couple of days. I need some facts, and above all I need some recommendations for action. This is an informal meeting: no minutes, no names, nothing for the record, therefore no need to protect any backs, yours or anyone else's – got it? Good. Jim, why don't you bring us up to date?'

He sat back stiffly in his chair and lit a cigarette. Through the screen of smoke, he stared down the table at Kay. She caught his eye briefly and he looked away. One of the officers rose and stood in front of the map.

'Right, sir, I think it's fair to say we were all rather lulled into a false sense of security in October, when the parachute landings at Arnhem forced the Germans to pull the V2 launchers temporarily out of the area around The Hague. That put London out of range of the rockets, and all they could do was fire missiles at Norfolk, to little or no effect. Unfortunately, when Operation Market Garden failed, they were able to reoccupy the coastal strip here' – he gestured to the map – 'at the end of October, and as a result November has been the worst month by far.' He opened his file. 'We recorded a total of twelve V2s hitting Greater London in the first week of November, rising to thirty-five in the second week, twenty-seven in the third week, and so far we're looking at about forty for this week.

'Just to give you some idea of casualties over the past seven days: we had nine killed in East Ham in one incident on Monday; twenty dead on Tuesday in Walthamstow, Erith and Battersea; twenty-four dead in Bethnal Green on Wednesday, plus another six in Chislehurst about fifty minutes later; two dead on Thursday; nineteen dead on Friday; and then, unfortunately, yesterday – the worst incident so far – a hundred and sixty dead in Deptford, and another seven elsewhere. We're still getting information about today, but so far it's more than a dozen killed.'

A square-faced officer with thick black eyebrows raised his hand. 'Sorry to interrupt, Jim, but if we're speaking frankly, and at the risk of sounding like a brute, at Bomber Command we're probably killing ten times as many Germans as all of that in a single night. In strictly military terms the rockets are a bloody nuisance, but they're not going to be a decisive factor in the war.'

Templeton said, 'That may be true. But any day now, one of those things could hit the Houses of Parliament or Buckingham Palace or Number Ten Downing Street and we're powerless to stop them. We can't just tell people to grin and put up with it. They've had enough.'

'Yes,' continued the officer at the map, 'we did have an airburst above the Houses of Parliament on Sunday evening two weeks ago – that caused a panic at Victoria station. And the other side to this, sir, apart from the casualties, is homelessness. Because the missiles hit so fast, they create craters up to thirty feet deep and the blast damage can be pretty devastating for an entire neighbourhood.'

'How many buildings have been damaged so far, do we have any idea?'

'About five thousand houses have either been destroyed or will have to be demolished, sir. In total, about a hundred and fifty thousand buildings have been damaged.'

A murmur went round the table. He returned to his seat.

Templeton said, 'Have we really not been able to lay a finger on these bastards at all? How many sorties have we flown in the last couple of days?'

'The weather's kept us grounded for forty-eight hours, sir,' said one of the other officers. 'We did put up four Spitfires from Coltishall this morning.' He stood in front of the map. 'They crossed the coast here, at Egmond, turned south and flew down the Dutch coast to the Hook of Holland. Unfortunately, the cloud base was three thousand feet. Even when they dropped to two and a half thousand, there was still too much mist to see anything. As soon as they went back up to twenty thousand – sod's law – they saw a V2 rising straight up through the clouds, but of course' – he gestured helplessly – 'they had no idea where exactly it had come from.'

Jim said, 'What time was that, do you know?'

'Around ten thirty.'

He consulted his papers. 'Must have been the one that hit Rainham.'

'If they're firing forty a week, surely we should be able to locate at least one of these damned launch sites? Les?'

Starr said, 'It's not for want of trying, sir. I've brought along some of the coverage of the area, just to give you an idea of what we're up against.'

He nodded to Kay. She stood and went around the table, distributing the photographs. Mike took his without even glancing at her. She resumed her place, watched him studying the image, frowning, irritated, turning it this way and that. He ought to wear his glasses but he would never put them on. He hated to be reminded of the poor eyesight that had ended his flying career.

Starr said, 'It's very difficult, sir.'

'Sure, I can see it's difficult. Everything's difficult. Even so, this has to rank as one of the greatest failures of photographic intelligence of the entire war.'

Starr flushed. His mouth flapped open. 'I can assure you we're working on it day and night, sir.' He looked around in desperation. 'Section Officer Caton-Walsh has been going back over the coverage to see if anything was missed. Kay, you can confirm that this presents us with unique difficulty?'

She was aware of all the men turning to look at her. She was so surprised to be asked to speak, she didn't have time to feel nervous. 'Yes, sir. I believe it wasn't until late September, when the V2 testing range at Blizna in Poland was liberated by the Russians, that we discovered the rocket requires an area of only twenty square feet to launch from. That's about half the size of this table. It's impossible for us to find something that small if it's hidden in trees.'

Mike said sarcastically – looking at the photograph rather than her, as if he couldn't bear to address her directly – 'Yes, but they have to get the missiles into the trees in the first place, I assume?'

'They do, sir, but they must be bringing them in by rail at night. By the time it's light enough to fly a reconnaissance sortie, they've already transferred them into the woods.'

Now at last he looked at her. He gave a slight slow shake of his head, which seemed to her to convey several layers of meaning all at once – reluctant admiration for the ingenuity of the enemy, irritation at the uselessness of Medmenham, and underlying that a certain rueful amusement, meant for her alone, that they should find themselves having such an exchange. He turned to the man from Bomber Command. 'Can't we just flatten the woods?'

'Obviously we've looked at that, sir. Two big drawbacks. One, we'd probably have to go in daylight, and there are heavy flak defences in that area: our losses would be unacceptable. Two, it's very close to The Hague. If we bomb from eighteen thousand feet, which is as low as we dare go, there's a grave risk of heavy civilian casualties, and no guarantee at the end of it that we would have knocked out all the launchers.'

The air commodore sank back in his chair and put his hand to his bandaged forehead. He looked paler than at the start of the meeting. Even from her place at the end of the table, Kay could see that he was sweating. A silence ensued. And then a small man sitting opposite her raised his hand. He was in his fifties, a wing commander according to his insignia, but most unmilitary-looking, with thick spectacles, a toothbrush moustache and a snowfall of dandruff on his collar. He might have been a bank manager in civilian life. 'May I make a suggestion, sir?'

Templeton squinted at him. 'Yes, please do. I'm sorry – I don't think I know you.'

'Knowsley, sir. Clarence Knowsley. Home Defence, Fighter Command. The Filter Room? We have met.'

'All right. Go on.'

'If I may?' He went over to the map. 'Last Sunday, the Filter Room created a forward radar base on the Continent. We deployed three mobile GL Mark Two units and two of the new experimental Mark Three high-looking radars to Belgium – here, to be exact, around the town of Mechelen. That's within about seventy miles of the launch sites, which is as close to the front line as we can get. The area's only just been cleared of Germans. Because of its position, and the lack of hills, it gives us a perfect side-on view of the missile's trajectory. These new radars have cathode-ray direction-finding displays, so not only can we pick up the rockets once they reach an altitude of about thirty thousand feet, we can also record their flight path before they pass out of range.'

'And that helps us, does it?'

'It could do, sir. When this all started, we rather hoped the V2 would turn out to be guided by radio signals, which we might at least have been able to jam. The Germans obviously anticipated that. They don't use radio guidance. We believe the missile to be purely ballistic – that is to say, the engine shuts off and it follows a perfect arc, similar to if one throws a cricket ball from the outfield. And that is a potential weakness we might be able to exploit.'

He broke off, obviously unused to speaking at such length. The air commodore made an encouraging gesture. 'Go on.'

'Well, a ballistic arc is mathematically calculable. If we have data giving us the missile's trajectory at the moment it becomes ballistic, and if we have the precise point of impact, then it should be possible, in theory, to work backwards and calculate the spot on the boundary from which the cricket ball, so to speak, was thrown.'

The officers looked at each other. Templeton sat forward in his chair. 'That's quite an interesting notion. The question is: can we exploit it operationally?'

'Obviously we've been thinking hard about that. Essentially, it becomes a race against time to put the two halves of the data together. The first half, from the MRUs in Belgium, can start to be collated on site a minute or two after launch. The second half can be supplied from Stanmore as soon as Home Defence radar gives us the point of impact – that's about three minutes later. So for the sake of speed, the calculating needs to be done as close to the mobile radars as possible.' He turned to the officer from Fighter

Command operations. 'How long does it take to get a Spitfire off the runway at Coltishall and over the Dutch coast? Twenty-five minutes?'

'About that. Give or take.'

'So if the planes are scrambled as soon as a missile launches, and the point of impact is reported to Belgium as soon as the V2 hits, we'd have about twenty minutes to make the calculation, locate the rough area of the launch site and get the coordinates radioed to the pilots while they're over the North Sea. In theory, we could bomb the target, say, thirty-five to forty minutes after launching, while there are still men and vehicles on site.'

Templeton turned to his aide. 'Did you get all that?'

The flight lieutenant was still writing. 'Yes, sir.'

'What does everyone think? Is it feasible?'

With varying degrees of enthusiasm, the officers agreed it was.

Templeton said, 'It gives us a chance, at least. And in the absence of any other options, it's certainly worth a try. Good. Let's start tomorrow.'

Knowsley looked alarmed. 'I'm not sure we can start as soon as that, sir.'

'Why not? You said yourself we have the radar units in place. And we have 303 Squadron at Coltishall. The pilots are familiar with that area of Holland.'

'We still need the personnel in Belgium to make the calculations.'

'Are the calculations difficult?'

'It's fairly sophisticated algebra. It requires an ability to use a slide rule, for a start. I've pulled a few girls out of the Filter Room and started training them – with somewhat mixed results, I have to admit.'

'How many do you need?'

'For round-the-clock coverage, to begin with, at least eight.'

'Come on, Wing Commander! There are a hundred and eighty thousand WAAFs in the country! It has to be possible to rustle up eight capable of using a slide rule by tomorrow, surely?'

Knowsley was more stubborn than he looked. 'It's a demanding job, sir – working under extreme time pressure, putting pilots' lives at risk, without any room to make an error.'

Templeton said, 'I don't care how you do it, but I intend to go to my office straight away and telephone the Secretary of State to tell him that we have finally come up with a plan that might just work, and that we'll have eight WAAFs on a plane to Belgium tomorrow. Is that clear?'

If Knowsley was minded to debate the issue further, he clearly thought better of it. 'Yes, sir.'

'Good. I'll leave you gentlemen to sort out the details.' Templeton gestured to the flight lieutenant, who retrieved his crutches from the corner and gave him his arm to help him stand. He looked completely done in, thought Kay as he hobbled past her, his eyes fixed straight ahead, his jaw clamped to contain the pain, his face damp and clammy-looking.

After he had been gone for a minute, and the others had started talking – 'Well, Clarence, you've really landed yourself in it now' – she got to her feet. Ignoring Starr – 'Kay, where are you going?' – she slipped out of the room, closing the door behind her.

She looked up and down the long, deserted corridor, uncertain which direction to choose. Suddenly the door to her right opened and the flight lieutenant emerged. He nodded briefly to her and walked away. She waited until he had disappeared around the corner, then stepped quickly to the office, knocked, and without waiting for a reply went in.

He was sitting behind his desk with his back to the window, a telephone in front of him, sipping what looked like a glass of whisky. It was growing dark outside. The room was filled with shadows. A lamp in the corner provided the only light. She could barely make out his face. She moved a little closer but stopped well short of his desk. He looked at her over the rim of his glass and sighed.

'Well that was pretty bloody. I'm sorry. Drink?'

She shook her head. 'How are you feeling?'

'A bit rough, but I'll mend.'

'Where's Mary?'

'Gone back to Bletchley.'

'So you're on your own? Where will you stay?'

'The ministry's got me a hotel somewhere.' He put down his glass. 'Look, Kay, do you mind? I'm not sure I can face this conversation right now. I've got a splitting headache and Downing Street's about to call.'

'Don't worry. I haven't come to make a scene. I just want to ask you for a favour.'

'Which is what?'

'After everything that's happened, I can't just go on sitting in the countryside looking at photographs – I need to **do** something.'

'It's important work, Kay.'

'I know it is. But it isn't the real war, is it? I'm good at maths. I know how to use a slide rule. Tell Wing Commander Starr you want him to let me join this unit in Belgium.'

He jerked his head back slightly in surprise. 'He'll never buy it.'

'Yes, he will – he will if you order him.'

'He'll say you're too valuable to lose.'

'Tell him it's only temporary, while they train up more WAAFs in England. Please, Mike – this may be my last chance to make a real difference. Besides,' she added, playing what she knew to be her trump card, 'wouldn't it be easier for you if I were out of the country?'

'Of course not.' But she could tell he was tempted as soon as he added, rather more weakly, 'That's entirely beside the point.'

Before she could reply, his telephone began to ring. In the quietness of the twilit office, the clamour sounded unnaturally loud. He studied it warily for a moment, flexed his fingers, then picked up the receiver and placed it carefully to his ear.

'Templeton.' He listened for a moment. She could hear the tinny, urgent jabber at the other end. He nodded. 'Very good. Thank you for letting me know.' He hung up. 'That was Stanmore. A V2 just hit north-east London. And then there were nine . . .' He looked at her briefly, then gazed out of the window. 'All right. Leave it with me. I'll have a word with Les, see what I can do.'

'Thank you.'

He called after her when she reached the door: 'Look after yourself, Kay.'

She didn't turn round. I am a stranger to him, she thought, just as he is to me.

The telephone started to ring again.

'Templeton . . . Good evening, sir . . .'

She closed the door quietly behind her.

7

AFTER TWENTY HOURS ON DUTY, Graf had lost track of time. His world had shrunk to testing bays and firing control vehicles, the smell of high-octane fuel and damp vegetation, the dripping silence of the woods punctuated by the pulverising roar of the launches. Occasionally he managed to find a quiet spot in the cab of an empty truck, or – as now – on a pile of discarded tarpaulins in the corner of a tent, and doze for a few minutes, but it was never long before he was shaken awake or heard his name being shouted.

'Dr Graf! They're ready to launch at site seventy-two!'

He opened his eyes to find a Wehrmacht motorcyclist bending over him.

'What time is it?'

'Just before nine, Doctor.'

'Morning or night?'

'Night.'

'Night. Of course.' He pushed himself to his feet and stumbled after the soldier, out of the tent and into the clearing.

Beneath the trees, the shadowed figures of the technical troops, with their headband lamps and flashlights, toiled like Nibelung. So much activity! The darkness was filled with their mysterious hammerings and shouts. The revving of engines was underscored by the continuous, monotonous throb of the generators. In one tent, its flaps drawn back, a pair of technicians bent over a prone missile linked by cables to a monitor. Further on, a rocket was having its nose cone bolted onto the end of its fuselage; the cylindrical plywood cover that had protected the warhead was being manhandled away by a couple of soldiers. Two missiles had failed their diagnostic tests and were being hooked up to tractors to be sent back to the engine shed at Scheveningen. Others awaited their turn for inspection, parked up on their trailers beside the lane. The big mobile erectors, the Meillerwagens, trundled back and forth between the field stores and the launch sites, churning up the ground. As soon as a rocket had been lowered onto its launch table, the tankers and bowsers closed in to begin the fuelling, and once the missile had been checked, the Meillerwagen returned to the technical stores to collect another.

Graf clambered into the motorcycle sidecar, stretched out his legs and grabbed the safety handles. The cyclist pulled down his goggles and kick-started the engine. They bounced over the grass and onto the road.

Number 72 was one of the launch sites furthest from the technical stores – beyond the Duindigt racetrack, in a wood on the outskirts of Wassenaar, quite close to the sea. The motorcycle flew along the highway and turned left, and was waved through the checkpoint. The beam of its headlamp played across the iron gates of the big empty villas; the houses thinned out, they crossed a field and then they were into trees again. It felt much wilder and more remote than the park-like forests around Scheveningen. In the fresh air, Graf felt his energy revive. They jolted to a stop.

The rocket, standing solitary on its launch table, was hard to make out. The brown and green stripes of its camouflage dissolved its sharp lines into the surrounding firs. Graf shone his flashlight from the tail fins up to the control compartments, across the umbilical cable to the electrical mast and down again. In their anxiety to launch a dozen missiles in a single day, he was sure the technical crews were rushing the test procedures. The launch had been delayed by another transformer failure. The part had been replaced. But there was no way of telling for sure if the avionics were functioning properly. Still, what could he do? He turned towards the firing control wagon and raised his arm. At 9.05 p.m., for the tenth time that Sunday, the discordant note of the klaxon brayed like a hunting horn around the woods.

He directed his torch beam onto the ground and made his way through the undergrowth to the slit trenches where the firing platoon were sheltering. The men shifted along to make room for him. He jumped down and shone his torch back in the direction of the V2, checking it once again, even though he knew it was pointless. A slight mist was rising from the forest floor, carrying a fragrance of wet earth and decomposing vegetation. The shape of a man appeared and seemed to wade through it, a cheerful voice said, 'Move along, Doctor!' and Lieutenant Seidel, the commander of the second battalion, slithered heavily down into the trench beside him.

'You sound happy.'

'Sturmscharführer Biwack is happy. Therefore the colonel is happy. Therefore I am happy. Therefore you should be happy too.'

'I'm never happy before a launch.'

'Nor afterwards, that I can see.'

The countdown started over the loudspeaker. Graf braced himself.

First the brilliant light that lit up the forest. Then the hot wind that seared his face. Twigs and leaves and loose earth whipped across the trench. He ducked and covered his head and felt a shower of debris patter across his arms and shoulders. He couldn't hear or think about anything except the roar of the rocket. The ground shook. The pitch of the noise deepened. With a tearing sound the missile shot skywards. Immediately the men all stood to watch,

Graf included. It was against the safety regulations to expose one's upper body until the all-clear was sounded, but everyone ignored them. He glanced briefly along the trench. In the reddish glare of the exhaust, the upturned faces were softened by a kind of childish wonder. Then abruptly the light was extinguished and the forest was darker than before.

'Ten gone,' said Seidel, in a tone of deep satisfaction. 'Two to go.'

'He really means to fire all twelve?'

'That was what he promised Biwack.' Seidel shone his torch on his wristwatch. 'But it'll be a while before the next one. Stock's battalion haven't started fuelling yet. It's quite a feat, I have to say. Did you ever expect to fire so many birds at the British in a single day?'

'Honestly, Seidel? I never expected to fire any.'

Graf clambered out of the slit trench and brushed the dirt from his coat. He picked his way through the vegetation back to the launch site. The stench of burned fuel turned his stomach. Here and there the undergrowth was smouldering. Small fringes of orange fire crept across the ivy. He stamped them out with his foot. He felt a sudden surge of self-disgust. He walked across the clearing to the other side and set off along the path into the woods. As soon as he was far enough away, he stopped and lit a cigarette and inspected his shaking hands. It took a few deep draughts of nicotine for his nerves to settle. He looked around him. The evening was cold and still, with a strong tang of pine and just enough of a moon to silhouette the tops of the trees against the sky. Behind him the platoon had already started dismantling the firing platform.

He listened to the silence. From somewhere nearby came a faint whispering sound, an indistinct rustle. On impulse, he started to walk towards it, picking his way along the track for a few minutes. The rustle grew louder, the forest thinned and he found himself climbing sand dunes, his shoes sinking into the soft ground. He pushed on to the top.

A fence of thickly coiled barbed wire barred access to the beach. A sign with a skull and crossbones dangled from it. **Achtung! Minen!** The low tide had exposed a wide, flat stretch of sand. Shallow pools reflected the moonlight. The rows of angled metal stakes that were supposed to stop the enemy's landing craft cast sharp shadows. Out at sea, the waves formed luminous soft lines of white.

He sat on one of the grassy dunes and lit another cigarette. The past, so long and so successfully held at bay, came flooding over the beach towards him.

I have spent the last ten years of my life by the side of the sea, he thought, always with the smell of pine in my nostrils and the taste of salt in my mouth, listening to the seagulls and straining my eyes at a wide sky.

They had set off in a convoy of trucks and cars from Kummersdorf just before dawn. That had been the first time: December 1934. So, yes – ten years, more or less exactly. He remembered he had sat in the cab of the lead truck, sandwiched between the driver and von Braun. Stowed in crates behind them were a pair of small rockets, just 160 centimetres long, officially known as Aggregate-2, but named Max and Moritz by the team, after the two naughty little boys in the stories they had all read as children. They were too powerful to be given their first test flights anywhere near a town, so they had to be taken to the seaside. What a lark! Even in the middle of winter, the whole expedition had had a holiday feel.

This was six months after Graf had joined the team at Kummersdorf, and he was lucky to still be alive. In July, Kurt Wahmke, a young physicist whose doctoral thesis had been on the outflow of gases through cylindrical nozzles, had decided to test his theory that they could dispense with mixing alcohol and liquid oxygen and could fuel the rocket much more simply instead with a ninety per cent concentration of hydrogen peroxide. On the day of the test, Wahmke had telephoned the mess to warn them there might be an explosion, in which case would they send help? Then he and Graf had smoked a cigarette in the company of two technicians. The pale blue hydrogen peroxide was suspended in a tank above the rocket motor, linked to it by a single pipe. They had stubbed out their cigarettes, opened the fuel line, and Wahmke had held a burning tin of kerosene to the nozzle. What had they been thinking?

The flame had shot straight up the pipe and blown up the tank. Graf had been the only one who had reacted quickly enough, flinging himself headlong behind the concrete wall. The charred corpses of the other three had stayed in his mind for weeks, the smell of roasted flesh seeming to clog his nostrils, although von Braun had viewed the remains with equanimity. His main concern had been that the test stand was destroyed. He was always able to take other people's tragedies in his stride. That was the mark of a leader, Graf supposed.

But poor Wahmke was already in the past, dead and buried – what was left of him – never to be mentioned again, certainly not during the long day's drive from Berlin to Emden carrying Max and Moritz. They spent the night in the port and the next day took a boat to the North Sea island of Borkum, about thirty kilometres offshore. It had been a horrible crossing in a high wind, and Graf had spent much of it crouched below decks, throwing up. Von Braun, needless to say, the Aryan Superman, was not only a proficient horse rider, pilot, concert-standard cellist, et cetera, but also an accomplished sailor. He spent the voyage on the bridge. Apart from a couple of dozen soldiers, there were five engineers in the Party as Graf remembered it: himself and von Braun; Walter Riedel (not to be confused with Klaus Riedel), whom they all called 'Papa' on account of his sedate manner; Heini Grünow, the mechanic from the Rocket Aerodrome; and Arthur Rudolph, an expert in jet propulsion from the Heylandt works, who had been with the racing driver Max Valier on the evening he was killed by an exploding motor. Rudolph was the only one of them who was a Nazi.

They installed themselves in a hotel on the beach and sat on uncomfortable cane furniture in a chilly, brine-streaked glass-enclosed veranda looking out at just such a view as this. They listened to the gale whistling around the gabled roof and waited for it to die away. And waited, and waited. That was Graf's first experience of winter on the northern European coast, when you might see seven hours of daylight if you were lucky. They stuck mostly indoors and scanned the monotonous grey vista for any signs that the weather might break. They played chess and bridge. They discussed space flight. They listened to von Braun's ideas for a two-stage rocket – the first stage to carry its captain beyond the earth's atmosphere and into orbit, the second stage with a booster to propel him to the moon or Mars: 'The vacuum of space will mean that only a relatively small amount of power will be required.' He showed them his calculations. When he claimed that the first man to walk on the moon had already been born, it was obvious he meant himself. Finally, over dinner on 18 December 1934, after a week of waiting and with Christmas approaching, he announced that they would launch Max the next day, whatever the weather; if it failed, they always had Moritz as a backup.

The morning of the 19th dawned clear and

blustery: cloud base 1,200 metres, wind from the east, gusts up to 80 kph. For the sake of secrecy, the local people, mostly fishermen and their families, were ordered to stay indoors and keep their curtains closed. Soldiers were posted to make sure they obeyed. The engineers carried Max to the dunes and erected the launch mast, connected the electrical cables to the measuring equipment, checked the gyroscopes and filled the fuel tanks with alcohol, liquid oxygen and compressed nitrogen. Graf took charge of the movie camera. He had to keep wiping sand from the lens. They waited for a lull in the wind, then von Braun lit the tin of kerosene at the end of the broom handle and applied it to the nozzle. There was a crack of thunder as the jet ignited, and Max shot upwards – up and up and up: they had to tilt their heads right back to follow him, until his exhaust flame had shrunk to a tiny red dot. He reached an altitude, they later calculated, of 1,700 metres – the greatest height ever achieved by such a rocket – before his fuel burned out and they watched him plunge silently into the sand about a kilometre away.

They whooped and hollered, pounded one another on the back and danced around the beach like wild men, even Papa Riedel. That night when they stood on the covered veranda looking out to sea, von Braun proposed a toast: 'Is it my imagination, gentlemen, or does the moon look closer tonight than she did this morning?' He turned to Graf and clinked his glass. 'To the moon!'

'To the moon!'

They were twenty-two years old.

When they got back to Kummersdorf in the new year of 1935, Graf spliced together the footage of the Borkum test and von Braun started hawking it around Berlin. He might have been made for the age in which they now lived. Aristocratic yet not at all snobbish, charming yet with an infallible command of technical detail, here was the embodiment of the New German spirit! Here was a prophet of the future! It was their great good fortune to have flown a rocket to a height of almost two kilometres just at the very moment that the resources of the German economy, on the Führer's orders, were being diverted to the military on an unprecedented scale. The army kicked in half a million marks immediately, enough for them to build two new test stands. The Luftwaffe offered him five million even before he had finished his presentation. When the commander-in-chief of the army came out to Kummersdorf to watch a firing, he turned to von Braun and simply asked him, 'How much do you want?'

How much did he want? What a question! He wanted enough to build a rocket city, exactly like the one in Fritz Lang's movie. He wanted something like Borkum, only bigger – a place on the coast, far from prying eyes, where a dedicated group of scientists and dreamers, drawing on unlimited resources, could safely fire their rockets undisturbed over ranges of hundreds of kilometres. That was what he wanted.

One of the Gestapo men who had interrogated Graf seemed much angrier than his partner. It was more than just a good cop/bad cop routine: Graf had the feeling that if it had been left up to this other man, the sessions would have involved fists and truncheons. Perhaps he had lost someone on the Eastern Front – frozen to death in the winter of 1941–2, or captured due to a lack of adequate equipment – because at one point he jumped up and pounded on the table.

You're all just a bunch of traitors! This 'army research centre' at Peenemünde is the biggest swindle in German history!

Graf replied that he had nothing to do with the decision to build the facility at Peenemünde. It was a matter far above his head.

The other Gestapo man consulted his thick file. **And yet according to Professor von Braun, you accompanied him on his original visit to the site?**

I went with him, certainly. Nothing more than that.

When was this exactly?

Graf pretended to think. They must have it all in the file. The whole thing was a charade.

I believe it was just after Christmas 1935.

In truth he remembered it very clearly. They had spent much of the previous year designing and building a new motor that produced over 3,000 pounds of thrust for a much bigger rocket – seven metres long, the Aggregate-3 – and he had been invited to spend part of the holiday on the von Braun estate in Silesia to continue working. The baron had lost his position as Minister of Agriculture as soon as Hitler came to power and had retreated to this ugly grey barrack-like building, simultaneously appalled at the vulgarity and violence of the Nazis and privately impressed by their results. His brilliant son's continuing obsession with rockets bewildered him. It did not seem an entirely appropriate occupation for a gentleman. He treated Graf with cool politeness – not the kind of person with whom he was used to associating; another symptom of the modern age to which he was too old to adjust.

One evening after supper, sitting in front of the fire, Wernher mentioned that he was looking for somewhere quiet and out-of-the-way on the coast to erect his rocket city. He had found the perfect spot on the Baltic island of Rügen. Unfortunately, the Strength Through Joy organisation had beaten him to it and were building a holiday resort for the Labour Front. 'But I know just the place,' his mother announced suddenly, looking up from her tapestry. 'It's right next to Rügen. Your grandpapa used to go duck-hunting there every winter. What was it called, Magnus?'

The old baron removed his cigar and grunted. 'Peenemünde.'

That was the first time Graf heard the name.

And so for the second time, he found himself heading north, this time just the two of them, in von Braun's new car. They stopped off overnight at Carmzow, near Stettin, at the ancestral home of von Braun's mother's family, the von Quistorps – a far grander property – and continued the next day for about fifty kilometres through the flat Pomeranian countryside until they crossed a bridge that spanned the narrow straits to the island of Usedom. For ten minutes or so the road curved through woods and marshland and ran along a narrow spit, with water sparkling on either side, taking them past pretty little fishing villages painted pink and yellow and pale blue, until at last it dwindled into a forest track at the northern tip of the island. They parked the car and completed the journey on foot.

That morning remained imprinted on Graf's mind as a visit to paradise before the Fall – ancient oaks and hundred-foot Scots pines, dunes and peat bogs, white sandy beaches with reed beds; silent, immemorial, not a human to be seen, only swans and ducks, warblers and cormorants, streams with otters, and immense Pomeranian deer crowned by dark antlers wandering among the heather, placid and unafraid. It took more than an hour to clamber along the coast to the point where the mouth of the river Peene opened out to the Oder Lagoon. Von Braun, the winter sun on his broad face and his blond hair blowing in the sea breeze, flung out his arms to embrace it all. 'This is fantastic, no?' He started gesturing to where everything could go, abolishing nature with a sweep of his hand. He saw test stands in the forest and launch pads on the foreshore; on the grasslands there would be workshops and laboratories, a factory to manufacture the rockets, chemical plants to make the methyl alcohol and liquid oxygen, a power station, an airfield where they could work on jet engines for the Luftwaffe, a railway station, a model town for the workforce.

'But you would need to bring thousands of people up here,' Graf objected. He couldn't help laughing. It sounded so absurd, like one of their boyhood fantasies. 'Who on earth would pay for such a place?'

'Oh, they will pay for it.'

'They?'

'Our masters in uniform. Believe me, they have so much money for rearmament right now, they don't know what to do with it. They're falling over themselves to spend it.'

'Come on! The costs would be unbelievable.'

'Don't worry about it. You'll see. I'll promise them such a weapon they won't be able to resist it.'

On their return to Kummersdorf, von Braun had sat down with Papa Riedel and the head of weapons development, Colonel Dornberger, to start sketching out the most advanced ballistic missile that might be technologically feasible based upon what they had achieved so far. Graf had always got on well with Dornberger. He was a congenial artillery veteran of about forty, clever enough and ambitious, whose obsession was the Paris gun that had shelled the French capital in the Great War. Von Braun played him as skilfully as he played his cello – flattering him, sometimes deferring to him, always allowing the older man to feel he was in control. Between them they came up with the specifications for a workable weapon: one that could be transported intact on a railway wagon to wherever it was required. The need for mobility limited its size to less than fifteen metres. Even so, it would be capable of carrying a one-ton warhead of either high explosive or poison gas over a distance of 275 kilometres. To accomplish this, Riedel calculated, would require a motor capable of developing twenty-five tons of thrust – seventeen times more powerful than anything they had achieved before. This would be Aggregate-4.

One morning at the beginning of April, Dornberger and von Braun were driven to the Air Ministry in Berlin to present their plans to General Kesselring of the Luftwaffe. Graf watched them go, sitting together in the back of the Mercedes with their briefcases on their laps like a couple of salesmen. He didn't know what was said, but by lunchtime, a Luftwaffe staff officer was in a fast car to Usedom, and by nightfall, the Air Ministry had rung Dornberger to say the deal was done: the Peenemünde site had been bought from the local council for three quarters of a million marks and the Luftwaffe would pay half the costs of construction.

The whole thing had an element of madness from the start. Indeed, there were a couple of times during his interrogation in Stettin when Graf had been tempted to throw up his hands and simply confess what he believed: that von Braun hadn't created Peenemünde in order to build a weapon so much as created a weapon in order to build Peenemünde. The audacity of it – the **risks** of it – was dizzying.

It wasn't until the third day that they finally asked him the question they had been leading up to all along.

Did you or did you not, on the evening of Sunday 17 October 1943, at a beach party in Zinnowitz, in the company of Professor von Braun, Dr Helmut Gröttrup and Dr Klaus Riedel, state that the war was lost, the rocket would not save Germany, and your aim all along had been to build a spaceship?

In the second or so that followed, even as his throat constricted and his heart seemed to hollow, his engineer's brain tried to work through every possible option to find the safest reply. What had the others said? If this, then that; if that, then this . . .

Gentlemen, I don't recall saying any such thing. I think there must be some mistake . . .

Listen to me, Rudi. This is the absolute truth. The road to the moon runs through Kummersdorf.

No, my dear Wernher, for all your genius, the road from Kummersdorf has not led us to the moon. It has led us precisely here.

He heard a noise behind him. His joints had stiffened in the cold. He stood and turned awkwardly.

Someone was coming up the track through the forest. Torches flashed between the trees. A dog barked. First one SS guard appeared, his gun aimed from his shoulder, then another, and finally the dog handler with a big German shepherd straining at its leash. Graf raised his hands. A torch shone straight into his face, blinding him. He tried to shield his eyes.

One of the shadowy figures shouted, 'Don't move!'

'I'm Dr Graf. I have authorisation.' He flinched and turned his head away. 'Can you get that thing out of my eyes?'

A second SS man said, 'It's the civilian from Peenemünde, Sturmmann. Don't you recognise him?'

'Yes, I know him. Papers!'

Wearily Graf reached into his inside pocket. 'If you recognise me, why do you need my papers?'

In the distance, a klaxon sounded.

He handed over his pass. 'That's a launch. I ought to be there.'

'Then what are you doing here?'

'Just get on and check it, will you?' He glanced into the trees as the guard went through the laborious process of shouldering his gun, transferring his flashlight to his other hand and directing it onto Graf's identification. Sensing Graf's impatience, he took his time.

'I asked you a question, Doctor: what you are doing in a restricted area?'

The boom of the V2's first-stage ignition rolled

across the forest. Graf swivelled in the direction of the sound. The SS men followed suit. It was impossible to say how far away the launch site was. A glowing hemisphere appeared in the darkness, lighting the pointed tips of the firs so that they seemed to extend like a sea in moonlight. Above them, a column of fire ascended slowly. It reached a height of perhaps fifty metres, then stalled. For several seconds it hovered, pulsing red and blue, before appearing to drift sideways. Still vertical, it slowly subsided on a diagonal line and disappeared out of sight. The wood lit up with the brilliance of a summer's day. Moments later came a roar as the fuel tanks exploded.

No one spoke, or made a sound – at least that was how Graf remembered it – and then he came out of his trance and pushed his way past the SS men, scrambled down the sandy track and started running through the trees.

He ran for a couple of minutes until he could see the fireball up ahead. **Not the warhead,** he prayed, **not the warhead.** Men were shouting. Figures were moving to and fro. He wanted to shout at them to keep back, but he was too far away. Behind him the SS guards were crashing through the undergrowth, almost on his heels. The dog was barking. One of them was blowing on a whistle – an action as pointless as it was irritating. He was just about to turn and tell him to shut up when the trees bent towards him and he ran head first into what felt like a wall of earth. It filled his mouth and eyes. The ground dropped away beneath his feet. He trod air. His arms flailed in panic. His back struck something hard.

When he opened his eyes again, the trees around him were on fire. Burning leaves and paper floated in the smoke. He crawled on his knees, then pulled himself up and staggered through the blasted trees towards the smouldering crater. Just before he reached it, the dog trotted past him, proudly carrying something in its mouth that only afterwards he realised was a hand.

8

IN THE GROUNDS OF DANESFIELD House, in the dormitory at the far end of the hooped metal Nissen hut, Sunday night turned into Monday morning to the accompaniment of nothing more noisy than a murmuring of snores. Of the four women, only Kay was awake – lying on her side, studying the luminous green markings of her travel clock with such concentration she convinced herself she could see the big hand edging forward with infinitesimal slowness.

Beside the softly ticking clock, on the chair that served as a nightstand, lay the papers that were to be her passport out of this place. The first affirmed that WAAF Section Officer A. V. Caton-Walsh of the Central Interpretation Unit, RAF Medmenham, had been temporarily reassigned to 33 Wing, 2nd Tactical Air Force, the transfer having been requested by Wing Commander C. R. Knowsley, approved by her commanding officer, Wing Commander L. P. Starr, and authorised by Air Commodore

M. S. Templeton, DFC. Attached to this chit by a paper clip was a second document: a crudely typed and duplicated movement order directing her to report to RAF Northolt by 0900 hours the next day. The rows of dots left empty for name, rank and serial number had been filled in by a careless hand in an indecipherable scrawl of blue ink.

She wondered how much aggravation it had cost Mike to pull rank and do her this favour – quite a bit, to judge by the way Starr had marched past her while she was sitting in the lobby of the Air Ministry and driven off without offering her a lift back to Danesfield House. Wing Commander Knowsley, lost in thought, had also ignored her. The bushy-browed officer from Bomber Command had given her a knowing wink. Finally, when the flight lieutenant who served as Mike's aide had descended the stairs half an hour later to hand over her orders – 'The Air Commodore asked me to give you this' – his manner had been one of cold distaste, like a footman sent down by his master to pay off a tart.

Word of this would spread, she thought. Starr would see to that. She wanted very much to leave before the others were awake, but she didn't dare set the alarm in case she disturbed them. She rolled onto her back and dozed through the night, occasionally hearing the cry of a waterfowl on the Thames or the hooting of the owls in the big elms. When she checked the clock for what felt like the twentieth time and saw that it was nearly six, she finally decided to risk it. She eased herself out from beneath her blanket and struck a match. The rasp sounded to her as loud as a gunshot. She lit a candle.

She had gone to bed half dressed. It took her only a couple of minutes to put on her skirt and jacket. She sat on the edge of the mattress and squeezed her stockinged feet into her shoes. The floorboard creaked. Someone stirred. A voice in the wavering shadows cast by the candle whispered, 'What are you doing?'

It was Shirley Locke – inevitably.

Kay whispered, 'Going to the loo.'

'Why are you dressed?'

'Never mind. Go back to sleep.'

She finished tying her laces, stood and put on her cap. Her suitcase was already packed. She shrugged on her heavy coat, closed the travel clock and slipped it into her pocket along with her papers.

'Are you eloping?'

'Don't be silly.'

She collected the candle, picked up her suitcase and fumbled with the door handle.

'When will you be back?'

'I'm not sure. Go to sleep.' She felt unexpectedly tearful at the thought of sneaking away from her friends like this after more than two years. 'Will you say goodbye to everyone for me? Give them my best?'

'Kay—'

She closed the door. By the light of the candle, she made her way along the passage to the far end of the hut and out into the morning. A cold gust of wind flattened the flame and blew it out. She threw away the candle and set off along the path.

The blackout at Medmenham was still strictly enforced, even though no German bomber had encroached anywhere near Marlow for years. The great house was entirely dark. It was impossible to imagine that behind its heavy curtains, at that moment, a hundred people were working.

She walked with her suitcase in her hand up the middle of the gravel drive, between the black masses of the rhododendrons, towards the guardhouse, conscious of a certain absurdity in heading off to war in such a fashion. Despite her years in the WAAF, she had never so much as sat in an aircraft, let alone flown in one. She hadn't even been abroad, not properly – not unless one counted a school trip to Paris in 1937. And yet precisely for that reason, she felt a great sense of exhilaration, as if she were breaking out of prison. After all, what had her life consisted of up to now? A sheltered Dorset village of ancient golden-stoned houses, a thatched cottage shared with her mother and her younger sister, the teaching nuns of Our Lady's Convent, a single-sex Cambridge college and then the seclusion of Danesfield House.

At twenty-four, she had only had one lover apart from Mike – a pilot her own age she had met during a Phase One debrief at RAF Benson, a relationship that had barely lasted a month before he was posted to Scotland. They had both been virgins. In some ways he was even younger than she was. But his descriptions of his solo reconnaissance sorties in an unheated Spitfire – swaddled in two sweaters, a leather flying jacket, two pairs of socks and a double layer of gloves; climbing alone over the North Sea through the tropopause into the dark blue stratosphere, where the temperature was minus seventy; the frost crystals forming on the Perspex canopy and the icicles in the tiny cockpit glinting in the brilliant sunlight; his terror that his oxygen might fail and he might pass out; switching on his camera and circling in the thin air eight miles above Berlin (so high that he could see the Baltic coast and the curvature of the earth) – his experiences of life were so far beyond anything she could imagine, she could not help comparing his existence ruefully to the littleness of her own.

At the main gate, a Bedford van was waiting, its engine running, the heater turned up full blast. The man behind the wheel was drinking from a thermos flask. She said, 'Are you waiting for me?'

The corporal in the guardhouse the night before had checked his rota and said he was sure he could fix up a lift for her: a driver had to make an early-morning delivery to Bomber Command HQ at High Wycombe before going on to the Air Ministry. 'He'll drop you off at Northolt in time, ma'am, no trouble.'

'Yes, ma'am. Morning. Hop in.'

He was middle-aged, Cockney, cheerful. She could barely make out his face. He cleared a space on the seat beside him. 'Tea?'

'That would be very kind.'

He refilled the cup. She resisted a prissy urge to wipe the rim. It didn't taste much like tea. It was weak and sickly with saccharine and made with dried milk. But she was grateful for it, and when he offered her a cigarette, she took that too, even though she didn't really smoke. She sat with her suitcase balanced on her knees, trying not to cough, staring through the windscreen at the empty road as the van climbed, gearbox grinding, through the woods towards High Wycombe. He talked away and she pretended to listen. 'That's right,' she said. 'Absolutely.' It was like being in a London taxi. She finished the cigarette, wound down the window and threw it out. Ten minutes later, they drove into the fake Buckinghamshire hamlet that concealed the headquarters of Bomber Command, with its mock manor house and make-believe church steeple. 'Just give me a mo,' he said.

She waited while he delivered a box of photographs. In the darkness she could just make out the building where she had briefed the planners about Peenemünde the previous summer. They had built a scale model based on her analysis of the photographs – the power station and the liquid oxygen plant on the west of the island, the main test firing area and the experimental workshops and factory to the east. They had been particularly interested in the housing estate, with its school and meeting hall, and the barracks, and when she had asked why, a solemn young man who reminded her of a curate had said that they planned to attack in the early hours of the morning, when the scientists and technicians would still be asleep, so that they could kill as many as possible: 'It's the personnel we're after as much as the facilities.'

The raid had been mounted on the night of the August full moon. At Medmenham they had been alerted an hour before the air fleet took off – six hundred heavy bombers, more than four thousand aircrew, two thousand tons of high explosive. None of the airmen was given the true reason for attacking an objective of which they had never heard. She had sat by the Thames as the sun went down and the moon rose and had imagined the Lancasters streaming out across the North Sea in tight formation. Mike had told her later that forty planes had never made it back. When Dorothy Garrod's section had analysed the post-raid reconnaissance photographs the following day, many of the test facilities were disappointingly unscathed, but the roofless houses and dormitories appeared through Kay's viewfinder like the ruins of Pompeii.

The driver returned from his errand. She closed her eyes and pretended to fall asleep to discourage his conversation, but after a few minutes the pretence became a reality and she didn't wake up until the van came to a sudden halt and she heard voices. She opened her eyes.

A day of sorts had dawned, it seemed reluctantly, over straggling suburban fields. Beyond the high chain-link fence, in the grey light, she could make out the shapes of aircraft hangars and a control tower. Behind them, on Western Avenue, a drone of morning traffic headed into London. The driver had his window down and was talking to an RAF policeman holding a clipboard. The policeman leaned into the cab and asked for Kay's papers. She passed them across. He studied them and flipped over a few sheets on his clipboard. It all seemed to take a long while – too long – and it occurred to her that even at this last minute, the ponderous bureaucracy of the Air Ministry could thwart her.

'That's fine, ma'am.' He handed back the papers. 'I'll take you over.'

'Thanks for the lift,' she said to the driver. 'And the tea. And the cigarette.'

She climbed out of the van and followed the policeman through the gate and onto the airbase. She had never been to Northolt before, but it felt very much like Benson – the same steady breeze across the wide flat space, the sweet pervasive smell of aviation fuel, the ugly and impersonal low buildings, a sense of transience made permanent, the distinctive cracking sound of the Spitfires taking off and landing. After the talkative Cockney driver, the policeman was mercifully taciturn. He led her round the back of the administration block, past bare flower beds separated off from the cinder path by whitewashed stones, through a narrow door and along a dark corridor to a waiting room with wooden chairs around the bare walls and a steel-framed window beside a door opening onto a concrete apron. Ground crew were fuelling a big twin-engine transport plane. She recognised it from the identification chart at Medmenham. A Dakota. In the distance, a dozen Spitfires were parked in a line.

She stood at the window watching the preparations. A Morris 8 staff car appeared, painted in the RAF's drab grey-blue, drove along the edge of the apron and parked in front of the plane. Out of the rear seat clambered the bank-manager figure of Wing Commander Knowsley. He contemplated the Dakota and tugged nervously at his tunic to straighten it. From the other side came a tall, thin middle-aged woman in WAAF uniform with the twin stripes of a flight officer on her sleeve – one rank up from Kay's. The driver began to empty the boot of wooden boxes and a couple of long tubes that looked like rolled charts. A bus rattled to a halt behind the Morris. A red-faced WAAF sergeant emerged, followed by half a dozen others, jolly-looking women in their twenties carrying their suitcases. After them came the section officers. Kay counted seven in all. She studied them uneasily. She had never been good at joining in with a gang, especially not one that had already formed. Something about the way they were laughing together reminded her of a school lacrosse team at an away match. She picked up her suitcase and went out onto the apron.

No one paid her any attention. The WAAFs were

already lining up to board the plane. The thin flight officer was supervising the ground crew, who were loading the boxes into the tail section. Knowsley had his back to her, talking to the pilot. She waited till his conversation ended.

'Wing Commander?'

He turned and peered in puzzlement through his thick spectacles.

She saluted. 'Section Officer Caton-Walsh, sir.'

Recognition spread across his face. 'Yes, of course. You were at the Air Ministry.' He returned her salute. 'Cicely!' he called to the flight officer. 'This is your new recruit.' The woman looked irritated at being interrupted. She came over, frowning. Kay saluted her. She had a hard, humourless, clever face. Knowsley said to Kay, 'Flight Officer Sitwell is our scientific observer. This is Section Officer Caton-Walsh from Medmenham.'

The woman ran a sceptical eye over her. 'Medmenham – so you can use a slide rule?'

'Yes, ma'am.'

'Logarithms?'

'Yes.'

'You have some grasp of mathematics?'

'Some, yes.'

'You've heard of Euler?'

'No, ma'am.' Kay already regretted her reply.

'Jacobi? Legendre?'

She shook her head.

'The theorem of the ballistic curve?'

'No.'

'Then you don't have much of a grasp at all!' Sitwell sighed. 'Well, I suppose you're probably no worse than the rest of them. You'd better get on board.'

'Yes, ma'am. Thank you.' Kay saluted.

The door was just behind the wing. Feeling vaguely humiliated, she climbed the steps and ducked her head into the gloomy, crowded cabin. Ten seats on either side faced one another. Almost all were occupied by WAAFs. There were a couple of army officers. Square windows behind the seats admitted a weak morning light. Everyone's luggage was at their feet. She picked her way awkwardly along the centre of the fuselage until she found an empty place on the left near the front.

'May I?'

'Yes, ma'am.'

The WAAF sergeant shifted along reluctantly, just enough to enable her to squeeze into the seat, then very pointedly turned her head away. Kay smiled a greeting around the other women. None would meet her eye, officers or sergeants. Clearly she was unpopular before she'd even started. Well damn them, she thought, with sudden irritation, and damn that dried-up old stick who's in charge of them. She dragged the two halves of her seat belt out from beneath the WAAFs on either side of her and clipped them together.

At the back of the cabin, Flight Officer Sitwell stooped through the doorway, followed by the wing commander. They took the last two seats. One of the ground crew stowed the steps and closed the door. The engines coughed into life. The propellers sawed the air. The pitch rose quickly to a roar, and with a lurch the plane began to trundle across the apron and onto the concrete runway.

It was too noisy to speak. They all stared straight ahead. Kay could feel the tension. The accident rate on these flights was notorious. There was always a chance, even at this stage in the war, of encountering a stray Luftwaffe fighter. The WAAF opposite her was moving her lips, and Kay realised she was saying a prayer. She turned away, embarrassed, to look out of the window. She felt her own anxiety clench inside her chest and tried to concentrate on the take-off. So this was what it was like – the pause at the top of the runway, the sudden acceleration that forced you off balance, the buildings and the trees flashing past, and then the transition to slow motion as the landscape fell away and your stomach seemed to fall with it. The Dakota shuddered and creaked as it turned eastwards. She glimpsed the traffic on Western Avenue, the red-roofed houses, and then all too quickly veils of cloud whipped across the window and the view disappeared.

They seemed to be climbing too steeply for the power of the engines. The cabin bounced and rattled. The WAAF who had been praying began to cry. Kay gripped the edge of her seat. It felt as if they were in a submarine trying to surface. After what seemed an inordinately long time but was probably no more than two or three minutes, they breasted the clouds and the cabin was filled with sunshine. The Dakota levelled off. Flying beside them about three hundred yards away she noticed a Spitfire. It was maintaining the same course and height as theirs. Through the window opposite she could see another. They must have been given a fighter escort. Either someone important was on board whom she had not recognised, or this was for the WAAF unit.

Once everyone had registered the Spitfires, the tension relaxed. The WAAF stopped crying. Kay searched her pockets for a handkerchief, unfastened her seat belt and leaned across the aisle to offer it to her. The sergeant gave her a grateful look. 'Thank you, ma'am.' She wiped her eyes and offered it back.

Kay waved it away. 'Keep it for now. I'm Kay Caton-Walsh, by the way.'

'Ada Ramshaw, ma'am.'

'Where were you before this?'

'Filter Room, Stanmore. Do you know where we're going, ma'am?'

'Belgium, I believe.'

The Dakota jolted violently, lifting her out of her seat. She refastened her belt. For the next fifteen minutes the plane threw them around like a fairground ride. A few places to her right, one of the soldiers was sick over his luggage, and the stench quickly filled the cabin. Kay felt her stomach coil. She put her hand to her nose and turned away to look out of the window again. The clouds were a sea of foam far beneath them. She wondered if they had crossed the English coast yet. She tried to visualise one of the maps from Medmenham. A straight course to Belgium would take them just north of Dover across the North Sea to Ostend. What was that? About a hundred and fifty miles? And what was the cruising speed of a Dakota? Two hundred miles an hour, more or less? The journey shouldn't take them too much longer.

It must have been about fifteen minutes later, when she sensed by the pressure in her ears that they were descending, that her eye was caught by a movement. What looked to be a thin white fountain was rising like a needle point at tremendous speed far in the distance at an angle of about forty-five degrees. As it climbed, its contrail broadened and in several places sheared as it was caught by the crosswinds, leaving behind a narrow broken arc of cloud. She watched it for a few moments, hypnotised, then shook the shoulder of the unfriendly woman to her left. 'Look! Is that what I think it is?'

The sergeant turned to follow her gaze. 'My God, it's a bloody rocket! Girls – there's a V2!'

Everyone on the left side of the Dakota pressed their face close to the window. Those on the right got up and bent over their shoulders to get a better view. The plane rocked. They slid into one another. The door to the cockpit was flung open. A man's voice shouted, 'Sit down, for God's sake, you're destabilising the plane!'

As people returned to their places, Kay crouched down in her seat and twisted her head for a final glimpse, but the V2 had already passed out of sight on its way to London.

9

GRAF WAS STANDING IN A slit trench in the Scheveningen woods, scrutinising the sky through a pair of binoculars, following what he estimated to be the trajectory of the rocket. It was more than a minute since it had vanished into the clouds. Its exhaust plume had been normal during launch; at four seconds into its flight, the start of the forty-seven-degree-tilt manoeuvre had been executed perfectly. Even so, he continued to train his field glasses in the direction of its low rumble. Around him the men of the firing platoon were still crouched with their hands over their heads: after the previous night's disaster, no one wanted to take any chances. Finally he lowered his binoculars. 'She's gone,' he announced. He tried to disguise the relief in his voice. 'It's safe.'

Slowly the soldiers straightened. The regiment was made up of two types of men, Graf had observed. The older ones, the cynical veterans of the Eastern Front, had seen so much death they regarded a tour in occupied Holland as a well-earned holiday; their priority now was to survive the war. The teenagers straight from training were more ideologically committed to the struggle, but also usually more frightened. To judge by the number of red eyes and slack white faces evident in both groups this morning, a lot of methyl alcohol had been drained out of the fuel tankers overnight and consumed in the barracks. Graf couldn't tell whether they were impressed by his display of confidence, or thought him a show-off, or simply resented him as one of the scientists who had landed them with such a dangerously unreliable weapon. Probably all three.

He hauled himself out of the trench. After the noise of the launch, his ears still felt as if they were wadded with cotton wool. It took him a moment to realise that someone was calling his name. He couldn't see who at first. Then he spotted Lieutenant Seidel's head protruding through the inspection hatch of the firing control wagon. The battalion commander was waving.

'Graf!'

'What?'

The battalion commander cupped his hands to his mouth and shouted something unintelligible. Graf spread his hands helplessly. 'I can't hear you.'

Seidel pointed his finger at the spot where Graf was standing. The gesture seemed to be telling him not to move. The lieutenant's head disappeared.

Graf stamped his feet and blew on his hands. It

was another cold November morning – dry for once, thank God, but freezing. The wood was rimed with frost, except close to the launch table, where the ice had melted. He glanced at it, then looked away. He couldn't rid his mind of the scene at launch site 76 – the six-metre-deep crater, the firing control wagon burning like a furnace, the human remains and fragments of uniform hanging from the blasted fir trees like grisly Christmas decorations. Twelve men – half the firing platoon – were dead or impossible to identify. He had stayed at the scene until the last of the wounded had been taken away. When he finally got back to his hotel room, it had taken him a long while to get to sleep, and when he did, he dreamed of Wahmke at Kummersdorf, in his white laboratory jacket, smoking a cigarette, turning to smile at him just before he touched the kerosene igniter to the jet of hydrogen peroxide, and he found himself running in a panic through the trees, the exploded test stand with the charred bodies and the night-time scene in the forest merging into one. He had woken to find his hands clutching his blanket so tightly they ached.

Seidel approached through the undergrowth, swinging his arms to loosen his stiffness after his confinement in the armoured car. 'Morning, Graf.' There was no nonsense from him about a Hitler salute. 'Did you sleep?'

'A little. You?'

'Me? I always sleep well. So – did you hear poor old Stock died this morning?'

'I didn't know that. When they took him away, he was still breathing.' As the vision came into his mind, Graf briefly closed his eyes.

'Well he's dead now, poor fellow. It was a mercy. His battalion will have to be reconstituted. Huber's called a meeting at headquarters. Your attendance is requested.'

'Requested?'

'Ordered, then, if you prefer.'

'For what purpose?'

'To determine what went wrong, I should imagine.'

'What went wrong?' repeated Graf. 'What went wrong was his insistence on firing twelve rockets in a day!'

'Well then, my dear Graf, you can have the pleasure of telling him that. In the meantime, he wants us to go and inspect the site for clues. Come – I'll give you a lift.'

They walked along the road towards the lieutenant's car. Once they were clear of the launch area, Graf pulled out his pack of cigarettes and offered one to Seidel, who accepted it at once. They halted while Graf lit them. They were ersatz, disgusting; it was like smoking sawdust. He took a drag and contemplated the glowing tip. He didn't much relish revisiting the crash scene. 'What kind of "clues" does the colonel imagine we're likely to find?'

Seidel gave him a pitying look. 'None. He just wants to cover his arse when he reports to Kammler.'

Kammler was the SS general in charge of the V-weapons offensive: by common consent, a madman.

Graf laughed, despite himself. 'You're such a cynic, Seidel.'

'I was a lawyer before the war. I'm trained to be cynical.'

Five minutes later, they were in Seidel's little Kübelwagen, with its flapping canvas roof and bucket seats, jolting towards Wassenaar. A brief interval of flat grey dune land stretching down to the sea yielded quickly to the inevitable trees. Unlike the woods closer to Scheveningen, this one was dotted with smart houses. The wealthy owners had been moved out a couple of years earlier to create a three-kilometre security zone along the coast. Seidel slowed down and turned left, towards the sea. They stopped at a guard post, showed their passes and were nodded through. On either side, high iron gates offered glimpses of the gravelled drives that had been hidden in darkness the previous night. They ran across overgrown lawns, through drifts of unswept leaves, up to big steep-roofed houses. Some were as large as palaces. All looked empty apart from one, Graf noticed, which had a staff car parked outside.

'What happens there?'

Seidel slowed and glanced over his shoulder at the open gate. 'That's the whorehouse.'

'What? You're joking? I thought the whorehouse was in Scheveningen.'

'Don't go there, whatever you do! That syphilitic hole is for the men. This one is for the officers.'

He put his foot down again. After the last house there was a strip of open ground that looked as though it might have been a pre-war golf course, and then the road became a track that ran into a hunting forest. This was what Graf remembered from the previous night: the sense of wildness. There was a sign: **Restricted Area! We will shoot without warning!** The security barrier across the road was up, the sentry post unmanned.

As the trees closed around them, Graf expected to see signs of activity – salvage, clearing-up – but it seemed that the launch area had been abandoned. In the centre of the wood the vegetation was scorched, the branches stripped bare of foliage, the ground ripped up, exposing roots. Already it felt haunted. The blackened stumps of the trees looked as if they might have been shelled. It reminded him of photographs of the Western Front. Seidel pulled up in the middle of the track and turned off the engine. The silence was absolute, unbroken by the usual birdsong or the hollow croak of wood pigeons.

They climbed out of the car and picked their way towards the launch site. Each footstep raised a cloud of ash and cinders. There was a toxic stink of soot and incinerated fuel. Fragments of the V2 were all around – blackened fuselage casing, pieces of pipe from the motor and fuel tanks, a turbo pump, exhaust nozzles. Part of an arrowed tail fin was embedded in a tree trunk. The launch table was melted and buckled. The heavy armoured control car, blown over by the exploding warhead and burned out in the subsequent inferno, appeared like a giant black stag beetle lying on its back.

'My God,' said Seidel. 'What happened? Did you see it?'

'Only from a distance,' said Graf. 'I was lucky.' He let his eye take in the bigger objects and avoided focusing on anything smaller. His imagination recoiled at the thought of what he might see if he peered too closely, or what they might be treading on. 'The rocket got just above tree height. Then it seemed to lose thrust. It sank back down and the fuel tanks exploded. Not long after that, the warhead detonated – over there. I'll show you.'

When they reached the lip of the crater, he put one hand in his pocket and the other to his mouth and nose and surveyed the tangle of earth and roots and metal fragments. In places, smoke was rising from fires still burning underground.

Seidel shook his head. 'It's a hell of a destructive thing you fellows made, Graf.'

'I know. I only wish we'd had the time to make it more reliable.'

He could not count how often he had seen the rocket fail at Peenemünde, but at least that had mostly been from a safe distance of a kilometre, and the missile had not been armed with a warhead. The engine would ignite and it would start to topple even as it rose; the gyroscopes would over-correct and it would weave its way into the air like a stitching needle. Sometimes it would level off and disappear over the Baltic to end up God knew where. Other times it would airburst in the distance like a red chrysanthemum. Or it would loop the loop and plunge into the sea or the forest. Or it would go up a few dozen metres and remain perfectly erect even as it edged shyly to one side. Or the casing would split and burning fuel sprout in flaming sheets from the rupture before it exploded. Or it would fall full-length like a swooning maiden. Or it would simply remain stationary on the launch table and blow itself up, taking the test stand with it. Oh yes, Graf was a connoisseur of failed launches.

Seidel said, 'So? Any theories?'

Graf shrugged. 'How many do you want? A bad weld. A frozen valve. An engine fault. A short-circuit in one of the control compartments. Perhaps there was a sudden gust of wind and one of the tail fins caught a tree branch. It looked as though there was a radio control failure and they couldn't cut the engine in time.'

In any saner time or country, the project would have been abandoned, or at least scaled down while the technical problems were solved. But von Braun had over-promised in order to gain funding, his promises had been believed, and Peenemünde had grown vast on his irrepressibly plausible optimism. By the second year of the war, in addition to the test stands and the offices and the workshops and the wind tunnels, there was an immense factory for mass production – it was supposed to be the first of three – that was larger than two football pitches laid side by side. Construction alone required a population of thousands. There was a town for the engineers and their families, with a school and a cinema. There was even a commuter railway to bring in the workforce, equipped with the same modern S-Bahn trains as Berlin – and all for a missile that had yet to fly.

Seidel said, 'Why don't you walk round in that direction, and I'll go this way? Then we can say we've inspected the whole scene and get the hell out of this place.'

He set off into the woods. Graf stared into the smouldering pit for a few moments longer – it was like peering into the crater of a volcano, he thought: a man-made Vesuvius – then turned and stepped into the blackened trees. He found one component intact. It was about the length of his arm and shaped like the blade of an oar – metal but surprisingly light: one of the graphite rudders that controlled the jet plume. That had been a breakthrough. He turned it around in his hands and examined it fondly. Before they hit on the idea of graphite, they had used jet vanes made of tungsten-molybdenum alloys, and they had been hopeless. He remembered the day they had finally made the rocket fly perfectly. A Saturday in October 1942. Four o'clock in the afternoon. A clear blue Baltic sky. The previous two attempts at a maiden flight – one in June and the other in August – had both been humiliating failures in front of a crowd of VIPs, and it was no exaggeration to say that if this try failed, the whole programme might well have been abandoned.

He had stood with von Braun and a group of engineers and army officers on the roof of the rocket assembly building, two kilometres from the launch site, staring through his binoculars at the missile shimmering in the unseasonal heat against the background of the sea. A television link showed live pictures on a nearby monitor. The countdown was relayed over speakers all across Peenemünde. Thousands were outside watching. There was a strange time lag between what they could see in hazy colour through their field glasses and in shaky black-and-white on the television screen – the searing flash of the motor igniting – and then the subsequent dull boom as the sound reached them. An agonising wait, and up she went.

A Doppler electronic signal carried over the loudspeakers climbed in pitch as the rocket rose. A calm, flat voice recited each second of the flight. At four seconds, she tilted. At twenty-five seconds, she broke the sound barrier and Graf held his breath. But she did not disintegrate against the compressed mass of air as many of the aerodynamicists had predicted. At forty seconds, a trail of white appeared in the blueness, and for a moment he was sure she must have exploded. But it was only her contrail, already shearing in the crosswinds. The rocket was still flying, a tiny bright dot at the tip of a white spear of vapour. The Doppler signal faded as she soared towards space.

As the reality of what had just happened sank in, there arose from the streets below the sound of clapping and cheering. Von Braun turned to him and shook his hand and clutched his elbow. His eyes were as blue as that searing Baltic sky, unnaturally wide and bright with moisture. A visionary's eyes. A fanatic's eyes. 'We did it!'

That night, Dornberger held a celebratory dinner for the leading engineers. They all got very drunk. Dornberger made a pompous speech, which afterwards he had printed and gave to them as a memento, along with the menu – just as well, seeing as none of them could remember what he'd said. Graf still had his copy somewhere. He knew it off by heart.

'The following points may be deemed of decisive significance in the history of technology. We have invaded space with our rocket and for the first time – mark this well – have used space as a bridge between two points on earth. We have proved rocket propulsion practicable for space travel. To land, sea and air may now be added infinite space as a medium of future intercontinental traffic. This third day of October 1942 is the first of a new era of transportation: that of space travel.'

It showed how far Dornberger – the solid, ambitious artilleryman who had started out wanting to build a better version of the Paris gun – had fallen under von Braun's spell. Even Hitler had succumbed. Von Braun and Dornberger had flown to the Führer's headquarters in East Prussia carrying a 35 mm film of the test flight, a file of blueprints and a crate of wooden models – of the rocket itself, the launch vehicles and a bunker the army proposed to build on the Channel coast, which at the time was how they envisaged the missile would be deployed against the English. This was not long after the defeat at Stalingrad, when Hitler was casting around for something – anything – that was huge enough and revolutionary enough to turn the war back in Germany's favour; another few thousand planes or tanks would not make a difference. The hour of the rocket had arrived.

'Weren't you nervous?' Graf had asked him.

'Not at all! We landed in the middle of a huge forest and were driven to his compound – incredible security: you've never seen the like. Zones within zones. In the middle of it was this movie theatre, very plush, with banks of seats. So we set out all our models on a table, our film was loaded in the projector, and then we waited for him to come. And we waited, and we waited. Hours went by. Then someone shouted, "The Führer!" and in he came with Keitel, Jodl, Speer and all their aides. I must say he looked pretty awful, hunched forward and pale as a sheet, and his left arm seemed to have developed a life of its own – when he sat down, he had to hold onto his wrist with his other hand to stop it shaking. He placed himself in the front row between Keitel and Speer, I stood beside the screen and I said, "Mein Führer, with your permission, we wish to report on the progress of Waffen Prüfen Eleven!" Then I clicked my fingers, the lights dimmed, and the film began to run. I talked him through every stage of it, and I could see him sitting further and further forward on his seat, and then when the rocket lifted off, his eyes grew wide and his mouth dropped open.

'After it was over and the lights came up, he sat there for a long time, staring at the empty screen, lost in thought. Nobody dared to utter a word. Then he stood and he said the following – these were his exact words: "Gentlemen, I thank you. If we had had these rockets in 1939, we should never have had this war. No one would have dared oppose us. From now on, Europe and the world will be too small to contain a war. With such weapons, humanity will be unable to endure it." Then he made me a professor on the spot.'

'Congratulations. And now what?'

'Now?' For the first time, von Braun had looked uncomfortable. 'Now he wants us to build ten thousand of them.'

'Graf!' Seidel shouted from somewhere through the trees. 'Have you finished? Shall we go?'

'Coming!'

The jet vane was perfectly crafted, an object of

beauty. He ran his hands over its smooth shape, feeling the fluted indentations that helped it to direct the plume of burning gas. His fingers came away coated with the sticky black residue of the explosion. Suddenly overcome with disgust, he turned from the crater and flung it into the scorched bushes.

Crouched on the ground, a figure watched him.

He was too startled to move. The figure also remained perfectly still – slight, a shadow, not much bigger than a boy, three paces distant, partly concealed by a tree. From beneath a workman's dark blue cap, a pair of eyes stared out of a dead white face.

Several seconds passed during which Graf's mind tried to assimilate these details. Was he a survivor from the launch platoon, accidentally left out overnight in a state of shock? Was he a ghost, even – not that he believed in them? He felt his hair stiffen on his scalp. He took half a step forwards and the apparition vanished – jerked behind the tree trunk, turned and ran. No ghost, then.

'Seidel!' he yelled. 'There's someone here!'

He set off in pursuit. Whoever it was, he was nimble, but not strong enough to force his way through the undergrowth, and Graf, crashing straight ahead, was soon close enough to make a grab at his jacket. He missed the first time, but the second time seized his collar and hauled him backwards, dragged him down onto the ground and squatted on top of him, pinioning his arms with his knees, as if it were a children's game. And that was what this wriggling creature was, he realised – a child: a teenage boy with a delicate, small, sharp-featured face. But when he pulled off the cap and saw the thick blonde hair, he realised he was sitting on a young woman of eighteen or twenty. He reached out to brush away her hair to get a better view of her face. She twisted her head and bit him on his thumb. He swore and snatched his hand away.

'Graf! Where are you?' It sounded as though Seidel was still some distance off.

At the sound of another man's voice, she bucked and writhed helplessly beneath him, then gave up and lay still. Her eyes were fixed on his – full of fear and wild defiance, like an animal's in a trap.

The lieutenant's voice came again, closer now. 'Graf! Are you all right? I'm over here!' He let off a round from his pistol. The crack of the gunshot rang around the wood.

Graf looked over his shoulder towards the place where the gun had been fired, then stared down at the girl. What should he do? If he handed her over to Seidel, the army officer would be duty-bound to turn her in to the SS. They would shoot her for sure. She was not much more than a child. The idea was intolerable to him. He put his weight on one leg and then the other, hoisted himself clear and carefully stepped away from her. She didn't move. Was she half-witted? Had he injured her? He gestured with his head and hissed: 'Go!'

She scrambled to her feet without a word and slipped away into the trees.

'Graf!'

'It's all right! Stay where you are! I'm coming!'

He hurried back through the undergrowth. The lieutenant was at the edge of the crater. His gun was drawn, his expression irritable. 'What the devil's going on? What were you shouting about?' He glanced over Graf's shoulder as if he suspected he might have been followed.

'I thought I saw someone. But it was nobody. I'm sorry. This place gets on my nerves.'

'I heard you running.'

'I was chasing a shadow.'

Seidel looked him up and down. For the first time Graf was aware of the dirt and leaves stuck to the front of his coat. He brushed them away. His hand was bleeding slightly from her bite. Some kind of explanation seemed to be required. 'I fell.'

'You fell?' It was clear from his tone and the way he raised an eyebrow that the battery commander did not believe him, but after a moment he returned his pistol to its holster. 'We should go.'

10

THE DAKOTA WAS DESCENDING FAST, shuddering so violently in the turbulence Kay could see its fuselage twisting. It didn't take much effort to imagine it shaking itself to pieces. In the last five minutes, two more passengers had vomited up their breakfasts. The smell in the unheated cabin was cloying, inescapable, contagious; she had to fight the urge to be sick herself every time the plane bucked and her seat belt cut into her stomach.

She forced herself to stare ahead through the window opposite at the dirty white gauze of cloud. Rivulets of raindrops crawled across the glass like drops of sweat. She gripped the metal seat struts. With a final vertiginous plunge that reminded her of an express lift, they dropped out of the cloud base. The colour in the window changed abruptly from white to grey. She turned to look out the porthole behind her. They were coming in low over a town. She could make out streets and red-roofed houses, several big square church towers in the distance, and beyond them a wide navigable river with docks and cranes, shaped like a mortise key with a long straight handle and stubby levers. The distinctive pattern was familiar to her from Medmenham, so that when the sergeant next to her said, 'Where are we, ma'am?' she was able to answer, 'Ghent.'

She had expected them to land at an aerodrome like Northolt, and as they lost height, she kept looking out for one, but at the last moment she realised they were coming down onto a field. Trees flashed past alarmingly close and she braced herself for the impact. They hit the ground once and bounced up again, then hit it a second time and a third before jolting at speed over the uneven ground. The Dakota braked suddenly and flung them forward. The engines cut.

'Christ,' drawled one of the army officers, 'that was bloody awful.'

Kay laughed with the others.

Never had she been more relieved to arrive anywhere than she was that November morning, carrying her suitcase the length of the fuselage, stepping out of the fetid cabin into cold fresh air and down onto the damp grass. The RAF airfield consisted of nothing much: a couple of big tents, a fuel tanker, two lorries, a staff car and half a dozen jeeps, one of which had a machine gun mounted on its back. But to her it was the primitiveness that was thrilling. She walked up and down and took a few deep breaths and pressed her shoe into the spongy ground. So this was Belgium – an enemy-occupied country less than three months ago. This was what it had all been about. This was **the war.** The fact that the other WAAFs still seemed to be deliberately ignoring her did not bother her in the least.

One of the section officers clapped her hands. 'Very well, listen, please. As you can see, our transport is ready. The sergeants are to travel on the lorry.' The announcement was greeted by a few good-humoured groans. 'Sorry, girls. Officers – you'll be travelling in the jeeps.'

Kay picked up her suitcase. The officers were arranging themselves into groups of three – two to sit in the back and one up front next to the driver. She didn't want to travel with the wing commander and Flight Officer Sitwell, so she hung around the rear of the column and waited for someone to take pity on her. Finally two women detached themselves from the others and came over to her – one quite tall, blonde, plump and pretty, with a wide, open face; the other thinner, shorter, dark-haired.

The blonde stuck out her hand. 'Hello, I'm Joan Thomas.'

'Kay Caton-Walsh.'

'And this is Louie Robinson.'

They shook hands.

'Front or back?' asked Joan.

'Whichever you prefer.'

'Why don't we go in the back and you take the front?'

The two women climbed into the jeep with their suitcases. Kay got into the front. There wasn't much space. She had to twist her knees to the side and clutch her suitcase to her chest. The driver nodded affably. 'Ladies.'

Louie said, 'We're officers to you, Private.'

'Sorry, ma'am.'

The jeep with the machine gun mounted at the back jolted past them and took up position at the head of the convoy. Kay said, 'We have an armed escort?'

'There are still a few Germans about,' said the driver. He started the engine. 'You'll need to keep your eyes open.'

The column moved off. Kay could see the pale faces of a couple of the sergeants staring out of the gloom from the back of the covered lorry. She didn't envy them. Not that the jeep was much more comfortable. It had a thin canvas roof and was open at the sides. She drew her coat together to protect her knees against the cold. They rattled off the airfield and onto a country lane, then turned left onto a main road.

The back seats were set higher than the front. Joan leaned forward and shouted in her ear, 'So where have you come from, Kay?'

She tipped her head back to answer. 'Medmenham. You're all Stanmore, I take it?'

'Yes, that's right – Filter Room.'

'I feel a bit of an outsider.'

'Oh, you mustn't say that! We're a very friendly lot, aren't we, Lou?'

Lou grunted.

'That's good to know,' said Kay. 'Thank you.'

'You're welcome.' Joan settled happily back in her seat. In the rear-view mirror Kay could see that the two women were holding hands. Well, well, she thought, and returned her attention to the road.

The Flanders countryside spread out exposed on either side, flat and bare, unprotected by the hedgerows she was used to in England. They passed isolated farms and barns, a big empty greenhouse with most of its windows broken, a line of leafless poplars like the teeth of a broken comb. There was little traffic, apart from the occasional old man on a wobbly bicycle. Nobody was working in the winter fields; there was no livestock. The vastness of the sky only served to depress the landscape further. Layers of monochrome clouds stacked up from the horizon. It began to spit with rain.

The first little town they came to seemed entirely shut. Outside a church, beside an elaborate 1918 war memorial of green oxidised copper, a group of children stood on the corner and held out their hands like beggars. The army vehicles swept past without slowing. The optimism of the autumn, when liberated civilians showered British tanks with flowers, looked to be long gone. Houses, shattered by bombs or shelling, stood roofless beneath the grey sky. The shop windows were empty. My God, thought Kay, with a stab of shock, this place is starving.

They drove eastwards for about an hour. Signs of war were everywhere – tanks on their transporters parked down a side road, the barrels of an anti-aircraft battery poking out of a palisade of sandbags, a stone bridge chipped by bullets and guarded by troops. Buildings seemed to have been burned out at random. One field was a moonscape of perfectly circular waterlogged holes. She wondered if it were true that there might still be some Germans in the area. It seemed unlikely. The battlefront must have swept on weeks ago. Perhaps it was just a story the driver had invented to unsettle them.

Around noon, she spotted a sign for Mechelen, and soon afterwards the convoy entered the outskirts of a town, thundering down a narrow cobbled street of small houses. The black, yellow and red stripes of the Belgian flag hung from a couple of the upstairs windows. Up ahead, rising over the roofs, were the twin spires of what appeared to be a large church.

The lorry with its trailing column of jeeps emerged from the street and drove onto a low bridge spanning a wide canal. In the distance, on what looked like waste ground leading down to the water's edge, two big, boxy olive-green vans with radar dishes and radio antennae on their roofs were parked behind barbed wire. The dishes were directed away from them, pointing northwards – towards The Hague, Kay guessed. She turned to the back seat to share her excitement, but Joan and Louie had already seen them.

Louie said, with an air of expertise, 'GL Mark Threes. The latest MRUs.'

At the end of the bridge a yellow road sign pointed left to **Antwerpen** and **Sint-Niklaas,** right to **Heist-op-den-Berg, Leuven, Brussel.** What Kay had mistaken for a church turned out to be a massive fortified medieval gate, on top of which a pair of ugly twin spires of dark slate had been stuck, apparently as an afterthought. The convoy swung around it, passed along a broad, handsome street of big flat-fronted houses and shops, and drew to a halt.

From the back seat, Louie sounded surprised. 'This is it?'

The driver nodded. 'It is, ma'am. HQ, 33 Wing.'

Kay had presumed the headquarters would be in some big country pile like Danesfield. Instead, they were confronted by a nineteenth-century provincial terraced house with an iron balcony – grand but nondescript. She swung herself out of the jeep and pulled the passenger seat forward to let the other two out. She noticed the lorry had disappeared.

'What happened to the sergeants?'

'They've gone straight to the barracks,' said the driver. 'HQ is officers only.'

Joan pointed to a sign in thick Germanic script

above the doorway: **Soldatenheim.** She gave a nervous laugh. 'You'd have thought they might've got round to taking that down!'

The WAAFs began to congregate on the pavement with their suitcases. It was raining harder now. An old-fashioned cream-coloured tram rattled past, half empty; a few curious faces turned to stare at them. Wing Commander Knowsley put his hands on his hips and gazed up at the three-storey building. His little moustache twitched slightly – like a mouse's whiskers, Kay thought. He looked pensive, just as he had at the Air Ministry the previous afternoon – a man who had perhaps offered more than he could deliver and rather wished he was back in north London. He stepped to the front door and rang the bell. Almost at once it was opened by an RAF sergeant. 'Welcome to Mechelen, sir.' He saluted. 'We've been expecting you.'

Kay let the others go in ahead of her. The sergeant was waiting in the dimly lit hall. 'If you'd leave your case at the bottom of the stairs, ma'am, you can collect it later. There's a cup of tea and a sandwich waiting on the first floor.'

Evidence of the previous tenants was everywhere – in the mezzotint pictures of Bavarian lakes and mountains that lined the staircase, in the Gothic signs on the doors leading off the first-floor landing – **Raucherraum, Esszimmer, Bibliothek.** German army announcements and instructions covered a noticeboard. The sergeant noticed Kay examining them.

'Sorry about that, ma'am.' He started taking them down. 'Been meaning to get round to it.'

In the large front room overlooking the street an aircraftman was pouring tea. A tin of evaporated milk stood on a table under the window, next to a pair of plates piled with fish- and meat-paste sandwiches. The two tasted indistinguishable. Kay stood at the window with her teacup and saucer and surveyed the street. On the opposite side, the army lorry had reappeared and was parked outside what looked to be a bank.

'Now come on, Kay,' said Joan. 'You mustn't hide in the corner. It's time you met the others.' She guided her by the arm into the centre of the room. Conversation ceased as five pairs of eyes turned to survey her. 'This is Joyce Handy . . . Barbara Colville . . . Gladys Hepple . . . Molly Astor . . . Flora Dewar . . .' Kay repeated their names as she shook hands in an effort to anchor them to an individual face. They were all her own age and type – middle-class, well-educated young Englishwomen, apart from Flora who sounded Scottish.

Barbara said, 'So you're the girl from Medmenham?'

'That's right.'

'You must be rather special.'

'Why's that?'

'We had to leave Evelyn behind to make room for you.'

So that was why they were so unfriendly. It hadn't occurred to her that someone else might have to be thrown out of the unit. 'I'm sorry to hear about that – I didn't know.'

Flora said mournfully in her Aberdonian brogue, 'The wee lass was terribly upset. She wasn't told she wouldn't be coming until she was about to get on the bus.'

'Oh dear, the poor thing! How rotten for her.'

Joyce said, 'Are you a mathematician, Kay?'

'No.'

'But you've plotted incoming enemy aircraft?'

'I'm afraid not.'

'Then I suppose it only goes to show,' said Barbara, with a smile like broken glass, 'how important it is to have friends in high places.' She was irritatingly good-looking, with a model's cheekbones.

Friends in high places . . . The innuendo hung in the air. They knew, or at any rate they'd heard a rumour. I must stand my ground, Kay thought, or go under. She said sweetly, 'Well, Barbara – it is Barbara, isn't it? – it sounded such a glamorous assignment – fish-paste sandwiches in Belgium in midwinter – that naturally I decided to pull every string I could to make sure I got it.'

A couple of the others laughed. Molly glanced over her shoulder and said quietly, 'They **were** rather frightful.'

Barbara frowned. 'I'm sure they're doing their best. We don't all have such refined taste.'

Flight Officer Sitwell came over. 'Are we getting to know one another?'

Kay, her eyes still fixed on Barbara, said, 'Yes, ma'am. Very much so.'

'Well I'm sorry to interrupt, but we have work to do. Leave your cases where they are and follow me.'

They returned their teacups to the table. Sitwell led them out of the room, down the stairs, out into the street and across the wide road. They walked in single file. Like a gaggle of grey geese, thought Kay. A few passers-by stopped to watch them. One elderly woman smiled at Kay, and she smiled back.

The bank, like the house, was nineteenth century, with a facade of heavy grey stone. A soldier guarded the entrance. They followed the flight officer inside and stood on the polished wooden floor in front of the tellers' counter. It was dusty, the air was stale. It felt as if it hadn't been used for years.

'Close the door,' said Flight Officer Sitwell. She waited until it was done. 'Right, from now on, every time you enter this building you will be required to show your identity card, so make sure you don't leave it behind.' She lifted a section of the mahogany counter and pushed open the low door. One of the rear windows had been opened to let in bunches of electrical cables that ran around the skirting board. The mobile radar vans were visible in the distance. The women followed her between the rows of empty desks and down a flight of stairs into the vault. The door to a big safe, lined with deposit boxes, was open.

In the dim light, beneath a low ceiling, the sergeants were at work: shifting tables to form a central workspace, setting up Anglepoise lamps, wheeling chairs into place, hanging charts, lifting a blackboard onto an easel, putting out wire baskets, graph paper, slide rules, books of logarithms. Wing Commander Knowsley was seated behind a desk in the corner with three telephones in front of him. Soldiers from the Signals Corps were unrolling cables around his feet.

Flight Officer Sitwell said, 'Gather round, ladies.' She waited until they were all in place. 'So this is where you'll be working from now on. We'll be reporting from here direct to 11 Group Filter Room. The GL Mark Threes parked between here and the canal are part of a detachment operated by a new mobile advance reporting unit. 105 MARU will alert us as soon as they detect a V2 has been launched. The watch team, consisting of two officers, will plot the first coordinates of its trajectory, exactly as we practised in England. In addition to radar, there will be backup data from parabolic sound mirrors, but these are to be regarded as a secondary rather than a primary source. If in doubt, use the readings from radar.

'As soon as Stanmore has the confirmed coordinates of the point of impact, it will be your job to extrapolate the parabolic curve back to the launch point. Each individual officer will work on her own, and then check her findings with her teammate. In case of a discrepancy, the calculations will be checked again, either with me or with Wing Commander

Knowsley, until we determine the true result. Team B, consisting of two sergeants, will then convert the data to a map grid reference, which will also be checked before being radioed to Fighter Command.

'Our objective is to complete the calculations within six minutes of receiving all data. That's the optimum time to enable our fighters to be over the targets before the enemy has time to fully disassemble their equipment. Every second is precious.

'Any questions so far?'

Her angular profile swung like a gun turret around the circle of WAAF officers. Louie Robinson raised her hand. 'When will we be starting, ma'am?'

'Oh eight hundred tomorrow morning. It will take us until then to get the system up and running. You'll be divided into four watches of two officers. Each pair will work a six-hour shift. Obviously our aircraft can only attack the launch sites in daylight, so priority will be given to those first two shifts, but don't despair if I put you on nights: according to the Dutch resistance, the Germans return to the same launch sites and use them again, so what we do overnight will provide targets for attack later.'

Barbara said, 'Where will we be staying when we're not here?'

'I'm afraid there's no room to sleep in headquarters, although you will be able to spend your rest hours there, and meals will be available. Besides, for security purposes we would prefer it if you were dispersed rather than gathered in a single location. Arrangements have been made for you each to be billeted with a separate family around the town, within walking distance of HQ. I cannot emphasise too strongly that the work you are doing here is most secret. Do not – I repeat, **do not** – talk about your reasons for being in Mechelen. Remember, the Germans were here for more than four years and only left a couple of months ago. We cannot take the loyalty of the local population for granted. Be wary of strangers, however friendly, and take particular care when you are walking between here and your billeted accommodation.

'Wing Commander? Would you like to say something?'

Knowsley was talking into one of his telephones. 'Hello? Hello? Can you hear me?' He shook the receiver and glared at it. He glanced across at the WAAF officers. 'Damn thing!' He slammed the receiver down hard in its cradle and came around from behind his desk.

The maps Kay had seen being loaded at Northolt had now been fixed to big cork noticeboards and attached to the wall beside the safe. One showed London and the south-east corner of England, a second the coast from Ostend to Amsterdam, taking in the territory to the south as far as Brussels; a third showed south-east England and the North Sea as far as the Dutch coast. The fourth – familiar to Kay from Medmenham – was a large-scale chart of Holland from the Hook of Holland to Katwijk aan Zee.

Knowsley picked up a box of coloured pins. 'Right. This is where we are,' he said, sticking a red pin into Mechelen, 'and somewhere around here is where the V2s are coming from.' He put a pin into The Hague. 'That's a distance of roughly seventy miles. As you can see, we're just seventeen miles south of the port of Antwerp, which is the only city apart from London currently being targeted by the V2. Both are receiving roughly the same number of missiles. For now, we're concentrating on the London attacks, but our aim in the next week or two is to extend our coverage to include the launch sites that are hitting Antwerp.

'So, although the street outside looks peaceful enough, never forget we're on a battlefield, which is why we're sitting below ground in a bank vault, and why you're going to be dispersed around the town when you're not on duty. This is a new kind of warfare – the warfare of the future, I dare say – and we're attempting something new as part of fighting it. The first rocket will hit London in five minutes. You have six minutes to stop the second. I want you to give it everything you've got. A lot of people are depending on us. All right?' He nodded around vaguely, as if embarrassed at his own theatrics. 'Good. Carry on.' He went back to his desk and his silent telephones with evident relief.

Sitwell said, 'All right, everyone. Find yourself a seat.'

Kay took one of the eight places around the pushed-together tables. Each had been neatly laid with a slide rule, a book of logarithm tables, graph paper, a notepad and two pencils. On the blackboard, the flight officer was making rapid marks in chalk. She stood aside to reveal:

$$\mathbf{y} = \mathbf{ax}^2 + \mathbf{bx} + \mathbf{c}$$

'We'll start with the basics.' She looked down the table. Her eyes rested on Kay. 'New girl – what is that?'

Kay felt her mouth go dry. She took a guess. 'It's the formula for calculating a parabolic curve, ma'am.'

'Thank God for that,' said Sitwell. 'Although you'd have to be pretty dim not to have worked that out, given why we're here.' She started writing again, in hard, jabbing motions that sent chalk dust sprinkling to the floor. 'So let's see if you can tell me . . . If the equation is this . . .' she gestured to the board:

$$\mathbf{f}(\mathbf{x}) = 2\mathbf{x}^2 + 8\mathbf{x}$$

'. . . what are the values of **a, b** and **c**?'

Once again she looked directly at Kay. She had a sadistic light in her eyes that reminded Kay of Sister Angela, one of the nuns who had taught her algebra at school and who would hit her on the hand with a ruler if she made an error. For a few long seconds her mind fogged with panic, until years of Sister Angela and days and nights in the Phase Three room at Medmenham came to her rescue.

'I would say . . . **a** equals two . . . **b** equals eight . . . and **c** equals . . .' She hesitated before adding uncertainly, 'Zero?'

'Congratulations.' The flight officer looked slightly disappointed. 'You have passed your entrance exam.' She wiped the board clean. 'Now, ladies, we shall work on some serious trigonometry.'

They worked on through the afternoon. For an hour they practised the basic algebraic calculations required to work out a parabolic curve. Then Flight Officer Sitwell produced a stopwatch and announced they would move on to dummy runs. She chalked up an imaginary set of height and velocity readouts provided by the radar unit, waited five minutes, then gave them the coordinates of the shot-fall of the missile. 'Go!' She started the stopwatch.

The sequence of calculations required to plot height and distance, to discover the apex of the curve, to calculate the launch position by converting the distance into miles, and then to locate the origin of the arc on the large-scale map and provide the grid reference – all of it required a level of concentration that made Kay's head swim. The slide rule became slippery in her sweaty fingers. 'Six minutes!'

barked the flight lieutenant. 'You should be done by now!' And then: 'Ten minutes! Come on, ladies! Those wretched Germans will be out of the woods and back in their mess drinking beer if you don't get a move on!'

She circled around behind them, passing so close Kay could hear the rapid ticking of the watch. Finally the bespectacled Joyce Handy raised her hand. 'Got it, ma'am!' The flight officer stopped the watch. 'Twelve minutes, eight seconds – useless!' She bent to check Joyce's calculations. The WAAFs all straightened. She turned on them at once. 'Don't stop, you silly girls! Keep going until you've all done it.' With an angry click, she restarted the watch. Kay put her head down again.

One by one over the succeeding minutes they finished and raised their hands. Kay was fourth. She sat back in her chair exhausted as Sitwell took her paper. Barbara, she was pleased to note, came in last. The flight lieutenant sorted through their answers.

'Well, at least you all got there in the end.' Her tone softened. 'Well done. But slow – too slow! Remember – pilots will be risking their lives on the basis of what you do. Imagine it's your brother or your boyfriend in that cockpit. Don't, for God's sake, send them on a pointless dangerous mission because you couldn't do your part in time.' She tore up the papers and dropped them into a waste basket. 'Right. We'll go again.'

The next time was better – ten and a half

minutes – and in the run after that Kay was the first to finish, in eight minutes and two seconds. Twice Sitwell fed them false coordinates and let them struggle to make sense of it before she stopped them. 'If the data is obviously wrong, for God's sake say so quickly, and we can go back to Stanmore and MARU and tell them to check.' By now, to her surprise, Kay realised she was enjoying it. There was a pleasure in the mental absorption, in the conjuring of arcs and map points from what looked like random numbers. There was a freedom, too, in not being able to think about anything else. She lost all sense of time and place and was almost disappointed when the flight officer announced that they had just concluded their last practice run, with their best time of the day: six minutes, fifteen seconds.

'Take a break, ladies, while I confer with the wing commander.'

Kay pushed back her chair and stood. Her neck and shoulders were locked with tension. She rotated her head. There was a satisfying, exhausted ache in a specific area of her brain that she associated solely with mental effort. She had not felt like this since her finals at Cambridge. Joan said, 'Well done, Kay. Do you fancy a fag?'

'I certainly fancy some fresh air.'

'Come on, then.'

'Do you think we should?'

'Why not? Let's ask.' She went over to Sitwell,

who was talking to the wing commander. 'Ma'am, is it all right if we stand in the street for a few minutes?'

'All right, but don't go far.'

They climbed the stairs. While they had been in the vault, the daylight had gone. Outside, a soft misty rain was falling. In the glow from the street lamp the tiny droplets swirled like smoke. Across the road, a few lights showed in the windows of the headquarters. Joan lit a cigarette. Kay stood in the middle of the pavement, took off her cap and let the dampness cool her head. She could hear the voices of some of the other women emerging behind them, talking in murmurs. She yawned and belatedly put her hand to her mouth. 'Sorry. I don't think I've ever felt so tired.'

'I call it the end-of-shift headache.' The tip of Joan's cigarette brightened as she inhaled. 'What did you do before the war, Kay, if you don't mind my asking?'

'I was a student. I was called up straight from university. What about you?'

'I worked at a stockbroker's in the City.'

'When did you start in the WAAF?'

'Nineteen forty. Just before the Battle of Britain. Never thought I'd end up here.'

Kay felt too exhausted to talk. She smoothed down her wet hair and replaced her cap. She thought of the German soldiers in the woods seventy miles away. They had never been able to work out at Medmenham how the V2s would be launched. In

July they had gone back over all the old coverage of Peenemünde trying to find a clue. Just beyond one of the giant elliptical earthworks was a fan-shaped stretch of foreshore, entirely bare, which they reckoned was the launch site. She had stared at it for a long time before the obvious fact had struck her. She had called out to Starr: 'Look at this, sir.'

He had leaned over her, his hand on her shoulder. 'What about it?'

'There isn't a rail line.'

'So what?'

'It must mean they can bring up the rockets by road. In which case, they don't need a dedicated bunker to launch from – any bit of old concrete or asphalt will do.'

The hardest thing to spot was often what was directly in front of you.

One of the other WAAFs came over. 'Can I have a cigarette, Joan? I'll pay you back.' It was Barbara. She looked at Kay. 'You seemed to get the hang of it pretty quickly.'

'God knows why. I suppose there's a lot of mathematics in what we do at Medmenham.'

Barbara inserted the cigarette between her lips and muttered, 'Sorry I was a bitch earlier.'

'That's all right.'

Flora Dewar appeared behind them. 'Flight Officer Sitwell wants us all downstairs right away.'

Barbara returned the unlit cigarette. 'Bloody Sitwell.'

They descended into the vault and took their former places around the central table. Kay exchanged nods with some of the others. Joyce, Gladys, Molly . . . It was the better part of wartime, how easily one made friends. It had been the same from the first day of her basic training. Women you would never normally have spent five minutes with became as close as family. Adversity bred intimacy. She was already starting to feel she had known them for years.

Flight Officer Sitwell was wiping the blackboard clean. When the last of the calculations had been expunged, she turned to face them. 'We'll follow the same shift pattern as we do in England. And we've arranged you into the following pairs.' She picked up a sheet of paper from the desk. 'Section Officer Colville and Section Officer Caton-Walsh will take the first watch, starting at oh eight hundred tomorrow morning.' Kay glanced across at Barbara, but she was staring straight ahead. 'Section Officers Robinson and Dewar will take the second shift, at fourteen hundred. Section Officers Hepple and Astor will take the third, at twenty hundred hours. And I'm afraid that means Section Officers Handy and Thomas will have the graveyard slot, from oh two hundred to oh eight hundred.

'If you have any questions, please remain behind. Otherwise, you are free to return to headquarters. There is transport waiting to take you to your billets. You will each be given a small amount of food, which you will take with you and present to the woman of the household. Remember, please, that many civilians in Belgium are close to starving. No doubt you are hungry too, but be tactful, and eat sparingly. By all means take your slide rule and logarithm tables and practise, practise until you can perform these calculations in your sleep. I shall see you all tomorrow.'

The Flanders evening was dark, wet, silent. Kay sat in the front of the jeep, her suitcase and the small box of rations stowed in the back. She had been given a name – Dr Maarten Vermeulen – and an address, with no other details. It was obvious as soon as they left HQ that the driver didn't know the way. He had a little hand-drawn map, and every so often he would stop and Kay would have to get out and squint up at the unfamiliar street names. They drove through an empty square and across a bridge. A lamp reflected weakly in the black water. Here and there, along a wide, deserted street, a few lights showed behind thick curtains. It was the old central part of town – that much she could make out. The tall, flat-fronted buildings with their patterned brickwork and elaborate windows summoned vague memories of Flemish paintings. It wouldn't have surprised her to see a nightwatchman with a lantern.

After doubling back a couple of times and passing the same church twice, they entered a cobbled alley with high brick walls on either side into which were set heavy, ancient wooden doors. The silhouettes of houses rose behind them. The driver pulled up, shone his torch on the map and then on the house number and announced they had arrived.

'Are you sure?'

'That's what it says here, ma'am.'

They clambered out of the jeep. He was flustered, in a hurry, muttering that he had other WAAFs to drop off around town. He retrieved her suitcase and the box of food, deposited them on the wet pavement, wished her goodnight and drove away. She looked around. She had no idea where she was, let alone how to find her way back to the bank the next morning. For the first time, she felt a twist of panic, which she at once suppressed. As dangers went, it hardly ranked with flying alone eight miles above Berlin. She turned the metal ring of the gate handle, picked up her suitcase, tucked the cardboard box under her arm and put her shoulder to the wood. The hinges squeaked and gave reluctantly.

A path of worn stones led across a small muddy garden to a front door. She rang the bell and stepped back to look up at the tall house. A crack of yellow light shone from a window on an upper floor, quickly extinguished as the curtain was closed. After a minute she heard a shuffle of feet on the other side of the door, the sound of bolts being drawn back, a key turned. It opened part way. One side of an elderly male face peered out at her over the door chain.

'Dr Vermeulen?'

'Ja?'

'I'm Section Officer Angelica Caton-Walsh of the British Royal Air Force.'

A single rheumy eye rolled in exasperation, exposing yellow whites. He said something angrily in Flemish.

Kay said, 'I'm sorry, I don't understand.'

'Je ne parle pas anglais!'

'Peut-on parler français?'

He gave a reluctant grunt. **'Oui.'**

For the second time that day, the teaching nuns of Our Lady's came to her aid. **'Je suis l'officier de section Angelica Caton-Walsh de la force aérienne britannique. Vous m'attendez?'**

He scrutinised her face, looked at the box of food and then at her again. **'J'ai dit à l'officier anglais: non!'**

I told the English officer: no. 'Did you indeed,' she muttered under her breath. She was starting to lose her temper, standing in the rain. She gestured to the sky. **'Je suis désolé,'** she said firmly, **'mais je suis ici!'**

He glared at her for a few more seconds, then sighed, unfastened the chain and opened the door.

The hall reminded her of her grandmother's house – a black-and-white tiled floor with a threadbare rug, heavy wooden furniture, a dinner gong, a metal crucifix, pictures of saints and various embroidered religious texts around the walls, the tick of a long-case clock, and an obscure smell of something . . . not dead exactly, but mouldy, ancient, of another time. It was colder than it had been in the jeep. She put down her suitcase but kept hold of the box of food.

Dr Vermeulen closed the door and locked and bolted it. He was bald and bony, sixty-something, with liver spots on his hands and skull. A bottle-green cardigan hung loosely from his sloping shoulders. He called up the stairs, 'Amandine!'

The wooden boards creaked and at once a woman began to descend. She must have been listening from the landing, dressed as if she was about to go out, in thick shoes and a dark coat. Her grey hair was cut in a mannish helmet. She inspected Kay through wire-framed spectacles. Vermeulen said something to her in Flemish, then turned to Kay and shrugged: **'Ma femme.'**

Kay held out the food. 'This is for you,' she said in French. 'I am sorry for the imposition.'

The woman took the carton and peered down into it. She looked up with a slightly friendlier expression and replied, also in French, 'You had better come into the warm.'

Kay followed them past the ticking clock and into the kitchen. Dr Vermeulen's slippers slapped against the flagstone floor.

A big dresser was filled with blue-and-white china. Two high-backed wooden chairs with cushions and blankets were drawn up in front of an iron stove. On the table was a pile of old cloth-bound books and some woollen socks that were being darned. Mrs Vermeulen pushed the sewing out of the way and set down the box. She began taking out the contents and examining them with an expression of wonder. Two red tins of Fray Bentos corned beef. An army-ration tin of meat and vegetable stew. A packet of tea. Three rashers of bacon wrapped in greaseproof paper. A tin of condensed milk. A small loaf. An egg box. A slab of chocolate. She lined them up carefully as if they were pieces of treasure. She opened the egg box to reveal three small white eggs and showed them wordlessly to her husband.

'It isn't much,' said Kay. 'I'm sorry.'

'Vous êtes très gentil,' said Dr Vermeulen. He looked forlorn. 'Forgive us,' he said suddenly in English. 'We told them we would prefer not to take you. My wife has – how do you say it?' He tapped his heart. **'Angine.'**

'Angina?'

'**Oui,** angina – of course, from the Latin. And my son is also not in good health. But, as you say, here you are, and we must make the best of it. Perhaps it will not be for long.' He gestured. 'Your coat, please. Sit. Be warm.'

She took off her coat and handed it to him, then perched on one of the chairs and held out her hands to the stove. So he could speak English after all, she thought, and quite well by the sound of it. She wondered why he had pretended otherwise.

There was a loud tapping behind her. She turned and let out a cry of surprise. At the window of the back door a man's distorted face was pressed close to the frosted glass.

'Do not be alarmed,' said Vermeulen. 'It is only my son.'

He unlocked the door. A young man limped in carrying a small sack. He dumped it on the table, turned immediately to Kay and took off his cap, releasing a mop of thick dark hair, cut short at the sides but long on the top.

Vermeulen said, 'This is Arnaud.' He said something quietly to him in Flemish.

The man bowed to her, took her hand and kissed it. He was about her own age, middle twenties, very pale but good-looking. His face was wet from the rain. Hunger had given him sharp features, she thought. His eyes were dark and full of life. In a thick accent he said in English, 'A pleasure to meet you.' He rummaged through the sack and held up four potatoes still covered in wet soil. He winked and smiled in triumph: **'Voilà!'**

Kay smiled back. He has stolen those from someone's garden, she thought.

At the prospect of food, the Vermeulens became almost merry. Arnaud took off his wet jacket, sat and started tugging off his boots. Mrs Vermeulen washed the potatoes at the sink, put them in a saucepan and set it on the stove. She opened the can of meat stew and tipped it into a second saucepan. The doctor went next door into what looked to be a freezing, darkened parlour and returned with a bottle of advocaat. He poured four tiny glasses and handed them round. He proposed a toast – **'À l'amitié!'** – and Kay clinked her glass with each of theirs. The sweet and eggy drink reminded her of custard, and therefore for some reason of Christmas, which made her briefly maudlin.

They sat around the stove and watched the potatoes boil. Vermeulen said bitterly, 'The Nazis took all our potatoes before they left – as if they don't have potatoes in Germany!'

Mrs Vermeulen served the stew and potatoes. The doctor poured another thimbleful of advocaat. They ate in hungry silence, Arnaud with his head down over his plate. When he had finished, his mother gave him what was left of her own meal and he wolfed that down as well. Once or twice Kay looked wistfully at the rest of the food she'd brought, but it seemed the Vermeulens wished to keep it for another day. At this rate of consumption, it would last them for a week. She reproached herself for even thinking about it: she could always find something at the officers' mess tomorrow. When they were finished, Mrs Vermeulen cleared the plates, then cut them each a square of the hard and milkless British army chocolate.

Arnaud said, in French, 'Why are you in Mechelen, may I ask, mademoiselle?'

'I'm afraid I'm not allowed to say.'

'But you are based somewhere close to here?'

'To be honest, I don't know where it is. I'm supposed to be on duty at eight tomorrow morning and I'm not even sure how to get there.'

'Why, then we can draw you a map! What is the name of the street – can you tell us that?' He grinned at her. 'Or is it also secret?'

'I believe it's called Koningin Astridlaan.'

'But we know it, of course! The main road in the south. That's where the Boche had their headquarters.'

'They're our headquarters now.'

A sheet of paper was fetched, a pencil produced, and the three Vermeulens – with occasional disagreements in Flemish – put their heads together and drew her a plan of how to get there.

She studied the neatly labelled streets. The route was arrowed. 'Is it far?'

Arnaud shrugged. 'A fifteen-minute walk – no more.'

'Thank you.' She folded up the map and stowed it in her pocket. 'And now, I think, as I have to get up early, I should go to bed.'

'Of course,' said Dr Vermeulen. 'Let me show you to your room.'

As she bent to retrieve her coat, she was aware of Arnaud eyeing her.

'Goodnight,' she said.

'Goodnight. Sleep well.'

In the hall, the doctor insisted on picking up her case. She looked around at the high ceiling, the religious artefacts, the big wooden doors. It seemed too formal for an ordinary home. 'Is this where you see your patients?'

He laughed. **'Je ne suis pas ce type de docteur!'** He opened the nearest door and turned on the light. She followed him in. It was a large study, of a sort familiar to her from Cambridge – a working library, with floor-to-ceiling bookshelves so crammed with volumes that they had overflowed into piles on the floor and desk. Heavy black velvet curtains, streaked with dust, were tightly drawn. There was a strong smell of old tobacco. 'I taught at the University of Antwerp before the war. I am a doctor of philosophy – much use though that is these days.'

'On the contrary, surely – we need philosophy more than ever.'

'That's true!' He smiled at her – the first proper smile he had given that evening. It changed his face entirely. He was not as old as he first appeared, she realised.

On the desk were a few family photographs in silver frames, dating back to the last century: prosperous, solid citizens in fine clothes. In one, two boys posed on a beach, holding a football. She picked it up. The older she recognised at once by his thick dark hair as Arnaud. He looked about eighteen. His companion was a couple of years younger. The resemblance between the two was striking; even their expressions, squinting into the sun, were the same.

'You have another son?'

She regretted her curiosity at once. His smile disappeared. He took the photograph from her. 'That is Guillaume. He was killed in the war.'

'I'm so sorry.'

'Thank you.' He laid the photograph face down on the desk and gestured to the door. 'Shall we?'

She followed his stooping back up the stairs to the first-floor landing. A second, smaller staircase led into the upper reaches of the house, but instead of climbing further, he led her along a gloomy passage. At the far end he opened a door and turned on an overhead light. The room was large and bare, with a rug, a brass bedstead, a nightstand, a plain chest of drawers, a simple wooden chair and escritoire, and a wardrobe. A pair of heavy velvet curtains, similar to those in the study, were drawn across the window. A crucifix hung above the bed. The pink tasselled lampshade provided a weak light. It felt as if the room had not been used, or even visited, for years.

'The bathroom is there.' Vermeulen set down the case and pointed across the passage. 'I am sorry: there is no hot water. But Amandine can heat a kettle in the kitchen if you like.'

'Really, there is no need. I am very sorry to put you to this trouble.'

He hesitated and managed a brief smile. **'Alors – bonne nuit.'**

'Goodnight. Thank you.'

She listened to his slippers shuffling away, along the passage and down the stairs. She closed the door and surveyed the room. It was dry, at least, unlike the hut at Danesfield House, and it was private, but she would have given a lot at that moment to be back in England with the others, gossiping after their shift. A stupid thought! She shook her head to clear it. She could forgive herself any sin except self-pity. She lifted her case up onto the bed, opened it, and began unpacking, transferring her spare uniform to the chest of drawers and wardrobe. She laid out her white cotton nightdress on the counterpane. The slide rule and logarithm tables she placed on the escritoire. She had brought no civilian clothes, no book or photograph to remind her of home. She wound up her travel clock and set the alarm for six thirty, then parted the curtains and cupped her hands to the window. She could make out nothing in the blackness.

She sat at the desk and opened the book of logarithms. Flight Officer Sitwell had given them a list of equations ('Homework, ladies') to practise on when they were off duty, and for half an hour she worked conscientiously with her slide rule until her eyes were too tired to focus on the tiny markings. A church bell sounded in the distance. She counted the chimes. Nine o'clock.

She removed her cap and unpinned her hair, took

off her jacket and hung it up. She carried her sponge bag across the hall to the bathroom, searched among her make-up for a bar of soap, then rolled up her sleeves and washed her hands and face, wiping them on the small, thin towel, which at home they would have used to dry dishes. She brushed her teeth.

Back in her room, she took off her tie, shirt and skirt, removed her shoes, and unrolled her thick stockings. Her skin puckered into gooseflesh in the cold. She unclipped her suspender belt. As she reached behind her to unhook her bra, she paused, remembering the way Arnaud had kissed her hand and eyed her up when he thought she wasn't looking. Should she keep her underclothes on, or even prop the chair against the door? She dismissed her fears at once. He had obviously been badly injured somehow. She could handle him. She took off her bra and the hideous WAAF-issue knickers, elasticated at the waist and legs, nicknamed Passion Killers, the sight of which had always made Mike groan. She wished very much he was with her now, lying in bed, watching her, waiting for her. She shook her head again. No point in thinking about him any more. She pulled the nightdress over her head, turned down the covers and piled the two thin pillows on top of one another. Then she went to the door, switched off the light and darted across the room into bed.

The unaired sheets smelled damp, like an old raincoat. She drew the blanket up to her chin. The ancient house was quiet. She could hear nothing, see nothing. Her head was a merry-go-round of algebraic calculations. She worried they would keep her awake. But within two minutes she was asleep. In her dreams, a rocket, at the tip of a spreading white plume of numbers and symbols, rose far in the distance against a pale blue sky.

11

'CHECK,' SAID SEIDEL.

He lifted his fingers from his knight and sat back in his chair with a smile of satisfaction. Graf leaned over the table to inspect the board. His legs were wide apart, his forearms rested just above his knees. His fingertips tapped nervously against one another. 'So, what do we have here?' Normally he was the victor in these regular contests, but tonight his mind was not fully engaged and he had allowed his position to deteriorate. His queen was gone. His king, with its little band of weak protectors, was besieged by Seidel's rooks and knights.

'Do you concede?' asked Seidel.

'Not at all.' Seidel was offering his knight to be taken by white's king, but the sacrifice would give him checkmate in three moves. 'There is always hope.' Graf moved his king behind the line of pawns.

'You do know you're only prolonging the agony?' But when the lieutenant leaned over the board again, he folded his arms and frowned, worried he might have missed something.

Graf settled back. The officers' mess was on the first floor of the Hotel Schmitt, in a small lounge that faced towards the promenade. The sea was invisible but noisy in the darkness beyond the drawn curtains. The atmosphere was sombre. Some evenings Colonel Huber would play the piano – 'The Gendarmes' Duet' or a selection from **The Merry Widow** were his stalwarts – but tonight he was sitting quietly with Lieutenant Klein and a couple of other officers. The gramophone was silent and untouched. The chair by the window where Lieutenant Stock liked to read his westerns had been left empty as a mark of respect. In the corner, Obersturmbannführer Drexler, smoking a cigar, was entertaining a pair of SS men who had driven over from their headquarters in The Hague. Sturmscharführer Biwack was with them. Occasionally he would glance over in Graf's direction. At the post-mortem into the accident that afternoon, he had demanded to know why Graf wasn't at the launch site when the missile exploded.

'Why? Would you have preferred it if I was incinerated?'

'Of course not. I merely wonder why an SS patrol reported that at the time of the accident you were in the restricted zone beside the sea some distance away.'

'Obviously, I was signalling to a British submarine.'

When Seidel had tried unsuccessfully to suppress

a snort of laughter, Biwack had rounded on him. 'There's nothing funny about this, Lieutenant!'

'I'm aware of that. Stock was a friend of mine. I require no lectures from you.'

'Leave it, gentlemen,' ordered Huber. He explained to Biwack: 'Dr Graf has been sent by Peenemünde as a technical liaison officer, because of the number of modifications to the missile. He is not required to attend every launch – it would be physically impossible.'

'I'm not suggesting Dr Graf was responsible, merely that if he had been present, he might have noticed a fault in the missile. Plainly there **was** a fault, was there not? Is it possible there could have been sabotage?'

'Most unlikely,' said Huber. 'Indeed, impossible. But security is the province of the SS.'

All eyes turned to the SS commander. Drexler far outranked the National Socialist Leadership Officer, and beneath his well-cushioned exterior was known to have a sharp temper, but Graf noticed he was careful to keep his tone polite. 'Security is very tight. The rockets are closely guarded from the moment they leave the factory – all the way from Nordhausen by rail – and then when they arrive here, they are never out of the custody of the technical troop. It's true that at the start of the campaign there was some evidence of sabotage carried out by foreign workers at the factory, but we took severe measures to deal with that, and nothing's been reported since.'

Severe measures, thought Graf. He preferred not to imagine what that might mean. He wanted to say, **Listen, gentlemen, are you all crazy? This rocket is the most technologically advanced feat of engineering the world has ever seen, and no one involved in designing it ever expected them to be rolled off a production line at the rate of one every ninety minutes.** Instead he said, 'The rocket is checked and rechecked by the technical troop from the moment it's delivered to the railhead, so unless Sturmscharführer Biwack believes there are saboteurs within the regiment . . .'

'I did not say that!'

'. . . then the accident was the result of a technical fault. Or, I should say, a **series** of technical faults that compounded one another. I have visited the scene with Lieutenant Seidel, but there is nothing physically detectable that can tell us what went wrong. We must just stick to our pre-launch procedures, and make sure these are never skimped in our understandable desire to fire as many V2s as possible each day.'

Huber flushed and glared at Graf but made no reply.

'Check,' said Seidel.

Graf looked down at the board. He was thinking of the girl in the Wassenaar wood. What **had** she been doing there? He didn't regret letting her go. If he had handed her over to the SS in their present mood, shooting would have been the least of it. He put his forefinger on the top of his king. He could move it again. Perhaps he would find a way out if he stalled for long enough. Seidel was not a strong player. But he couldn't be bothered. He tipped the piece over.

'I surrender.'

'Finally!' Seidel started clearing the pieces, as if he feared Graf might change his mind. 'Another?'

'Sorry. I'm too tired.'

'A drink then?' He signalled to the orderly. 'Two cognacs.'

'We have no cognac, Oberleutnant.'

'What do you have?'

'Curaçao.'

Seidel wrinkled his nose. 'It had better be that, then.'

After the orderly had gone, Graf said, 'That brothel this morning . . .'

'What of it?' Seidel was putting the pieces back in their box.

'Who are the girls?'

'Oh, all sorts. Some Dutch. Some French. Some Polish. It's quite above-board. The army runs it.'

'Where do they get the women?'

'Prisoners from the camps, mostly. A few professionals from before the war. Why?'

'Sounds grim.'

Seidel shrugged. 'Everyone is just trying to survive.'

'You've been?'

'Once or twice.'

The orderly returned with two glasses of bright blue liquid.

Graf said, 'It looks like copper sulphate.'

'Smells like it, too.' Seidel took a sip. 'Actually, it's not so bad. Try it.' He waited while Graf put the glass to his lips. 'What do you think?'

'It's like gasoline with a twist of orange.' He downed it nevertheless. He played with the empty glass for a moment, then set it on the table. 'Shall we go?'

'Where?'

'This brothel.'

Seidel laughed. 'My dear Graf, you surprise me every day! Are you serious?'

'No, not really.' He felt embarrassed. 'Forget I said it.'

'But now you've put the idea into my head.' Seidel drained his glass. 'Why not? Let's at least get out of this morgue.'

Graf was conscious of the others watching as they walked towards the door.

Huber called after them. 'Goodnight, gentlemen!'

They descended the staircase, past black-and-white photographs of pre-war holidays, and went out onto the deserted promenade. The breeze was stiff with the scent of brine and seaweed. A canopy was flapping somewhere. A steel cable clinked a hollow beat against a metal pole. The massive hulk of the Palace Hotel, with its towers and high domed roof, loomed like an ocean liner run aground. A defensive concrete wall topped with barbed wire screened the view of the beach.

Seidel's Kübelwagen was parked alone on the empty forecourt. He switched on the shaded headlamps, started the engine and executed a sweeping loop over the wet asphalt. Graf put his hand out of the side and felt the spray.

Seidel said, 'There must have been some women at Peenemünde?'

'Naturally. Hundreds.'

'And? What were they like? Young? Old?'

'Young mostly. Secretaries. Assistants. Some mathematicians. The senior engineers were allowed to bring their wives and children.'

Seidel fell silent for a moment. 'Are you married – do you mind if I ask?'

'No. Are you?'

'Yes. Why?' He shot Graf a sideways look. 'Do you think it matters if I go to a brothel?'

'Not to me.'

Seidel laughed. 'If there were hundreds of women, even you, Graf, must have found one, surely?'

'I did.'

'Go on.'

'Her name was Karin. She died in an air raid.'

'Ah. I'm sorry.'

Graf leaned out of the window and put his face into the breeze. In the month or more he had been in Holland, it was the first time he had mentioned her name.

*

The RAF's attempt to destroy Peenemünde, code-named Operation Hydra, was mounted in near-perfect conditions under a cloudless full moon on the night of 17–18 August 1943. At 11 p.m., eight Mosquitoes dropped target flares and two dozen bombs over Berlin to trick the Germans into believing the capital was to be the main focus of the attack. The Luftwaffe scrambled 150 fighters to meet the threat. While they searched the empty skies above the city, and 89 flak batteries fired more than 11,000 rounds at the imaginary attackers, just after midnight, 200 kilometres to the north, 600 heavy bombers crossed the coast.

Peenemünde's population that night was nearly twenty thousand: engineers, scientists and technicians with their families; mechanics, clerks, secretaries, typists, guards, cooks, teachers, construction workers and foreign slave labourers, mostly French and Russian. The evening of the raid, a Tuesday, had been hot and still. The slaves were locked in their wooden barrack huts behind electrified wire. The Germans strolled through the fragrant pine woods and sat on the sand. A game of volleyball was being played on the beach within sight of the rocket assembly building.

Graf swam out and lay on his back with his feet pointing towards the setting sun, buoyed by the salinity of the water. He had only to rotate his arms occasionally to float without effort. The surface was warm after the long summer, but he could sense the great chilly depths beneath him, could feel the pull of the current carrying him eastwards out to sea, the motion of the waves flexing his body to their shape. He surrendered to the drift for as long as he dared, then rolled over and swam hard against the current, back towards the shore, where Karin, her slender figure haloed in his memory by the sunset, waited with a towel.

He had met her in the spring. She was the new personal assistant to von Braun's deputy, and Graf's immediate superior, Dr Walter Thiel. Her duties covered everything from scheduling her irritable boss's meetings to helping look after his two children. Everybody liked her; she was beautiful; she had a gift for spreading calm. When he asked her out and she accepted, he was amazed. After the war, she wanted to teach kindergarten. She was twenty-three. He had already decided he wanted to marry her, was intending to ask her – might have done so that night, in fact, if things had gone differently. But she hated it when he swam out so far and her anxiety had put her in a rare bad mood.

He emerged dripping and breathless. She handed him the towel, turned away with a frown and went back up the beach to pack away their picnic. He changed out of his trunks beneath the towel, wobbling first on one leg, then the other. A brief kiss on her warm cheek, a last taste of salt from the sea, and abruptly she was gone, walking in the direction of the old pre-war hotel where most of the single women lived.

Irritated, his good mood spoilt, Graf made his way back along the forest road in the humid twilight, through the security gate to the Experimental Works compound. His bachelor apartment, one of a dozen allotted to senior engineers, including von Braun, was on the second floor of Building 5, next to the main offices. He showered in cold water in an effort to cool off, draped his trunks on the bathroom windowsill to dry, and lay naked on his bed under a single sheet.

He had expected an enemy air raid sooner or later. Several times that summer he had looked up and seen a thin line of vapour, like the scratch of a fingernail, high in the cloudless cobalt blue. He suspected they were being photographed by the British. Even so, when the air raid siren woke him just after midnight, his first instinct was to stay in bed, listening out for the usual drone of the enemy formations as they streamed overhead down 'Berlin Alley' on their way to bomb the capital. He waited for the all-clear. Minutes passed. Then came the rapid **thump-thump-thump** of anti-aircraft fire. He sprang out of bed and went to the window. The full moon was brilliant. In its quicksilver flood, the buildings cast sharp shadows. Beyond the workshops and laboratories, a spray of multicoloured flak was rising from the harbour battery like a strand of glass beads. Strange configurations of lights –

red, green, yellow – seemed to hang in the sky like Christmas decorations. White flares descended slowly by parachute. Machine-gun fire rattled from the rooftops. It all seemed to be happening towards the south of the island. He watched for a while, then it occurred to him he ought to get to a shelter. He was still pulling on his shoes when a huge detonation blew out the window where he had been standing a moment before.

He ran along the corridor of the apartment block and down the stairs. The front door lay across the steps, blown off its hinges by an aerial mine. It rose and fell like a see-saw as he stepped across it into the swirling rosy fog created by the artificial smoke screens. The scene was surreal, dreamlike. Here and there the chemical gauze flickered pink and red from the burning buildings. The full moon seemed to be hurtling through gaps in the mist. He could see a wash of stars, the brilliant narrow beams of the searchlights duelling across the sky. The bombers were invisible, but he could hear their heavy engines, very low and loud, in between the deafening crashes of explosions shaking the ground. Shadowy figures ran past him in panic. For perhaps a minute, he stood transfixed, as if he were merely a member of the audience at some fantastical son et lumière. Only when he became aware of the intense heat did his residual fear of an explosion bring him to his senses. He set off quickly down the street, around the corner, towards the air raid shelter.

At the bottom of the steps, in the low concrete chamber, a dozen figures crouched around the walls. It was newly dug out; it stank of lime. The overhead lamp swung with each detonation. The light flickered. He recognised the faces of some of the engineers. Nobody was speaking. They were looking at the floor. Gradually the time between the explosions became longer, and after five minutes of silence, Graf decided to go in search of Karin.

In the bright moonlight he could see that the headquarters building had been destroyed, and the design block and the mess hall, but the wind tunnel and the telemetry labs were untouched. He went out through the security gate and set off down the road. It was covered by fine white sand, as if a storm had passed through. He could still hear a lot of aeroplanes overhead. Tiny pieces of aircraft debris, shrapnel fragments and spent bullet casings were pattering like hailstones across the road and through the trees. A Lancaster bomber with one of its engines trailing fire streaked low across the sky and disappeared in the direction of the sea. One of the rocket storage buildings in the production area was in flames. But it was the accommodation buildings that seemed to have been worst hit. Parts of the housing estate and the slave labour camp were on fire. Several hundred prisoners in their striped uniforms were sitting in a field beside the road with their hands on their heads, guarded by SS men with machine guns.

As soon as he reached the compound where Karin

lived, he knew she must be dead. The big hotel was windowless, roofless, gutted. A row of corpses, some badly charred, lined the path. He steeled himself to look at the faces but there was no one he knew. Perhaps she was alive after all. People were wandering around. 'Karin Hahn, have you seen her? Has anyone seen Karin Hahn?' He stood with his hands on his hips and tried to think what she would have done when the bombs began to drop, where she might have gone. He retraced his steps back towards the housing estate.

'I need to find Dr Thiel. Is the Thiel family safe, does anyone know?'

He found them ten minutes later, laid out in the school hall. Their house, he discovered afterwards, had suffered a direct hit. The slit trench in front of it where they had been sheltering was a crater. They had been buried alive in the soft sandy soil. Thiel looked different without his glasses, but unlike the bodies in the women's camp he at least seemed peaceful, and mercifully undisfigured. So too did Martha Thiel, and their children, Sigrid and Siegfried; and so, lying a little way apart from them, her head tilted slightly quizzically to one side in a mannerism he knew well, did Karin.

They stopped at the checkpoint that guarded the entrance to the Wassenaar street and waited with the engine running. An SS man shone his torch in their faces and then onto their identity papers. When he returned them, he gave a slight wink. 'Have a good evening.' Another guard raised the barrier.

Graf was beginning to regret the whole undertaking. He would have suggested abandoning it. But Seidel was like a hunting dog who had picked up a scent. He was sitting on the edge of his seat, his head hunched over the steering wheel, straining his eyes to follow the unmarked cobbled road. Each time they came to a house, he would slow and take a quick glance at it. He muttered to himself, 'It's so damn easy to miss in the blackout . . .'

Behind their gates and overgrown hedges, the mansions succeeded one another – silent, dark, abandoned – each quite different: some rustic, some modern, a few elaborate, like mini-Versailles. There was a lot of money here, Graf thought. Decades of it; centuries, probably. He said, 'I'm surprised they haven't been looted.'

'Don't you believe it. One of my men got caught with a Vermeer under his bed. A fucking Vermeer, for God's sake! They sent him to a punishment battalion on the Eastern Front.'

'Isn't that a death sentence?'

'As good as. Discipline, my dear Graf. Discipline! The army's very keen on protecting local property; local people – less so. Ah, here it is!'

He swung the steering wheel and they turned into a gravel drive. The house, so far as Graf could make it out in the weak headlights, was nineteenth century – square, three storeys, built in the French style, with shutters and a high roof. A couple of staff cars were parked in front of the door. Drifts of leaves had piled up around the entrance. The windows were blacked out, and when Seidel turned off the engine, there was a deep silence.

'Are you sure this is the right place?'

'Of course. Are you still up for it?'

'Why not?'

He followed the lieutenant up the steps. Seidel rang the bell. Without waiting for an answer, he pushed open the heavy door. They stepped into a large hall, dimly lit by red-shaded lamps. A staircase rose straight ahead. Doors on either side of the passage. A faint sound of music somewhere. Graf suddenly wondered if he had brought enough money. 'How much does this cost, by the way?'

'A hundred. Plus a tip for the girl. Or girls.'

One of the doors opened and a woman emerged – forties, plump, dark-haired. Her freckled breasts strained against a low-cut black velvet dress. Graf removed his hat politely. She recognised Seidel, or pretended to, and threw out her hands. 'Lieutenant! So good to see you again! A kiss for Madam Ilse.' Her German was thickly flavoured with an Eastern European accent Graf couldn't place. She proffered her face to Seidel. He kissed her twice, on either cheek, as if she were his aunt. 'And who is this?'

'This is my friend, the doctor.'

'A doctor! Let me take your coat,' she said to Graf. He unbuttoned it and handed it to her, together with his hat. Seidel gave her his cap. She hung them carefully on a rack. There were five other caps, Graf noticed – three grey Wehrmacht, two black SS – and a leather greatcoat. 'So! Come.'

She led them through a door into a bar. Thick strata of cigarette smoke hung motionless in the reddish half-light. A gramophone was playing a sentimental song by Mimi Thoma. Four or five men sprawled in comfortable chairs, booted legs outstretched, their jackets open, smoking. A couple of girls perched on the arms of their chairs. An SS man, his chin on his chest, appeared to have passed out on the sofa with his arms around two women, one on either side of him, who were whispering behind his head. There were more women in a huddle around the bar. A waitress, naked from the waist up, carried a tray of empty glasses. Ilse showed them to a shadowy corner where a pair of armchairs faced one another, and beckoned to the waitress.

'What will you drink?'

Seidel said, 'Do you have cognac?'

'Of course we have cognac.' She sounded affronted.

'You see,' he said to Graf, 'we were right to come.'

'Cognac,' said Ilse. The waitress moved away. 'Have you had a chance to look yet? Do you find anyone to your liking?'

Graf glanced around. He couldn't see the girl from the wood. Seidel said, 'That redhead, Marta – is she still here?'

'I'll see if she's free. And your friend?' she said, turning to Graf. 'What is the doctor looking for?'

He was straining his eyes at the bar. 'A blonde. Young. Quite small.'

Seidel laughed. 'You're a deep one, Graf! Do you have a shoe size you prefer?'

The madam nodded judiciously. 'I believe I have the perfect girl.'

She went over to the bar. Seidel took out a pack of cigarettes and offered one to Graf. The cognac came. Graf downed his straight and held out his glass for another. They sat back in their chairs. The lieutenant closed his eyes and conducted the music with his forefinger. He started to sing along with Mimi Thoma. **Sleep, darling, sleep, and dream a fairy tale . . .**

Ilse returned with a tall young woman with curly copper-coloured hair, who made an effort to seem pleased to see Seidel. Behind her, tiny in comparison, was a doll-like girl dressed in a sleeveless tight red satin sheath. Her scarlet lipstick and heavy mascara rendered her almost unrecognisable. The moment she saw Graf, her professional smile vanished. She stopped, and swayed back slightly on her high heels. Marta climbed into Seidel's lap and put her arms around his neck. Ilse steered the blonde girl forward by the shoulders, like a mother presenting a child for inspection. 'This is Femke.' Graf stood. 'See how polite he is, sweetheart,' she murmured into her ear, 'a real gentleman! Look at the way he's staring at you – I can tell he likes you. Why don't you take him upstairs?'

The girl hesitated. Ilse gave her a firm push. 'Go on, darling.'

Slowly, reluctantly, looking past Graf to some point beyond his shoulder, Femke held out her hand. He took it – there was no grip in her thin cold fingers – and followed her out of the bar and into the empty hall. The moment they were out of sight of the drinkers, she snatched it away and stood with her back pressed to the wall. Quietly, in German, she said, 'What is this? Are you Gestapo?'

'No.'

'You're dressed like one.'

'Well, I'm not.'

'Where's your uniform?'

'I don't have a uniform. I'm an engineer.'

'If you're not Gestapo, what do you want?' She sounded almost irritable, as if he were wasting her time.

'You're asking **me** that?' He showed her the marks in the flesh at the base of his thumb. 'What do you think I want? I want to talk to you.'

She opened her mouth to reply. A door slammed above them. They both looked up. Heavy footsteps stamped across the landing. A man began to descend. A pair of jackboots appeared, then black trousers, and finally an SS officer, buttoning his tunic across a fat belly. He stopped at the foot of the stairs and inspected himself in the mirror, smoothing down his hair. He turned and saw them, nodded affably to Graf, then went past them into the bar. Femke waited until he had gone. She looked at Graf, then began to climb the stairs. When she was halfway up she leaned over the banister. 'Well?'

She waited until he was behind her, then continued on ahead of him, a slim, straight, almost sexless figure in her red dress, precariously balanced on her high black heels. Eighteenth-century portraits lined the stairs. The eyes of the prosperous burghers followed them with disapproval. On the landing was a table with a Roman bust. She went past that and up a smaller staircase to the second floor. She threw open a door and stood aside to let him enter. The room was candlelit, seductive. She switched on the overhead light, dispelling the effect, closed the door and leaned her back against it. She was shaking slightly. When she saw that he had noticed, she folded her skinny bare arms to hide it.

'Well? What now? Do we fuck, or what?'

She looked so young – so tiny and fierce – that he almost burst out laughing. 'No, don't worry. No offence – but I don't want to.'

He felt very tired suddenly, and quite drunk. He went over and sat on the edge of the bed. From the room next door came the sound of bedsprings creaking, and the rhythmic knock of a headboard striking the wall. A woman cried out. He swung his legs onto the mattress and lay full length. It was much softer than his bed in Scheveningen. The room seemed to spin. He closed his eyes once more. He could hear the girl moving around. When he opened them again, she was standing over him, pointing a kitchen knife at his throat.

'If you're going to report me, I might as well kill you – at least I'll take a fucking Boche with me.'

'If I was going to report you, I would have done it by now. Put it away.' He closed his eyes again. He felt as he had on the evening before the Peenemünde air raid – disconnected from the world, as if he were drifting over deep cold water. Presently he heard her moving away from the bed, the sound of a drawer opening and closing. 'How old are you?'

There was a pause.

'Eighteen.'

'What were you doing in the woods this morning?'

'I heard the explosion in the night. I wanted to look when it was light.'

'Why?'

'I was curious. The soldiers had gone.'

He opened his eyes and propped himself up on one elbow. She had her back pressed against the dressing table, watching him. 'Femke, right? Is that a Dutch name?' She didn't reply. 'You must have been very curious, to risk getting shot. You're not that stupid. I'm not sure I believe you.'

She pouted at the floor.

Wearily he rolled over and planted his feet on the carpet. He looked around the room. It was like a time capsule from another world. A little armchair, upholstered in pink. Pink curtains. The wallpaper was patterned with pink-beribboned poodles – prancing, playing, standing on their hind legs. He went over to the wardrobe and opened it, ran his hands over the dresses. There was a small riding jacket. Lined up neatly on the wardrobe floor were girls' shoes, riding boots, a pair of ballet pumps. He closed the wardrobe and went over to the chest of drawers, started opening that – blouses, socks, underwear. He left the drawers hanging open, got down on his knees and looked under the bed. Nothing. He stood.

He gestured to the dressing table. 'Move out of the way, please.'

She hesitated. He put his hands on her thin shoulders and gently pushed her to one side. She watched him as he opened the drawer. Beside the knife, and a packet of Wehrmacht-issue condoms ('Vulkan Sanex'), laid out neatly on a sheet of newspaper, were half a dozen small pieces of the V2 rocket motor, none bigger than his fist, all blackened by fire. He recognised part of the turbine exhaust pump, a cooling nozzle from the combustion chamber, a stop valve from the alcohol tank, various other bits and pieces.

'What on earth did you think you were going to do with those?'

'I was interested.'

'Oh, come on! Tell me the truth!'

She shrugged. 'I thought maybe someone would pay me for them.'

'Who? The English? They can pick that stuff up off the streets of London any day of the week.'

'Who said anything about the English?'

'You're in the resistance, right?'

She looked away without answering.

'They get you to listen to the rocket officers when they're drinking? Pillow talk? Pass on what you hear?'

The faint thumping of the bedhead through the wall increased in tempo. This time the woman shrieked. The thumping stopped abruptly. Dear God, he thought, what has become of us?

He started stuffing the rocket fragments into his pockets. 'I'm taking these away. If you get caught with them, you'll be shot, no question.'

'Why should you care?'

He closed the drawer. His hands were blackened with soot, his pockets bulging. 'What is it you want to know?' he asked abruptly. 'I can tell you something that's actually useful, if you like. The missile is unreliable – at the moment we have a failure rate of about one in ten. But the real problem is the shortage of liquid oxygen. Our main production plant in France has been overrun. There are seven plants in Germany, producing two hundred tons a day, which is only enough for twenty-five operational launches. Tell your friends to warn the British that if they want to stop the rockets, not to bother trying to bomb the launch sites, but to concentrate on the liquid oxygen factories and the railways.'

She frowned at him. 'Are you crazy, or what?' He

made a move towards the door, but she blocked him. 'If you go down too soon, they'll be suspicious.'

'All right.'

He lay back on the bed. She sat in the armchair. For a couple of minutes neither spoke. To his surprise, it was she who broke the silence.

'We all thought Germany had lost the war. The rockets left, and then they came back. What does it mean? Are you winning again?'

'No, we're losing.'

'When?'

'Soon. Next year, maybe. How long have you been in Wassenaar?'

'Three months.'

'Where were you before?'

'In a camp – for stealing.'

'Where's home?'

'Groningen.'

'That's in the north?'

She nodded.

'Is there any way you could make a run for it? I could borrow a car. You could hide in the back.' He knew it was ridiculous even as he said it.

She shook her head. 'It's too far.' There was a sound of movement from the neighbouring room. A door opened, slammed shut. They listened to a man's footsteps receding down the passage. 'I should go to her and see if she's all right. You can leave now.'

At the door, he pulled out his wallet and counted out two hundred marks.

She shook her head. 'Pay Ilse.'

'No, this is for you.'

'I haven't done anything.' She opened the door.

He stood, uncertain. 'Well, then. Good luck.'

He put the money back in his wallet and went downstairs.

12

THE THING TO BE SAID for Kay's alarm clock, which she had been given by her mother on the day she was called up to the WAAF, was that it had never failed to wake her, however deeply she was asleep. It had a piercing percussive ring, as if a drill had been inserted into her ear. She flung her hand across the unfamiliar surfaces, fumbling to turn it off. In the blessed silence that followed, she brought the luminous dial up close to her face. Six thirty.

She flopped back on her thin pillows. The room was utterly dark. It took her a moment to remember she wasn't in England about to start her shift, but in Belgium – and at war! She eased her way out from under the blanket and felt around the wall for the light switch. The sudden brightness made her wince. She slipped her greatcoat over her nightdress and picked up her sponge bag. Cautiously she opened the door and listened. The house was silent.

She scampered on tiptoe across the icy corridor to the bathroom.

She was too anxious to avoid being late to linger over her usual morning rituals. Besides, it was too chilly. She splashed her face in the freezing water, and cleaned her teeth, and dragged her brush so savagely through her tangled hair it felt as though her scalp was bleeding. Back in her room, her clothes were stiff, as if they had been starched by the cold, her fingers were numb and clumsy as she tried to fasten her buttons and knot her tie. Finally, when she was fully dressed, she remade the bed and studied the map beneath the lampshade. A route that had looked complicated when the Vermeulens had sketched it out the previous night appeared now quite indecipherable. How would she find her way through the blacked-out streets when she didn't even have a torch?

She made her way along the corridor, hands outstretched like a sleepwalker. On the landing, to her relief, there was a faint gleam rising from below that enabled her to descend the stairs, and when she reached the hall, she saw a crack of light from the kitchen.

Arnaud was at the stove. A kettle was heating. He was dressed in the same outdoor clothes as the night before. He straightened as she came in and turned, smiling. **'Bonjour, mademoiselle. Voudriez-vous du thé que vous nous avez donné?'**

Somehow she managed to dredge up sufficient

French to reply. 'Thank you, but I'm afraid I have no time for tea. Could you point me in the right direction for this street I have to reach?'

'I can do better than that – I can take you there myself.'

She hesitated. At Medmenham they had been taught to be wary of showing people where they worked. But it was hard to see the harm in it, and she doubted she would be able to find the way on her own. 'Are you sure?'

'I insist. There's a curfew, but no one will stop us, not with your uniform. Really, you have plenty of time for tea.'

'Even so, I would prefer to leave now, if you don't mind.'

He shrugged. 'As you wish.' He lifted the kettle off the stove and unlocked the back door.

A brick path, slippery with frost, ran down the side of the house. There was some moonlight, and a few stars – sufficient to show the outline of the garden wall and her breath flickering in the cold. He limped ahead and opened the gate. Beyond it, the cobbled street gleamed faintly. He closed the gate behind them and gestured to the left. 'We go this way.'

Mechelen was silent, medieval in the darkness, foreign to her in a way it was hard to define – some slight smell in the air that was different to England, an unfamiliarity in the twisting streets and in the shapes of the tall terraced buildings. She tried to memorise the route so that she could find her way alone in future. Left, right, left, they zigzagged their way through the sleeping town.

She said, 'Are you normally up this early?' She wasn't interested in the answer; it felt rude to say nothing.

'Yes, quite often.'

'Do you work?'

'Of course.'

'Whereabouts?'

'Oh, various places. Sometimes in the furniture factory. Sometimes in the brewery, when they have the malt and the hops. Sometimes unloading barges. They are short of labour. Most men of my age were forced to go to Germany to work. My leg got me out of it.' He glanced at her. **'Ma bénédiction est ma malédiction.'** He put it in English for her, as if he was proud of the poetry of the phrase. 'My blessing is my curse.'

'Were you injured, do you mind my asking?'

'Not at all. I had polio when I was a baby. "Crippled from birth", as they say.'

'I'm sorry. That's bad luck.' Once again she had the feeling she had been tactless. Even so, she added, 'I was sorry to hear about your brother.'

'Why be sorry? There really is no need to apologise for things that are not your fault.'

They entered a wide street with shops on either side. A man was taking down the shutters on a bakery. There was a yeasty smell of fresh bread. Arnaud patted his stomach. 'That makes me hungry.'

'You are often hungry?'

'Always!'

At the end of the street was a large building with pillars and an arched glass roof that reminded Kay of a grand Victorian railway station. He said, 'It is quicker to cut through here.'

The vast empty space was dimly lit by the moon through the glass roof. A sudden clatter of pigeons echoing from the iron rafters made her heart jump. She was glad she was not alone. 'What is this place?'

'The food market – when there is food, that is.'

Once they were out the other side, he said casually, 'I saw the radar vans beside the canal last week.'

'Really?' She was on her guard at once.

'Is that what your work is – radar?'

'I told you last night: I can't discuss it.'

'Forgive me. I didn't know it was so secret. Now you see I am the one who must apologise.'

He sounded offended, and lengthened his stride, swinging his damaged leg angrily, his powerful shoulders rocking from side to side. She was careful to stay just behind him to avoid further conversation, and when they came to the bridge over the river, and the twin spires appeared faintly ahead, she said, 'I'm fine now, thank you, Arnaud. I know the way from here.'

He halted at the edge of the water. 'Are you sure? You go down to the Brusselpoort, and then turn right. The Boches' place is on this side of the road.'

'I remember.'

'What time will you leave? If you want, I can meet you and bring you back again.'

'No need. I can find my own way now, I think.'

'Good, then.' He stuck out his hand. She took it. Once again he raised her hand to his lips and kissed it.

'Au revoir,' she said, **'et merci.'**

She walked on. After half a minute she glanced over her shoulder. In the slowly dissipating darkness he was still watching her from the bridge. She raised her hand. He waved back, then turned and disappeared into the town. She quickened her pace, circling the old city gate and heading down the broad road. An army lorry went past, soldiers leaning out of the back. One of them wolf-whistled. She put her head down.

It was a five-minute walk to the bank, but when she reached it, she found the door was locked. She crossed the road to the headquarters, where the lights were on, and knocked. When nobody appeared, she went inside. There was an enticing smell of frying bacon. Upstairs in the mess, a couple of lieutenants from the Survey Regiment were helping themselves to tea from an urn. A pile of bacon sandwiches stood on a hotplate beside it.

'Tea?' One of the lieutenants insisted on pouring her a cup.

The other handed her a sandwich. 'Are you one of the calculators?'

'That's right.'

'Sandy Lomax.'

'Bill Duffield.'

'Kay Caton-Walsh.'

They balanced their plates on their cups and shook hands awkwardly.

Bill, who had a Yorkshire accent, said, 'Why don't you come and join us?'

They took the table furthest from the door. Transport must have arrived. At any rate, the room had started to fill with yawning, bleary-eyed officers. Wing Commander Knowsley stuck his head around the door, apparently looking for someone, and then withdrew it.

Kay said, 'When did you arrive?'

'Wednesday. Sorry.' Sandy put his hand to his mouth and finished chewing. 'Wednesday. You?'

'Yesterday.'

She held her sandwich in both hands, savouring the moment, then took a bite. It seemed to her the most delicious thing she had ever tasted. There were no napkins. She wiped the grease from her chin as discreetly as she could with the back of her hand.

Bill was watching her. 'Hungry?'

'Starving.'

'Whatever you do, don't touch the local food.'

'Why?'

'Apparently they fertilise the crops with human waste – sorry to be crude about it. A couple of the men have already gone down with something nasty.

They're practically living in the latrines. Stick to stuff from cans. And don't drink from the taps – bottled water only. In some of the towns the Germans poisoned the water.'

'Right.' She finished her sandwich and eyed the hotplate, wondering whether it would be greedy to go back for another, but the conversation had rather put her off.

The door banged open and Barbara Colville breezed in. 'Oh, thank Christ, I thought I was late! Morning, all. That smells good.' She threw her slide rule and logarithm tables down on the table and went over to the urn.

Kay looked at the slide rule in dismay. Sandy offered her a cigarette from a silver case. She shook her head. 'No, thanks.' The two lieutenants lit up.

Barbara came back with her tea and sandwich and sat down opposite Kay, who was still staring at the slide rule. 'What's up with you?'

'I'm an idiot. I was in such a panic about being late, I left my stuff back in my billet.'

'Oh, don't worry about it. There are bound to be spares.' She bit into her sandwich. 'What're your digs like?'

'Spartan. Yours?'

'I've struck lucky, actually. I'm with a widow who seems to have decided to mother me. She made me a vegetable pie.'

Bill said, 'I hope you didn't touch it.'

'Why?'

'Bill has heard some rumours about the local food.' Kay introduced the two lieutenants to Barbara. As Bill repeated his lugubrious warnings, and Barbara made dutiful expressions of horror, she sipped her tea and cursed her absent-mindedness. She imagined Dorothy Garrod whispering in her ear, as she had when she'd first arrived at Danesfield House: 'Concentrate, Kay, dear. **Concentrate.**'

Barbara took a cigarette from Sandy, leaned in to the flaring match. Kay noticed how she briefly touched his hand. She sat back and exhaled a jet of smoke through her nostrils. The door opened and Flight Officer Sitwell came in, followed by a major with a handlebar moustache. The three smokers quickly stubbed out their cigarettes in the ashtray. They all stood and saluted.

The major said, 'Right then. Let's get this show started.'

Sitwell looked with distaste at the smouldering ashtray, and then at Kay and Barbara. 'Good morning, ladies.'

'Ma'am.'

'When you're ready.'

They left the mess together and went out into the street. It was starting to get light. A few pedestrians were on their way to work. In the bank opposite, the windows were now lit. A sentry had taken up position beside the door. They showed their identity cards and went inside. The group separated with mutual wishes of good luck. The lieutenants followed the major left across the lobby – to a rear exit, presumably, allowing them access to the waste ground behind the bank where the radar vans were stationed. Kay and Barbara trailed Sitwell to the right, through the counter and down the steps to the vault. Knowsley was at his desk, talking on the telephone. At a table beside him sat a Signals Corps corporal. On the other side of the room three WAAF sergeants were already behind a row of desks. Kay and Barbara took their old seats in the centre. Kay was relieved to see that their places had already been set with slide rules, logarithm tables, pencils, notepads. She slipped off her coat and hung it over the back of her chair.

Sitwell stood in front of the blackboard. Behind it, an old-fashioned station clock showed two minutes to eight. She said, 'All we need now is a V2. And while we wait, we practise. Let's see how much you've forgotten.' She turned and began chalking rapidly on the board.

As the morning went on, the vault began to get busier. WAAF sergeants came and went. Messages arrived by motorcycle courier. A colonel of the Survey Regiment, immaculate in his uniform, stiff as a guardsman, conferred with Knowsley then prowled around the room. He checked the maps and the telephones, looked at his watch, sat in the corner for five minutes and finally got up and left. Knowsley came over and perched on the edge of the central table, watching Kay and Barbara as they worked their slide rules, leafed through their logarithms, filled sheet after sheet with calculations. Sitwell timed them with her stopwatch: seven minutes twenty – no good. Six minutes fifteen – better. Five minutes fifty-two – that's more like it. The wing commander lit a pipe and clamped it between his teeth. Pungent clouds of blue smoke drifted across the maps. His foot tapped nervously against the table leg.

Just before ten o'clock, Flight Officer Sitwell announced that they had practised enough. 'Take a break. If you need the lavatory, go now. It's upstairs. But one at a time. Be quick about it, and don't leave the building.'

Barbara said to Kay, 'Do you want to go?'

'In a minute. You go first.'

Barbara hurried up the stairs. Kay stood and stretched, rotated her head. The room had gone very quiet. There was no sound except the ticking of the clock. Knowsley looked pensive. 'They seem to be taking their time today. Normally they've launched by now.'

'There's no pattern to it, sir?'

'None. Sometimes there are three or four hours between launches. Sometimes they send up two, more or less at the same time.' He sucked on his pipe and inspected the bowl. He was fiddling, Kay realised, to calm his nerves, talking to fill up the silence. 'I don't know what their thinking is, operationally. I guess they have a lot of technical problems and just have to fire when they're ready.' He had smoked all his tobacco. The pipe made a whistling noise. 'I'd love to watch one take off.'

'Would you really?'

'Oh yes. It must be a hell of a sight. Wouldn't you?'

'I've never really thought about it.'

'How odd. Perhaps it's just a male thing. Freudian, and all that.'

A telephone rang. They both swung round to look at it. The Signals Corps corporal snatched up the receiver, listened for a second, covered the mouthpiece with his hand and called out, 'They've launched!'

An electric bell began to ring. Just like school, Kay thought. Everybody moved quickly back to their places. She could feel her heart thumping. Barbara clattered down the stairs and rushed to her seat. She made a face at Kay across the table. 'Bloody typical – it has to happen while I've got my knickers round my ankles.'

'Quiet!' shouted Sitwell.

Kay sat with her pencil poised above her notepad. A few seconds passed. The corporal was listening intently. He had his hand held up, like a marshal with a flag at the start of a race. 'Contact bearing two six zero; altitude thirty-one thousand; velocity three two four seven feet per second . . . Contact bearing two six zero, altitude thirty-nine thousand, velocity three eight six two . . .'

'There she goes,' muttered Knowsley.

'. . . Contact bearing two six zero, altitude fifty-seven thousand, velocity four zero three eight . . .'

around the desk to examine it. The red bead – like a drop of blood, she thought – was positioned precisely in the centre of the Scheveningen Wood.

On the corporal's desk, the telephone rang. All eyes turned to watch him as he reached to answer it. He listened, nodded, covered the mouthpiece.

'They've launched again.'

'My God, the speed of her . . .'

Sitwell said, 'Has anyone got the positions for the y-axis yet?'

One of the WAAF sergeants was writing rapidly. 'Yes, ma'am.'

The corporal announced, 'Contact lost.'

'She's already out of range,' said Knowsley. 'Well!' He shook his head and let out his breath. 'Now we wait.'

One of the sergeants sat with the phone tucked under her chin, on an open line to Stanmore, a pencil in her hand. Another stood by the large-scale map of London and south-east England holding a tin of pins.

The room fell silent again. Minutes passed. It was sinister to contemplate the rocket soaring towards space, Kay thought, the curve of its flight path flattening, the gradual turn, the speed of its descent. **There will be someone on the ground in London just like I was, someone going about their life on a normal Tuesday morning, full of plans and trivial concerns, entirely unaware that the mathematics of the parabolic curve have already condemned them.** She looked down at her sheet of paper – at the pencilled figures representing the values of bearing, height, speed and position. The integers of death. She remembered how she had just pulled her dress over her head in Warwick Court when something changed in the atmosphere, as if the air had been sucked away, and then came the crack of the sonic boom, the express-train roar of the incoming rocket, all of it swallowed by the rumble of the collapsing building.

'Report of impact,' called the WAAF sergeant with the phone. Her voice pulled Kay back to the present. Another pause, while the radar operators in Home Defence in England made their calculations. 'Latitude bearing fifty-one point thirty, three one point six one four six. Longitude zero, zero, thirty-seven point eight seven nine two.'

The sergeant put a red pin in the map. Kay picked up her slide rule. All thoughts of what was happening in London evaporated. She was surprised at her own calmness. Her mind bifurcated, one part concentrating on the procedure that had to be followed, the other making sure her calculations were accurate. The window on the slide rule moved back and forth, comforting in its precision. The world reduced to numbers. After exactly six minutes, she raised her hand and passed her notebook across the table to Barbara. Knowsley and Sitwell gathered at Barbara's shoulder to watch her check Kay's calculations against her own. Kay studied their faces. Now she was nervous. She would have liked a cigarette. After a minute, Sitwell took the notebook over to the map that showed London and the North Sea all the way to the Dutch coast. She measured off the distance.

'Latitude bearing fifty-two point seven, four point two seven zero two. Longitude four point one seven, fifty-two point three zero nine eight.'

'Latitude bearing fifty-two point seven . . .' One

of the WAAF sergeants, in the polished accent of a BBC announcer, repeated the coordinates clearly and calmly down the line to Fighter Command.

Barbara smiled across the table at Kay. 'Don't worry, sweetie, you got it bang right.'

At RAF Coltishall, nine miles north of Norwich, four Spitfire pilots – members of 602 (City of Glasgow) Squadron – who had been sitting in their cockpits for several hours, were ordered to scramble. Their warplanes were brand-new Type XVIs, only received from the factory that month, specially modified to serve as bombers. For several days the squadron had been studying high-altitude reconnaissance photographs of The Hague, familiarising themselves with the Type XVIs and practising dive-bombing. Straining under the weight of two 250-pound bombs, one under either wing, they roared down the runway and took off into low cloud. Flying in tight formation, they turned east, crossed the long sandy beach between Waxham and Winterton-on-Sea and headed over the North Sea towards the Dutch coast, 120 miles away. The attack coordinates were radioed to them by the control tower. At a maximum speed of just over 300 mph, they would reach their target in twenty-five minutes.

Sitwell moved to the large-scale map of The Hague carefully rechecked the bearings, and pressed a pin into the corkboard. Kay rose from her seat and wen

13

AS FAR AS GRAF WAS concerned, the first missile of the day had gone off without a hitch. A minute after it had disappeared into the clouds, the crew had emerged from their slit trench and started rolling up the electrical cables. The firing control vehicle had lumbered out of its burrow and reversed up to the launch table. Afterwards, when he looked back on it, he would concede that perhaps there hadn't been quite the sense of urgency there should have been. But it was so long since the men had seen an enemy aircraft – **Jabos** they called them, from **Jagdbomber:** fighter-bomber – that a certain laxity was understandable.

A sergeant leaned out of the half-track's window. 'Do you want a lift?'

'Thanks, but I've got to check on Schenk's platoon.'

Like a doctor making house calls, Graf moved on from one rocket to another. About five hundred metres to the west of the first launch site, a second V2 was standing on its platform, ready to take off. Yet again there had been a fault in the transformer, and the launch had been delayed for two hours while a replacement was fitted. Sergeant Schenk, the veteran of the Eastern Front who had left his frostbitten ears behind in a field hospital near Leningrad, was standing at the base of the missile. The control compartments were shut. Condensed air was venting from close to the liquid oxygen tank. She was ready to go.

Schenk said, 'Do you want to stay and watch?'

'I'll pass, if it's all the same to you. I need to get back to the base.'

'No problem. Your signature's enough.' He held out his clipboard for Graf to confirm that the repair had been carried out. 'I hear they're burying Lieutenant Stock and the others tomorrow morning. Should be quite an occasion.'

Graf wondered if the remark was meant to convey reproach, but he could see no evidence of it in the sergeant's battered face. 'So I understand.' He signed the chit and handed back the clipboard.

'That's war, isn't it? Some of these kids are so wet, they still have their mothers' milk on their lips.'

'Well, nobody knows this war better than you, Sergeant.' He was keen to avoid one of Schenk's horror stories about fighting the Russians. 'I'll see you around.'

'That you will.'

He set off down the road.

The morning was quiet, cold, grey. He was on the same stretch of road that he had walked with Biwack on Saturday morning, running east to west across Scheveningen Wood, with its view down to the lake. No one was about. He was glad of the solitude. He slowed his pace so he could enjoy it longer. From behind him came the roar of a rocket motor igniting. He stopped and turned to look. A second later, Schenk's missile shot clear of the trees. 'Go on, tilt, you bastard,' he muttered, and as if on cue, the V2's trajectory flattened just before it vanished into the ceiling of cloud. Good. There would be no more launches for an hour or two. He noticed a park bench overlooking the lake and decided to take a rest.

He still had a hangover from the previous night. A combination of curaçao and cognac and the memory of his conversation with the girl in the brothel weighed heavily upon him. Had he really told her all that stuff about the rate of misfires and the shortage of liquid oxygen? He took off his hat and rubbed his forehead with the back of his hand. **I must be going crazy.** He promised himself he would keep away from the brothel. But her image kept returning. Seidel had said, as they were driving away, 'She was a funny, skinny little thing. What made you choose her?'

'I don't know. Maybe she reminded me of someone I used to know.'

The explanation seemed to satisfy the lieutenant's

curiosity. 'Fair enough. Each to his own. I always ask for Marta exactly because she **doesn't** remind me of anyone.'

Graf lit a cigarette and stretched out his legs, his arm resting along the back of the bench. Because the ground fell away slightly towards the lake, he had a good view. There was something melancholy about a lake in winter that suited his mood. He had disposed of the fragments of the burned-out rocket motor that morning, dropping them at intervals in the woods. He supposed he had made himself Femke's accomplice. Once again he toyed with the idea of trying to rescue her, driving her back to her home town. But they were bound to be stopped. Perhaps there was someone in the resistance who could hide her in The Hague. He could drive that short distance, surely? That was feasible. Maybe he would go back after all, and suggest it.

He was still turning the idea over in his mind when the wail of the air raid siren carried from the direction of the town.

It was the first time he had heard the warning for weeks. His immediate thought, just as it had been at Peenemünde, was that it was most likely to be a drill. He was only about three hundred metres short of the tented base of the technical troop. But instead of running up the road to take cover in its air raid trenches, he stayed on the bench and scanned the sky. Judging by the way the V2s had disappeared that morning, almost as soon as they began to tilt, he reckoned the cloud cover must be high, maybe as much as 3,000 metres – dangerously high, now he came to think about it. Suddenly, against the grey, he saw tiny smudges of black erupting, like puffs of squid ink, followed by the distant **pom-pom-pom** of the anti-aircraft batteries opening up from their positions in Oostduinen.

That brought him to his feet.

The tactics of a Spitfire formation on a bombing run were to approach from a height of around 8,000 feet, identify the target, roll onto their backs and dive in line very steeply, at an angle of 75 degrees, to an altitude of 3,000 feet; release their bombs from an almost vertical position, the leader first; and then pull back hard on their joysticks and climb away at full throttle. This was the manoeuvre that 602 Squadron had been practising above the fens of East Anglia over the past few days, and this was the spectacle Graf witnessed that November morning: four dots dropping out of the clouds to the north, in perfect file, swelling rapidly in size and noise, the whining note of their dives rising to a crescendo, heading straight towards him. The precision of it was so extraordinary – the loud piston-crack of the famous Rolls-Royce Merlin engines so unlike anything he had ever heard – that the engineer in him remained riveted to the spot, even as he saw the bombs detach from beneath the warplanes' wings. Only when he heard the whistle of their descent did he realise the danger.

He threw himself full-length, pressed his face into the wet grass and covered his head with his hands just as the boom of the explosions started rolling across the lake. Each detonation vibrated through his stomach. He felt horribly exposed with his back presented to the sky. He imagined the pattern of the bombs creeping closer. He counted eight in all. When the last of the reverberations died away, he lay for another minute listening to the drone of the Spitfires' engines dwindling in the distance, pursued by the rattle of heavy-calibre machine-gun fire.

He picked himself up. A shroud of black smoke was rising above the woods on the opposite side of the lake. Some of the thin pines close to the shore were on fire from top to bottom, like burning brands.

Was it really over? At Peenemünde the bombing had gone on for the best part of an hour, wave after wave of it. He squinted at the sky, but there was nothing to see except a few dirty wisps of brown smoke, the residue of exploded shells, already fading.

He set off up the road. As he rounded the curve, several dozen men in grey overalls began emerging from the side lane that led to the technical troop's tents. They crossed the street and gathered to stare across the lake. A Kübelwagen appeared behind them, sounding its horn to clear a path. Colonel Huber climbed out of the front seat, followed by Lieutenant Klein from the driver's side. Biwack jumped out of the back seat. Obersturmbannführer

Drexler emerged after him, twisting his body to lever himself through the narrow gap. Huber lifted a pair of binoculars and scanned the fire. Graf was debating whether or not to join them when Drexler noticed him and beckoned him over.

'Dr Graf – are you all right?'

'Yes, I'm fine. Was anyone hurt?'

'That is what we are trying to determine.'

Huber was still peering through his binoculars. 'Half a kilometre closer and they would have wiped us out.' He turned to Klein. 'Do we have any stores in that area?'

Klein said, 'Not that I recall, Colonel.'

Huber resumed his inspection of the fire. 'There's no one over there that I can see.' He gave the binoculars to Drexler. 'We should go and make sure.' He spotted Graf. 'You should come too.'

They clambered back into the Kübelwagen. Graf squeezed into the rear seat next to Biwack. Perhaps it was his imagination, but the National Socialist Leadership Officer seemed to be ignoring him. Klein, who had been a mechanic before the war, drove skilfully but quickly, throwing them around. Graf hung onto the door. Just before the SS checkpoint, the lieutenant swung the wheel hard over to the right. They left the main road and descended the grassy slope towards the lake. From here, they got a much better view of the fire. Spurts of orange flame stood out brilliantly in the grey morning. As they drove around the water's edge, they could hear it crackling, devouring the vegetation. Smoke and ash drifted on the wind across the water. The bombs had fallen on the little island as well as on the opposite shore.

Klein said, 'It looks as though they may have dropped some incendiaries, Colonel.'

'No point in trying to put that out,' said Huber. 'Safer to let it burn. Stop here.'

They got out and stood on the shore, surveying the fire from a distance of a hundred metres. Graf had a turn with the binoculars. One of the bombs had left a deep crater, as if a giant thumb had gouged out the earth. When the wind shifted in their direction, he could feel the heat.

Klein said, 'I don't think we can have had anything stored there, Colonel. If we had, it would have exploded by now.'

Huber nodded. 'We were lucky.'

Biwack said, 'Has this happened before?'

'It never happens,' said Huber. 'The **Jabos** hit our old launch site at Rijsterbos about six weeks ago, but only after we'd pulled out of the area to come here.'

Biwack frowned. 'Then why has it happened today, I wonder?

'Who can say?'

Klein said, 'Perhaps an RAF patrol spotted something.'

'What is there to spot?' said Huber. 'The missiles are only moved from the railhead when it's dark.

The Luftwaffe have checked our camouflage security from the air. It's first-rate. We're undetectable.'

Biwack had taken out his notebook. 'Except during a launch, presumably.'

'True.' Huber eyed the notebook irritably. 'But we never launch if there are reports of enemy aircraft within fifty kilometres.'

'Then perhaps our location was betrayed by someone on the ground?' He looked at Drexler.

'Impossible,' said the SS commander. 'We have the entire area sealed off. The local population are long gone. There are no Dutch civilians within at least four kilometres.'

'Dr Graf?' said Biwack. 'What do you make of it?'

'Me?' Graf looked at him in surprise. He had been thinking of the girl in the brothel. 'Why would I have an opinion? I only know about the engineering. Security is nothing to do with me.'

'It could have been a coincidence,' suggested Klein. 'A routine patrol decided to dump their bombs before turning for home.'

'It didn't look much of a coincidence to me,' said Biwack. 'It looked very precise, in fact.'

'Let's not over-think it, gentlemen!' said Huber sharply. 'It's hardly a disaster. Look! All they hit were trees!' He folded his arms and stared at the column of smoke. 'Let's treat it as a wake-up call. Perhaps we have become complacent. We should tighten up the launch procedures, make sure we evacuate the sites within ten minutes of firing. Why don't we—'

The wail of the air raid siren stopped him in mid-sentence. For a moment, nobody spoke. They looked from one to another.

Biwack said pointedly, 'Another coincidence?'

'They can't be coming back,' said Drexler. 'They already dropped their bombs. It must be a second wave.'

'Or a false alarm,' added Klein.

Huber said, 'Whatever it is, we should take cover. They might use the fire as an aiming point.' He glanced around. They were out in the open. There was nowhere to shelter. 'Let's get back to the technical troop. And we'd best be quick about it.'

They crammed back into the Kübelwagen. Klein threw it into reverse before Graf even had time to close the door. They shot backwards, braked and lurched forward in a spurt of mud as he spun the car round. By the time they had bounced back up the slope to the road, they could already hear the rapid boom of anti-aircraft fire.

'Stop!' ordered Huber. He cocked his ear, listening – the old artilleryman. 'That's coming from the coastal battery at Rijnsoever. Forget the technical troop. Let's go back to HQ.'

Klein turned right. When they reached the SS checkpoint, he struck the horn with the heel of his hand and left it there until the guard climbed out of his slit trench and lifted the barrier. The main road into town was deserted, abandoned vehicles parked up haphazardly on the kerbside as their occupants sought shelter. They drove at speed past the empty guest houses and hotels towards the seafront. Outside the Hotel Schmitt, Klein braked sharply and they all pitched forward. Huber was the first one out. He stood on the pavement and studied the sky through his binoculars. 'Looks like they're hitting Wassenaar. Where's the damned Luftwaffe?' He adjusted the focus. 'Ah yes, here they come!'

Away to the south, above the rooftops, Graf could see the British planes – four of them again – coming in from the sea, plunging in line almost vertically. The howl of the high-performance engines cut through every other sound. Glittering lines of tracer fire waved against the clouds. He noticed that a couple of other planes had appeared in the sky above the **Jabos.** It was curiously remote and unthreatening, like watching flies buzzing around. The heavy thud of exploding bombs carried over the pounding of ack-ack fire. The hotel windows rattled. Again Graf found himself counting the detonations – eight in all.

Biwack said, 'Shouldn't we get to the shelter?'

'No need,' said Huber. 'They've dropped their bombs.'

'How do you know there won't be more?'

'Because they hunt in packs of four and it's obviously the launch sites they're after. They have no interest in the town, or they'd have bombed it by now.

But do go down to the cellar if you wish, my dear Sturmscharführer. I'm going to my office.'

The colonel turned and strode into the hotel, followed by Drexler and a smirking Klein. After a brief hesitation, Biwack went with them. Graf lingered on the pavement for a moment, reluctant to tear himself away. He could still hear the drone of the planes even though they were no longer visible. The flak and the anti-aircraft from the batteries continued to pound away, but only sporadically. Once again his mind went back to Femke and her meagre collection of debris. It seemed unlikely she had a direct connection to any of this. But what did he know? Perhaps it was the resistance, passing intelligence to the British? He felt suddenly uneasy, complicit.

The colonel's office was on the ground floor at the back of the hotel, and by the time Graf reached it, Huber was already seated at his desk, talking on the telephone. Behind him was a framed photograph of the Führer in a grey tunic with his arms folded, staring moodily off-camera. Graf couldn't remember seeing it before. He wondered if it had been hung for Biwack's benefit. Drexler was also on the telephone, at a corner desk. A couple of junior officers had come up from the shelter. Biwack was studying a large-scale map of The Hague that showed the positions of the regiment's launch sites – with the locations they had used in the past marked with green pins and those in current use marked with red – from the Hook of Holland and Loosduinen in the west, all the way along the coast to Scheveningen, the Haagse Bos and Wassenaar, a strip of more than twenty kilometres.

'Yes, yes,' Huber was saying. 'Good. Understood. Call me when you have more information.' He hung up and went over to the map. 'Well, it seems we were lucky again. Seidel says the bombs hit the woods here, at Duinrell.' He tapped his finger on the map. 'That's about a kilometre from our launch positions. What the devil are they playing at?'

Biwack said, 'Isn't it obvious? They must be receiving intelligence from the local population.'

'Well, if they are, it's not very good intelligence! We've never launched from Duinrell.'

Drexler put down his receiver. 'One of our SS patrols has picked up a kid in the woods nearby. Claims to be the son of a farmer. They're bringing him in for questioning.'

Huber grunted. 'You think he's responsible? A farmer's son? It doesn't seem likely.'

'He was in the restricted zone.'

The colonel's telephone rang. One of the staff officers moved quickly to answer it. He listened for a moment, then came to attention. 'Yes, Herr Gruppenführer. I'll put him on at once.' He held out the phone to Huber. 'It's Gruppenführer Kammler, Colonel.'

The temperature in the room seemed to drop several degrees. Huber regarded the receiver as if he were being offered a hand grenade with the pin removed. He tugged down on the hem of his tunic to straighten it, walked over to his desk and sat. He took the receiver and covered the mouthpiece.

'Will you all leave the room, please?' He waited until they had filed out. From the passage, Graf heard him say, 'Yes, my Gruppenführer, it's Huber here,' and then the staff officer pulled the door shut after them. Klein gave Graf a grim look and passed his finger across his throat.

They wandered into the lobby. Klein flung himself down into an armchair and lit a cigarette. Graf took the chair next to him. He wasn't sure what he was doing there. The two SS men went into the corner and stood in quiet conversation.

Graf said, 'What does this all mean, do you think?' He didn't know Klein as well as he did the others, although he recognised his type – the mechanic, more at home with engines than people. He was said to be popular with his men.

'Nothing good.' Klein contemplated the end of his cigarette. 'You know Kammler?'

'Of course.'

'Then you know that anything is possible. Did you ever hear the story of what happened to the regiment at Rijs?'

'No.'

Klein switched his gaze from the cigarette tip to Graf, and took a moment before he spoke. 'We were stationed there for about three weeks, while the fighting was going on at Arnhem. Kammler had pulled us out of The Hague, in case the Allies took it, which meant the rockets couldn't reach London any more, so he told us to fire at eastern England instead. When he decided it was safe for us to come back, he said he was worried our security had been compromised in Rijs, because the local people had seen what we were doing.' He stopped, frowned. 'You're sure you haven't heard this before? I thought everybody knew it.'

Graf shook his head.

Klein glanced over at Biwack and Drexler, then he leaned forward, and said quietly, 'Kammler ordered the colonel to round up every civilian in the area – that's about five hundred people – and shoot them. His exact words were "Your men must finally learn to see blood flowing." '

'Good God! What did Huber do?'

'He ignored the order. We pulled out that night and came here under cover of darkness. The following day, the RAF hit the woods at Rijs. So maybe we **were** betrayed by the locals – who knows?'

'Did Kammler ever say anything?'

'Not a word, as far as I know. He probably just forgot all about it – you know how he is, leaping from one crazy impulse to another. But anyway, that's why the colonel gets a bit jumpy around the SS, and our friend from the NSFO in particular.'

Graf looked over at Biwack. He was still conferring with Drexler, wagging his finger to make a point. Klein suddenly stubbed out his cigarette and gestured with his head. Huber had appeared in the passage. They both got to their feet.

Huber was rubbing his hands uneasily. 'Drexler and Biwack – the Gruppenführer wants to speak with you. He's still on the line in my office.' The two men hurried away. Huber watched them go, waited until they were out of sight and the door had closed. 'So, gentlemen, it turns out the Gruppenführer is in Holland. He's at Hellendoorn, inspecting the SS 500.'

'Ah,' grunted Klein, with some contempt, 'his favourites!'

SS Werfer Battery 500 had been set up as a rival to the Wehrmacht's V2 regiments – 'to show the army how it should be done' – but had so far failed to fire as many rockets, much to Kammler's irritation.

Huber continued, 'He's decided to pay us a visit and assess the situation for himself. He intends to address the men at the funeral tomorrow, to raise their morale, he says – that was Biwack's idea, apparently. And this will interest you in particular, Doctor, bearing in mind our conversation over dinner the other night. He has Professor von Braun with him.'

14

IN THE BANK VAULT IN Mechelen, it had been quiet for several hours.

Wing Commander Knowsley had left his desk and gone upstairs. Flight Officer Sitwell was writing up a report on the morning's activities for the Air Ministry. The WAAF sergeants and the corporal from the Signals Corps were staring into space. Barbara's head was nodding forward. Occasionally she raised it and looked around to check if anyone had noticed, then almost at once it drooped again. She had completed the last calculation in six and a half minutes, just ahead of Kay, and when it had checked out she had clasped her hands above her head like a boxing champ.

Kay sharpened her pencil and studied Barbara's thick blonde hair. The colour was natural, as far as she could tell. What she wouldn't give for hair like that! She gathered the pencil shavings into the palm of her hand, trickled them into the ashtray and went back to doodling circles and chequer boards around the edges of her notepad.

At Medmenham there had always been something to do. On the days when bad weather grounded the reconnaissance flights, the interpreters went back over the earlier coverage to see what they might have missed. It was like being stuck indoors on a rainy day in a country house filled with hundreds of uncompleted jigsaw puzzles, and it was during those lulls that some of the most significant breakthroughs had been made in the analysis of Peenemünde. But in this job, if the V2s didn't launch, one could only sit idle. She wondered who it was who had first said that war was long stretches of boredom punctuated by moments of sheer terror. People were always repeating it. Someone must have said it first.

She heard footsteps behind her descending the stairs. Louie, the short-haired, mannish WAAF officer, and the Scottish girl, Flora, appeared.

Sitwell looked up at the noise and frowned.

'Ma'am.' They saluted.

'Is is two o'clock already?' Sitwell swung round in her seat and peered up at the clock. 'All right, ladies – shift change.'

Kay leaned across and touched Barbara on the shoulder. 'Barbara? We've finished.'

Her eyes half opened. 'Was I asleep?'

'You could sleep standing up,' said Louie.

Flora took off her coat and cap. 'How did it go?'

'Two launches,' said Kay. 'I think we finished

the plots in time. It's hard to tell. What are your digs like?'

'Would you keep the chit-chat down?' called Sitwell. 'We **are** still on alert, you know.'

Kay retrieved her coat from the back of the chair and Flora slid into her place. 'Ooh, lovely and warm,' she whispered.

'Wait a minute, ladies!'

Knowsley trotted down the steps and strode to the front of the room. 'Before you go, I have some news I'd like to share with you. Everybody!' He clapped his hands to get their attention. 'None of what I'm about to say is to be repeated. This is strictly classified – I hope that's clear.' He tried to look stern, but he couldn't help breaking into a smile. 'I just got off the phone to Stanmore. As a result of our efforts this morning, two attacks were mounted on the launch sites in Holland. All our planes returned safely, and Fighter Command is reporting that both targets were destroyed!'

A murmur of excitement went round the room. Kay looked over at Barbara and mouthed, 'Well done!' She gave her a thumbs-up.

'And well done you!'

Knowsley beamed at them. 'Yes, jolly good show, the pair of you. You're both off duty now, so why don't you go over to the mess bar and have a drink on my tab?'

Barbara said, 'That's very kind of you, sir. Do you know, I think we might just do that!'

'For the rest of you, I'm afraid, it's back to waiting.'

There was a good-humoured groan.

Out on the street, Barbara threw her arms round Kay and hugged her. 'I can't believe we did that!'

'I know. Isn't it marvellous.' Kay patted Barbara's back. Over her shoulder she could see a couple of Belgians looking at them. 'We probably ought not to make too much fuss in public.'

'Oh, right. Good point.'

They crossed the road and went into the headquarters. Upstairs in the bar, Kay studied the small shelf of bottles. 'What do you think we ought to have? A beer?'

'Beer? We can do better than that! Two gin and tonics,' Barbara said to the barman. 'Doubles. On Wing Commander Knowsley's tab.'

'Yes, ma'am.'

'And can we get some food? We've just come off duty.'

'I'll see what the cook's got.'

They carried their drinks over to a table by the window. Barbara lit a cigarette. 'I could almost get to like this place. Two direct hits! We're winning the war between us, darling.'

They clinked glasses. The gin and tonic was warm and oily, too strong for Kay's taste, especially in the middle of the day, but she drank it anyway. **Two direct hits? In two raids?** She wasn't sure she believed it. In her experience the RAF always exaggerated their successes. But she didn't want to spoil the mood. A kind of warm loosening seemed to spread through her head. She nodded at the cigarettes. 'Do you think I could have one of those? I'll pay you back.'

Barbara lit it for her, and they sat back contentedly. The room was empty. Everyone else must be on duty, Kay thought. She had a sense of playing truant. Barbara said, 'What did you do before the war?'

'Nothing. I was at university. You?'

'Oh, boring. I worked in a gallery.'

Kay examined her through the cigarette smoke. Yes, that fitted. She could imagine her in one of those expensive Mayfair galleries, decorously drawing in the wealthy clients; it was harder to picture her in Stanmore. 'Was there any maths involved in that?'

'In the gallery?' Barbara laughed. 'Are you pulling my leg? No! After I was called up, I just found I could do it – whoever would have thought it? – so they sent me on a course to train as a filter officer. Where were you?'

'Medmenham. Photo reconnaissance.'

'I was on Chain Home Radar for a year, in some freezing bunker in Suffolk, plotting altitude and angles of approach. It's annoying, don't you think, the way the Filter Room makes us just look like croupiers in a casino, moving tokens around with a rake?'

The soldier from behind the bar arrived, carrying two steaming plates of steak and kidney pudding, the suet crust split at the side and leaking gravy over a few pale and watery tinned carrots and a couple of potatoes. He set them down with unnecessary force. Barbara pulled a face at his retreating back. 'I don't think he likes waiting on women very much.'

They stubbed out their cigarettes and started to eat, Barbara eagerly, Kay more gingerly, breaking up the pudding with her fork and trying to pick out the few pieces of steak from the chunks of kidney. She felt homesick all of a sudden. Perhaps it was the drink. Finally she pushed her plate away. 'Can I ask you something?'

'Go ahead.'

'What did you mean yesterday when you said I had "friends in high places"?'

Barbara carried on chewing for a while, her head over her plate, as if she hadn't heard. 'Forget it. I shouldn't have said it.'

'Tell me. I don't mind.'

'God, this is disgusting!' She cut a carrot in half and ate it. Finally she looked up. 'All right, since you ask. There's a rumour that the only reason you're here is because you're having a fling with some senior bloke in the Air Ministry.' She made a shrugging gesture with her knife and fork. 'What can I say, darling? People are mean. **Women** are mean, actually – speaking as one myself. I'll make sure they all know it isn't true.'

Kay looked out of the window. A tram went past. Across the street, the sentry outside the bank was talking to a couple of civilians leaning on their bicycles. The balance in her mind between discretion and honesty, so long weighted on one side, suddenly tilted the other way, and she blurted out, 'I'm afraid it is true. Or it was.'

'**Was** true? So it's over?'

'Oh yes. It's definitely over.'

'Well go on. You might as well finish now you've started.'

She hesitated, and then, to her surprise, found herself telling the whole story for the first time, and to a woman she barely knew – Mike's first visit to Medmenham (although she was careful not to mention his name), and then his second visit with the Churchills, and their drink in the pub, and their assignations in the countryside, and the disastrous decision to spend the weekend in his flat, and the V2 . . .

'No!' interrupted Barbara, her blue eyes wide. 'You mean you were actually hit by one of the beastly things?'

. . . and the way he wouldn't let her go with him to the hospital, and the nightmare meeting with his wife in the lobby of the Air Ministry . . . 'So I decided the best thing was actually just to get out of the country and **do** something, and this seemed the perfect chance, and I called in a favour.'

'And he was just as keen to get you out of the way, I bet.'

'He said he wasn't, but I could tell he was.'

'Well then, if you'll forgive me for saying so, darling, he sounds a complete and utter **shit.**' Kay laughed at the ferocity with which she pronounced the word. Barbara looked at her. 'I tell you what, why don't we get out of this dump and see if we can find a proper drink?'

It was only just after three, but already the day was fading, the temperature dropping, the lights in the buildings opposite standing out brightly in the dull winter afternoon. Kay stood on the step outside the headquarters and wrapped herself more tightly in her greatcoat. She didn't much want to go looking for a bar. She would have preferred to go over to the bank to see if there had been any more launches. But Barbara had already set off up the street. She turned, walking backwards, and beckoned to her. 'Are you coming?'

'But what if something happens? What if they need us?'

'Don't be a bore, Kay. They won't. Come on.'

Kay hurried to catch up. Barbara threaded her arm through hers and they wandered together towards the Brusselpoort, then turned left towards the river. The wide cobbled street was lined with shops, half of them shuttered, the rest offering mostly empty windows. Outside a butcher's, a group of quite well-to-do-looking citizens, including an elderly lady in a fur coat, were picking through the dustbins.

Further on was a café – a seating area on the pavement, the chairs all folded, the parasols down –

obviously closed for the winter. Even so, Barbara hammered on the door and peered through the glass into the darkened interior as if they might open up specially for her.

'Bugger it,' she muttered. 'This whole place is shut.'

'Why don't we just call it a day and go back to the mess?'

'Let's give it another ten minutes.'

They started across the bridge into the old town. A barge passed beneath them, rusted and empty. The big market square was surrounded by ancient tall, thin buildings, all crooked and squashed together, like an illustration from a Grimms' fairy tale, crowned by a profusion of turrets, stone urns, weathervanes and golden balls. The tower of a cathedral loomed behind them. In the centre of this cobbled expanse, a couple of British army lorries were parked. Squaddies stood around smoking, watched by a group of children. One of the men whistled as the two women went by, and Barbara turned and blew him a kiss. They pressed on up a side street. Kay glanced back at the square, which seemed to her a more promising spot for a bar than wherever they might be heading. She stopped.

Barbara said, 'Is something wrong?'

'I just think this is a waste of time.'

To their right was a pair of huge closed wooden doors with **Seminarium Archiepiscopale** written in faded gold paint above the lintel. To their left, a narrow alley. Barbara said, 'Let's try this way. I have a good feeling.'

Kay peered along it doubtfully. 'Really? I don't think we'll find anything up there.'

'Just give it one last go, all right?'

The street was narrow, twisting, medieval, enclosed like a tunnel on either side by dilapidated buildings of red brick and crumbling stone. At the end of it, entirely unexpected, was the cathedral. Kay thought she heard footsteps behind them and glanced over her shoulder. Barbara started to say something, but Kay held up her hand to quiet her. She halted and tilted her head, listening, but as the silence lengthened, she decided she must have imagined it.

Barbara was grinning. 'Don't tell me you think we're being followed, darling? How thrilling!'

'I'm not sure.' Kay felt slightly foolish. 'We were told to be careful, remember? The Germans have only just left, and we're pretty conspicuous.'

Barbara looked at her in amusement for a few more seconds, then shook her head and moved on.

Kay said, 'Where are you going?' She hurried to catch her up.

'We might as well look inside now we're here.'

The first door they tried was locked, but a little further on, the handle of the second turned and it opened with a clatter that was amplified by the deserted space inside. They stood on the threshold of the giant nave – pillared, vaulted, hushed, chilly with the smell of incense – a universe unto itself. For a moment even Barbara seemed awed. 'Well, we won't find a drink in here,' she said.

Kay laughed and took a few steps up the aisle towards the altar. Her footsteps echoed on the polished stone floor. Out of habit, she genuflected and made the sign of the cross. She glanced around at the statues of the saints. Now she came to think of it, she vaguely remembered a St Rumbold of Mechelen – an Irishman, supposedly, which must have been why the sisters made such a fuss of him. How odd that she should find him here! Offertory candles flickered beneath an icon on a table close to the door. On impulse she went over and lit one; she might even have got down on her knees and said a prayer if she hadn't been conscious of Barbara watching her sceptically, her arms folded.

'You're praying for **him,** aren't you?'

'No, I am not!' But she realised to her dismay that she was about to. 'You're right. That's enough piety.'

They stepped back out into the gathering dusk. An old-fashioned lamp had come on, attached to the building on the corner of the alley. And then: an odd thing. As they turned into the narrow passage, they heard the sound of running feet, and a woman darted round the corner clutching a loaf of bread. She ran between them, knocking them out of her way, and as she passed, Kay caught a glimpse of her face, grimacing with terror. A second later came the pounding of more footsteps, and suddenly the alley was a mass of running people – twenty or more, men mostly, with a few women and some children tagging along at the rear. The WAAFs had to press themselves into a doorway to avoid being trampled. The mob disappeared around the bend; as abruptly as it had filled, the passage was empty.

Kay looked at Barbara. 'What was all that?'

'God knows. It looked like they were trying to kill her.'

'Maybe she stole the bread.'

They stared in the direction the crowd had run.

Kay said, 'Had we better go and see?'

Now it was Barbara's turn to be uncertain. 'It's not really any of our business, is it?'

'No, but . . .' Kay hesitated. 'We should at least check she's not being murdered, shouldn't we?'

'I suppose.'

They retraced their steps back down the alley, past the cathedral doors, around its massive walls and into an open space, cobbled at the edges, with grass and trees in the middle. Under the trees, a crowd had gathered in a circle. They seemed to be watching something. More people were joining all the time, hurrying from the side streets. Instinct warned Kay to keep back; curiosity propelled her forward. Barbara caught her sleeve – 'Don't get involved' – but they went on together anyway, over the grass, shouldering their way through the wall of turned backs, until they reached the centre of the crowd.

The woman was on her knees. Her coat had been dragged halfway down her back, pinioning her arms. Not that she was offering any resistance. Her hands hung limply by her sides, her eyes were closed, her expression resigned. Behind her, a man was wielding a large pair of scissors, grabbing her hair in handfuls and cutting it off. He worked fast, professionally, roughly, as if he were shearing a sheep. The loaf lay in the mud beside her. Each time he seized her hair, the woman's head jerked backwards. The crowd was silent.

Kay said loudly, in English, 'Can we stop this now?' She felt weirdly detached from it all. Listen to yourself, she thought. You sound like a nanny. She stepped forward with her hand outstretched. **'Arrêtez!'**

For the first time, the crowd began to sound angry.

'Putain anglais femme!'

'Occupe-toi de tes oignons!'

One man gripped her arm. Another blocked her path. The half-shorn woman opened her eyes and looked at her, imploring her to go away. Kay thought: she doesn't want your help; you're only making it worse. She could hear Barbara shouting her name. Even so, she struggled to get closer, until another hand, much stronger, grabbed her from behind and pulled her roughly backwards. She turned, outraged, and saw that it was Arnaud.

'They are right,' he said quietly, 'It is none of your business.'

She tried to shake him off. He tightened his grip

and steered her away. Barbara took her other arm. Finally she surrendered, and allowed herself to be marched off the grass. The wall of backs closed behind them. Arnaud didn't let her go until they were clear of the open area and in a side street. She leaned against the wall and covered her face with her hands.

Barbara was rubbing the top of Kay's arm. 'Are you all right, darling?'

'Who was that woman?' She lowered her hands and looked at Arnaud. 'Do you know her?'

'No.'

'What had she done?'

'They thought she was a collaborator.'

'They **thought**?'

'They're not usually wrong.' He shrugged. 'Someone said she had had a child by a German soldier.'

'God!'

'You mustn't be too hard on them. They suffered a lot.'

'Were you part of it?'

'No!' He seemed angered by the suggestion.

'Then what were you doing there?' When he didn't reply, she said, 'Were you following us?'

He paused for a moment or two. 'Yes, as it happens,' he answered calmly. 'I saw you crossing the square. I thought to myself: those two could get into trouble. And I was right.' He looked back at the crowd. It was starting to break up. People were walking in their direction. The cathedral clock chimed the half-hour. 'We should get away from here. Where would you like to go? Back to your headquarters?'

Barbara said, 'Is there a place where we could get a drink?'

He led them on a circuitous route through the back streets to the river. It was dark by the time they reached it. A flight of worn stone steps led down from the bridge to a quay. Barges were moored up close to one another, mist rising off the water. He held out his hand to help them.

They would never have discovered it in a year of searching. From the outside it looked like a derelict warehouse, with a block and tackle hanging above a pair of doors with a smaller entrance cut into one of them. Inside, the smell of beer and tobacco was so strong it was like walking into a wall. A dim light cast by naked electric bulbs showed sawdust on a bare brick floor, a long counter with wooden kegs behind it, chairs and tables that did not match, a game of shuffleboard in progress in one corner, and an entirely male clientele. They turned to stare at the two Englishwomen in their uniforms.

Arnaud found a table and pulled out two chairs. Kay said, 'This is Barbara Colville, by the way. Barbara, this is Arnaud Vermeulen. I'm billeted on his family.'

He kissed her hand. **'Enchanté.'**

He went over to the bar, said something to the

barman and then started talking to a man who was drinking on his own, perched on a stool. Barbara said, 'He seems charming. Rather attractive, from the knees up. Like Byron with his club foot. "Mad, bad and dangerous to know." ' She pulled out a powder compact and checked herself in the little mirror, then quickly applied some lipstick.

Kay watched her uneasily. 'We can't stay long, you know. There **is** a curfew.'

'All right, don't fuss. You're the one who almost got us involved in a fight.' She offered Kay the lipstick.

'I'm fine, thanks.'

Most of the men had gone back to their drinks and their games of cards, but a few were still staring at them. Kay doubted if any other British servicewomen had ever been seen in Mechelen. It was not official policy to send women abroad. She felt exposed, embarrassed. It had been naive of her to try to intervene earlier. Stupid. What had she been thinking?

Arnaud came back. 'I've ordered us beer, if that's all right.' He sat across the table from them.

'Heavenly.' Barbara offered him a cigarette. He took one and she lit it for him.

He said to Kay, 'You shouldn't judge us harshly. If England had been occupied for four years, the same would have happened in your country.'

'Absolutely,' said Barbara. 'I'm sure I would have lost all my hair.'

Kay laughed. Arnaud didn't. 'When the British

soldiers first came, they made the collaborators kneel in the Grote Markt and clean their boots. I watched them do it.'

There was an awkward pause that was only ended when a waiter in a dirty white apron came over and set down three glasses of beer.

Barbara said brightly, 'What shall we drink to?'

'Happier times?' suggested Kay.

'Good,' nodded Arnaud. 'That we can agree on.'

They clinked their glasses. The man Arnaud had been talking to earlier slid off his stool and approached their table. He said something to Arnaud in Flemish, and then, to them all, in English, 'May I join you?'

'This is Jens Thys,' said Arnaud, 'an old friend of mine. This is Barbara, and this is Kay.' The stranger bowed to each of them in turn, and sat. He looked to be the same age as Arnaud, but more smartly dressed, in a suit and tie. 'Jens is a teacher,' said Arnaud.

The other man added, 'We used to be colleagues.'

Kay said, 'But I thought you did manual work?'

'That is now. Before, I was a teacher.'

'And what are you doing in Mechelen?' asked Jens.

Barbara said, 'Oh, it's all very hush-hush – we're not allowed to say.'

'Hush-hush?' He looked bewildered.

'You know – top secret.'

'It's just administration,' said Kay quickly. 'Typing, filing, that kind of thing. Very boring.'

'Women's work,' added Barbara sarcastically, to show she had been joking.

'But you are being modest, surely? I can see from your uniforms that you are officers.'

'Darling,' said Barbara, 'in the Women's Auxiliary Air Force, **everyone** is an officer.'

They all laughed.

After that, the evening became convivial. To Kay's relief, there were no more questions about what they did. They complimented Jens on his English and he told them about a holiday he had spent in England: 'In Guildford, do you know it?' Barbara said her family had a place in a village nearby. Jens insisted on ordering more beer. The shuffleboard came free – **sjoelen,** they called it in Flemish – and Arnaud suggested they should play. The men's attempts to explain the rules became the focus of their conversation. Indeed, for half an hour, Kay almost entirely forgot the war. She was conscious of Arnaud standing close to her, of the way his hand covered hers as he showed her how to slide the wooden discs. Jens did the same with Barbara. The beer was strong, the flirtation mild, so that when she looked at her watch and saw that it was nearly seven, she was not only surprised by how much time had passed, but sorry to call a halt.

'Barbara – we ought to go.'

'Really? You're such a prefect.'

'What's a prefect?' asked Jens.

'Someone who stops other people having fun.'

'She's right,' said Arnaud. 'It will be the curfew soon.' Kay looked around. Without her noticing, the bar had already half emptied.

Jens said, 'I'll walk you back, Barbara. Where do you live?' She told him the street. 'Oh, that's easy. It's only ten minutes from here.'

The two men went over to the bar to settle the bill. Kay whispered, 'Do you think we ought to offer to pay our share?'

'Of course not. You'll offend their manly honour. Besides, we haven't any Belgian money.'

'And are you sure you'll be safe going back with him?'

Barbara gave her a pitying look. 'A teacher? Please! Anyway, he's rather good-looking, don't you think?'

'Oh God!'

'We should definitely see them again.'

Arnaud limped back from the bar, smiling. He gestured towards the door. 'Shall we go?'

Jens and Barbara left first, and Kay was just about to follow when someone shouted, 'Hey, Arnaud!'

She turned at the same time as he did. A man at the bar clicked his heels together and shot out his arm in a Nazi salute.

Arnaud pretended he hadn't noticed. They walked along the quay and up the steps and said goodbye to the others on the bridge. 'See you tomorrow,' said

Barbara with a wink. 'Don't do anything I wouldn't do.' She set off in one direction with Jens; Arnaud and Kay went the other.

They walked in silence for a while. The curfew had emptied the streets. Eventually he said, 'Your friend is very funny.'

'Isn't she? I only met her yesterday. I like her a lot.' She glanced at him. His jaw was clenched. He was staring straight ahead. His earlier good humour had entirely gone. 'Is something the matter?'

'Not at all.'

'The business at the end, just as we were leaving – the Nazi salute – what was that about?'

'Nothing. Just a stupid joke.'

'Then why are you angry?'

'I'm not.'

Two British soldiers were walking along the pavement towards them, carrying their rifles across their chests. They blocked their path. 'Your papers, please.'

Kay pulled out her identity card. Arnaud did the same. One of the soldiers shone a torch on their photographs and then on their faces. The other said, 'You're breaking the curfew.'

'I'm sorry,' said Kay. 'We're on our way back now.'

'Not you, ma'am. Him.'

'I can vouch for him. I'm billeted on his family.'

'Arms up,' said the soldier. He gestured with his rifle. Arnaud raised his hands. The soldier patted him down. 'Turn around.' Wearily Arnaud turned to face the wall.

Kay said, 'Is this really necessary?'

'He knows the rules.'

The soldier finished his search. 'All right, we'll let you off this time, seeing as you're with a British officer. But don't let us catch you again.'

Their papers were returned. The soldiers resumed their patrol.

Kay said, 'I'm sorry about that.'

'Why? The Germans were rougher.' He tucked his identity card back into his inside pocket. She could sense his resentment and humiliation.

They continued across yet another of the town's seemingly endless succession of squares. The night was freezing. Already frost was beginning to rime the cobbles, glittering in the glow of the street lamps. Above the pointed roofs a couple of stars had appeared. Suddenly Arnaud stopped, gripped her arm and pointed. A shooting star, travelling very fast, was descending directly in front of them. They watched it for a second or two, and then it vanished.

He said, 'You know what that was?' He was still holding her arm. She could feel the rise and fall of his chest.

'A meteor?'

He shook his head. 'A German rocket, hitting Antwerp. I have seen them twice before. They have the ingenuity of the devil.' He looked at her.

She said carefully, 'That is terrible. Those poor people.'

He seemed to expect her to say something else.

When she didn't, he turned away. 'Well,' he muttered, 'the bastards will lose the war soon enough, rockets or no rockets. We should get on. We're nearly there.'

It took them another five minutes. When they reached the gate in the garden wall, he pretended to fiddle with the latch for a few seconds, then turned and kissed her. She had guessed it was coming. She had even rehearsed her response in her head while they were walking: a gentle push away, a polite 'No, I can't, I'm sorry', perhaps to be followed by a prim 'I'm not that sort of girl'. But now it came to it, it turned out she **was** that sort of girl. The unfamiliar intimacy of having a different man's mouth on hers felt unexpectedly natural. He tasted sweetly of beer. His skin was smooth, not bristly like Mike's. Damn Mike, she thought suddenly. She cupped Arnaud's head gently between her hands and kissed him back. For the second time that day she seemed to observe herself from a distance. She started to laugh.

'What's funny?' He broke away from her, half smiling, uncertain.

'Nothing. Come here.' She kissed him again. He undid the middle buttons of her coat and put his hands around her waist. She shivered. 'Can we go inside?'

They walked up the path to the front door. It was locked. He reached up and felt around the lintel and took down a key.

Inside, the hall was in semi-darkness. The usual

light shone from the kitchen. She could smell bacon frying. As the day had begun, so it ended. The door to the study was closed.

Arnaud put his finger to his lips. She took his hand and led him upstairs to her room.

15

A LITTLE AFTER NINE THAT evening, Dr Rudi Graf stood stripped to the waist in front of his bathroom mirror in Scheveningen, his fingers held in the tepid rusty trickle beneath the hot tap, listening to the clanking of the hotel's pipes as the water made its tortuous progress around the building. It wouldn't get any warmer. His razor blade was six months old and it was hard to whip up much of a lather out of his thin bar of soap. Still he jutted out his chin and scraped away methodically at his day's growth of beard. One had to maintain standards.

Colonel Huber had announced over dinner that in view of the increased RAF activity, the regiment would, from tomorrow, aim to launch seventy per cent of its rockets at night. His officers had looked at their plates. Launching was a much slower and more frustrating procedure when undertaken by torchlight with numb fingers in the freezing woods, the liquid oxygen coating the pipes with a sheath of frost. For once Graf had turned down Seidel's offer of a game of chess. He wanted an early night.

He rinsed his razor under the tap and was just drying his face when he heard the sound of fists hammering on doors and voices shouting.

He went out onto the landing and peered over the banister. From below came a thump of boots on the stairs. A couple of helmets appeared. Light glinted on the barrels of a pair of rifles. The tops of the men's shoulders were clad in SS black.

He stepped quickly into his bedroom and closed the door. The suitcase full of microfilm rolls was still on top of the wardrobe. He looked around. There was nowhere he could hide it, and no time anyway – the door was already being struck by a rifle butt. He grabbed his shirt and called out, 'Wait!' but the door was flung open and the SS soldiers stamped in. One put his rifle to his shoulder and covered Graf, who immediately raised his hands, while the other threw open the wardrobe door and stabbed at his clothes with the barrel of his gun. He ducked to search under the bed, prodding at the dust, then went over to the window and drew back the curtains, raised the sash and stuck his head out into the night. He withdrew it and turned to look at Graf. He was young, no more than eighteen.

'You are alone?'

Graf still had his hands up. 'As you can see.'

'And the other men in the building – have you seen them bring in women?'

'I haven't seen anyone all evening.'

The SS soldier frowned at him. His gaze swept the room again. Abruptly he turned on his heel and the two men left.

Graf lowered his hands and quickly finished buttoning his shirt. He put on his tie and jacket, grabbed his coat and hat and hurried down the stairs. A couple of NCOs were standing in their vests and underpants on the next landing. On the ground floor the doors hung open and the passage was crowded with outraged rocket troops. He bumped into Schenk, who was in his shirtsleeves, his braces dangling round his knees. 'Fucking SS!'

'Did they find anyone?'

'No. Arseholes!'

Out in the street were maybe twenty SS men – standing in the middle of the road with machine guns, going in and coming out of the hotels. Some had dogs. A searchlight was mounted on the back of a lorry. Its beam moved methodically up and down the buildings. Graf set off round the corner. From the boarding house that served as the other-ranks' brothel, the women were being led out, shivering in their flimsy dresses, carrying their suitcases. One by one, occasionally prodded by a rifle barrel, they climbed up into the back of a lorry.

'Oh God,' muttered Graf. 'Oh God, oh God . . .'

He turned around and headed in the direction of the seafront. SS men had sealed off the Hotel Schmitt. He had to show his pass to get through.

In the officers' mess, Huber stood at the windows with Seidel and Klein and a couple of others, looking down into the street.

Graf said, 'Are they searching here as well?'

'They're searching everywhere,' said Huber. 'On Kammler's orders, given to Drexler on the phone. They even searched **my** room! As if I'd be hiding a spy under my bed!'

'They've gone crazy,' said Seidel. He was still watching out of the window. 'Look at Party Comrade Biwack over there, directing operations. Anyone would think he was flushing out reds on the Eastern Front!'

Graf said, 'They're taking away all the girls from the brothel. What's going to happen to them?'

For a moment nobody spoke.

Huber shook his head. 'It's a bad business.'

Graf turned to Seidel, 'Do you have your car outside?'

'Yes.'

'Can I borrow it?'

Seidel stared at him. 'Don't even think of it!'

'Please.' He held out his hand.

The lieutenant's expression was incredulous. He sighed. Reluctantly he put his hand in his pocket and took out the keys.

The SS had first started seriously sniffing around Peenemünde as soon as it became apparent that the rocket was going to work. Two months after the successful test flight, in December 1942, the Reichsführer-SS, Heinrich Himmler, had made the trek up to the Baltic to watch a launch. Graf had been present. It had been a fiasco – the rocket had crashed after four seconds – but that didn't deter Himmler. 'Once the Führer has decided to give your project his support,' he told General Dornberger, 'your work ceases to be the concern of the Army Weapons Department, or indeed of the army at all, and becomes the concern of the German people. I am here to protect you against sabotage and treason.'

'I am extremely interested in your work,' he added, just as he was getting into his aeroplane to fly back to Berlin. 'I may be able to help you. I will come again alone and spend the night here, and we can have a private talk with your colleagues. I will telephone you.'

Such, at least, was what Dornberger told von Braun he had said, and such was the gist of the conversation that von Braun relayed to Graf the next day. 'It was all very polite, according to Dornberger. But I can't help feeling it sounds like a visit from a gangster, offering protection.'

'So the SS are going to be involved in production?'

'There's no way of stopping them. They're into everything these days.'

And Graf, to be honest, had not voiced any objections to receiving SS help. He had been as keen as the rest of them to get the test facilities and the missile factories built. Nevertheless, it had been quite a shock to him the following May when a camp of barrack huts had suddenly sprung up in the woods, encircled by an electrified barbed-wire fence; and an even bigger one a few days later to see a column of five hundred prisoners in their heavy striped pyjamas and caps being marched along the road by SS guards with machine guns. **Slaves in the middle of the twentieth century? What are we becoming?** That had been his instinctive response in the morning. But by the end of the afternoon, God forgive him, such was his obsession with fixing the faults in the rocket's design, he barely noticed the slaves, just as he barely registered the number of black uniforms that started to spread like spoors across the island in the weeks that followed – manning checkpoints, patrolling perimeters, guarding the building sites – as hundreds more prisoners, mostly French and Russians, were shipped in.

In June, Himmler came again – entirely alone, as promised – driving himself in his heavily armoured but modest car. Dornberger gave a dinner for him in the officers' club to meet some of the senior engineers, and Graf was invited. Did he object now, at last? Did he refuse to go? He did not. He was not even shocked when von Braun put on his SS uniform for the occasion. It was a hot evening, not long after the summer solstice, and the Baltic daylight extended for hours. Himmler sweated profusely – slender, damp, pink in his thick black tunic, like a mollusc in its shell. He talked quietly, listened a lot, and when they moved from the dining room to the hearth room for drinks after dinner, he relaxed back in his armchair, refused all alcohol, pressed his fingertips together and gave them a **tour d'horizon** of the post-war world after a German victory.

'The Führer thinks and acts for the benefit of Europe. He regards himself as the last champion of the Western world and its culture . . .'

On and on he went: the need for Germany to lead western Europe, the threat posed by the Soviet Union if she ever switched from armaments to the production of consumer goods, the fact that Germany could only support sixty per cent of her population on her own soil and hence the need to transfer the remaining forty per cent to the Ukraine. 'Obviously a fall in the birth rate over there will have to be brought about in some way. We have enough settlers. We shall arrange for the young German peasants to marry Ukrainian girls of good farming stock, and found a healthy new generation adapted to conditions out there. The Führer calculates the population of Germany will be a hundred million in ten years. We must bear in mind the greatness of our mission and simply force people to accept their good fortune. European industry must work for the great cause. The whole wealth of labour we now control must be enlisted in the life-and-death struggle . . .'

All this was delivered in a tone of calm reasonableness. It was four o'clock in the morning by the time he finished, and still not entirely dark. As they walked back to their apartment block, von Braun took off his tunic and slung it over his shoulder. 'Was I dreaming, or was that insane?'

'Not merely insane, surely? Monstrous.'

'Yes, I suppose it was.'

The first launch they laid on for Himmler the next morning was yet another disaster. The rocket failed to tilt properly and flew at a height of two hundred metres westwards right across the island to the airfield, where it blew up on impact, destroying three planes. The second, in the afternoon, launched perfectly. Himmler promoted von Braun to Sturmbannführer.

Two months later, the RAF bombed Peenemünde, and a week after that, while they were still trying to clear up the worst of the damage, von Braun called Graf into his office. He was haggard from lack of sleep, too exhausted even to rise from his desk. He waved Graf into a chair. 'I just had a call from Dornberger in Berlin. Himmler has spoken to the Führer, and it seems we are to abandon plans to manufacture the rockets on the island, in view of our vulnerability to air attack.'

'So that's it? It's over?'

'Not at all. Production is to be moved underground. The SS have a mountain site in Thuringia that Himmler says is perfect for our needs. Their chief of construction will be in overall charge of building the factory.' He studied his notepad. 'Brigadeführer Dr Hans Kammler.'

*

Graf turned on the ignition. The Kübelwagen sprang forward and stalled. He put his foot down on the clutch and tried again. This time he moved off slowly, but when he tried to change up to second, he couldn't find it. The grinding of the gearbox was loud enough to draw the attention of an SS soldier, who emerged from the shadows at the back of the hotel and waved him to a halt.

'Nobody is permitted to leave.'

'I am Dr Graf of the army's Special Weapons Department.' He took out his identity card and held it up. 'I have to get over to Wassenaar immediately. There's an emergency.'

'All personnel must remain in place until the security action is completed.'

'A rocket is on fire! Do you want to be held responsible for a disaster?' Graf leaned out of the window and peered up and down the promenade. On the corner, a group of SS men were watching them. 'Where is Obersturmbannführer Drexler?'

'I don't know.'

'We need to find him. What's your name?'

The man looked uncertain. 'Schumacher.'

'Right.' Graf leaned across and opened the passenger door. 'Get in, Schumacher.'

'Why?'

'I want you to tell your comrades that this is an emergency. Hurry up.'

The man obediently climbed into the front seat.

Graf told himself not to drive too fast. The group of SS men stepped in front of the car and waved him down.

'Tell them quickly, Schumacher.'

One of the men bent to talk to his comrade. 'Who's this?'

'He says he's one of the rocket engineers. He needs to get to Wassenaar. There's a fire.'

'All right.' The man stepped back and waved them through. The same thing happened a hundred metres down the street: 'He needs to get through: it's an emergency.' The SS man seemed to be enjoying his sense of importance. Graf drove past the railway station. After that, the road ahead looked clear. He pulled over. 'You can get out here, Schumacher. Thank you. I'll be sure to mention you to the Obersturmbannführer.'

He pulled away. When he looked in his mirror, the soldier was standing by the roadside staring after him. He turned left, towards Wassenaar.

Graf flew with von Braun and a couple of engineers to visit the proposed rocket factory at the end of August 1943. Von Braun piloted the plane himself, descending over the forests and mountains of the Harz and landing, with delicate precision, on a grass runway next to the pretty town of Nordhausen, with its roofscape of high church towers. Bluish in the distance rose the swell of the Kohnstein – not so much a mountain, it turned out, as a gently elongated wooded hill. Kammler had thoughtfully sent a car to pick them up.

It was late summer; harvest time. They drove in the back of an open-topped Mercedes, swatting away the thunderflies rising from the fields, through a haze of heat towards the square mouth of an enormous tunnel. A shadow fell across the car. The temperature dropped. After the dazzling golden light of the afternoon, it took a minute for their eyes to adjust to the gloom of the electric bulbs.

Brigadeführer Dr Hans Kammler – his doctorate, they discovered later, was in civil engineering – was waiting for them with his staff officers. He was in his early forties, good-looking to the point of prettiness, taut, trim, immaculate – a clockwork-toy SS figure with an extraordinary rapidity of movement and expression. He led them on foot along the tunnel, dashing off facts and statistics with the proud air of a country landowner showing off his estate.

The roof was high enough for a rocket to stand upright, or to lie horizontally across it and not touch either wall. This vast gallery extended as far as they could see – more than a kilometre, Kammler assured them, right the way through to the other side of the mountain. This was Tunnel B. Tunnel A, which ran parallel to it, was almost completed. Cross-tunnels linked the two galleries. The place had been a gypsum mine before the war, and after that a storage site for fuel and poison gas. The first task would be to clear it thoroughly, and that phase was already under way. In the semi-darkness, phantom figures in striped uniforms staggered under the weight of cement sacks, steel girders, wooden prop supports, metal drums. The showering white sparks of the oxyacetylene cutters, dismantling the gasoline storage tanks, spurted at intervals in the gloom. Next, continued Kammler, they would dig and blast out further cross-tunnels and lay a rail line, build a railway station. Eventually the components for the missiles would be brought in by locomotive at one end of the complex, and finished rockets would be taken away on flatbed trucks at the other. The production capacity would be nine hundred missiles per month, the entire process to be undertaken three hundred metres beneath the mountain, invisible to the enemy's reconnaissance flights and impervious to his bombers. Production would be the responsibility of General Degenkolb, the railway tsar, who had made his reputation mass-manufacturing locomotives.

'And when will production begin?'

'January.'

One of the engineers whistled. Von Braun said, 'The rocket is an extremely complicated mechanism, Brigadeführer. The machine tools require high precision and skilled machinists. Tomorrow is the first day of September. How can a factory be completed at such speed?'

'By the utilisation of the one resource in which Germany possesses an undoubted surplus capacity.'

'Which is what?'

'Manpower.' Kammler clapped his hands and laughed at their dumbfounded expressions. 'Come now, gentlemen! If the pharaohs could build their pyramids two and a half thousand years before the birth of Christ, I can assure you the SS is capable of constructing a factory in the middle of the twentieth century and having it fully operational within four months.'

'How much manpower are you contemplating?'

'For the construction of the factory and the eventual production?' Kammler's hand circled the air. 'Twenty thousand men. Thirty thousand.' He shrugged. 'However many it takes. The reservoir is inexhaustible.'

As they walked back towards the tunnel mouth, Graf asked him if he had ever built anything else of similar size under such pressure of time. 'Oh yes. In the East. The reception centres for the Jews.'

That had been his first encounter with Kammler.

His second came six weeks later, towards the middle of October. He had not wanted to go back to Nordhausen. 'Must I?' he complained to von Braun. 'There is so much to be done here.' After the death of Dr Thiel, he had taken over most of his responsibilities in the propulsion department, where they were still trying to solve the problems with the turbo pump steam generator system that had driven the excitable Thiel to the edge of a nervous breakdown.

'You have to come,' von Braun told him. 'We have to get the rocket ready for mass production.'

Once again von Braun flew the plane himself, and

this time as they descended towards the airfield he took them directly over the Kohnstein hill. Amid the dark green forests of pine, the abandoned gypsum quarries stood out like vivid white scar tissue. In the flat area to the south-west of the hill a big prison camp was under construction. Graf stared down at it uneasily. None of the barrack blocks had roofs, he noticed. If Kammler had brought in all these thousands of foreign labourers, where were they housed?

The answer was obvious as soon as they drove into Tunnel B. They lived underground, along the walls of the cross-tunnels, in tiers of rickety wooden bunk beds stacked four high like rabbit hutches. Half-barrels with wooden planks laid across the rim served as latrines. In some of the hutches men lay prone, skeletal; one with his eyes wide open was plainly dead. The stench of it. And the noise of it – the rumble of cement mixers, the ring of pickaxes, the muffled boom of explosions as further tunnels were excavated, the roar of the generators, the clank of railway trucks moving up and down the line, the barking of the guard dogs, the shouts of the SS overseers. And the sight of it, wherever one looked in the eerie dim yellow light: the moving sea of striped uniforms, an undifferentiated mass unless one made an effort to fix one's eyes on one of the pale, emaciated figures that were hurrying everywhere – always hurrying, never moving at a normal pace. And amid it all, the immaculate figure of Kammler, attended by his black-capped officers, striding along the middle of the newly completed Tunnel A, pointing out this or that achievement. In a month and a half, it had to be granted, he had worked a dark miracle. The lineaments of a giant production line were already beginning to appear: cranes, workshops, assembly areas, test stands, repair shops. He conducted the engineers right the way through the mountain and out the other side into the clear autumn afternoon light.

'Well, gentlemen, what do you think?'

Graf lit a cigarette.

Arthur Rudolph, the only one of them who had been a Nazi right from the start – even from before Hitler came to power – said immediately, 'It's fantastic.'

Klaus Riedel, the liberal utopian who had learned to keep his political opinions to himself, stared at the ground and muttered something about being overwhelmed.

Von Braun said, 'I wouldn't have believed it possible.'

'Dr Graf?' Kammler looked at him expectantly.

'I'm speechless.'

'I shall take that as a compliment! Now, let us go to my office in Nordhausen and have some refreshments, and we can discuss the production plans in more detail.'

As they walked towards the waiting cars, Graf fell into step beside von Braun. 'I should go back to Peenemünde. I'll be of more use there.'

'No. We have come a long way to reach this point. None of us is turning back now.'

He strode ahead. Graf stopped and looked back at the mouth of the tunnel, then up at the sky. He felt himself to be like one of the rockets – a human machine, launched on a fixed trajectory, impossible to recall, hurtling to a point that was preordained. He finished his cigarette and flicked it away, and walked on to join the others.

The night was clear. There was no traffic. Low above the black mass of trees, seemingly far out over the North Sea, a bright crescent moon lit the road ahead. Now that he was out of Scheveningen, Graf put his foot down. The moon seemed to keep pace with him. **Frau im Mond.** They had kept the movie company's cheerfully erotic symbol painted on the fuselage of the rockets all the way through the tests at Peenemünde. Only when the missiles went into mass production did such whimsy become impossible.

He reached the outskirts of Wassenaar and slowed down, looking out for the turning. He spotted it, braked and swung left. He was stopped at once by the barrier. The inevitable SS guards emerged from their hut.

He showed his identity card and pass. 'I need to get through to the launch site.'

'No one is allowed beyond this point.'

'This is an emergency.'

One of the SS men laughed. 'I'm sure it is! If you're trying to get to the brothel, forget it.'

The other said, more sympathetically, 'Leave it, Doctor. There's nothing you can do.'

From somewhere in the woods came a long burst of machine-gun fire – fifteen or twenty seconds. The SS men turned to look. For half a minute there was silence. Then came another, shorter burst, followed by half a dozen single shots.

Graf rested his forehead on the rim of the steering wheel. The guards went back to their hut. He stayed like that for a while, feeling the ticking-over of the engine vibrating through his skull, before wearily reversing onto the main road and returning the way he had come.

16

KAY WOKE, TURNED OFF THE alarm, rolled over and glanced at the other side of the bed. It was too dark to make out whether he was still there. She reached under the blanket and put out an exploring hand. The mattress was cold. He must have left a while ago. She couldn't remember him going.

She slipped naked from beneath the covers and felt her way along the wall to the light switch. The room was in a mess that told its own story. Her shoes, coat and jacket were in a heap next to the door; her shirt and skirt at the foot of the bed; her underwear and stockings strewn across the bedspread along with her tie, which he had struggled to unknot and which had been the last thing to go. She went around gathering it all up. In the bathroom she dashed her face and neck with freezing water and considered herself in the mirror.

He had been tender, passionate, anxious. Once, when she made a noise, he had put his hand over her mouth and stopped to look at the ceiling, listening. The floorboards creaked above their heads. It had given her a fit of the giggles. 'Poor Arnaud,' she whispered, 'aren't you allowed to have a girl in the house?'

'My parents are very old-fashioned,' he whispered back, 'very religious. They would be appalled.'

She smiled as she brushed her hair. The more nervous he was, the bolder she had become. What a game it had been.

Once she was dressed, she inspected the bed for any telltale traces, smoothed the sheet and tucked in the blankets. If there was one skill she had learned in the WAAF, it was how to make a bed perfectly. She turned off the light and let herself out of the room. In the darkness she moved cautiously to the end of the passage. On the landing, she paused. The doors were all closed. She wondered which room was Arnaud's. Was it on this floor or the one above? The deep, chilly silence was disturbed only by the ticking of the long-case clock in the hall.

It was hard not to make a noise descending the old wooden staircase. When she reached the ground floor, she saw the familiar faint light shining from the kitchen, but when she went in, it was deserted. A kettle was boiling on the stove. She lifted it off the hob and looked around. Dirty dishes were piled in the sink. A chair was pulled back from the table. A cupboard hung open, its shelves bare. She couldn't see any sign of the food she had brought. The key was in the back door, but she didn't need to turn it: the door was unlocked.

As she stepped outside, she thought she could smell cigarette smoke. She stopped and called out quietly, 'Arnaud?' She glanced over her shoulder, then continued down the path along the side of the house. In the middle of the garden she stopped again, and repeated, more urgently, **'Arnaud?'** She was sure she could sense him watching her. She picked her way across the rough grass to the gate in the wall and out into the street. The pre-dawn sky cast a greyish light over the empty cobbles. He was not here either, she realised with dismay. It was as if he was embarrassed by what had happened and was trying to avoid her. She would have to find her own way across town.

The bell of the cathedral chimed seven, and that at least gave her something to aim for. She moved off down the street and into the twisting side roads. The town was slowly waking up. Lights were coming on in some of the houses. A dog barked as she passed. Occasionally she stopped and checked behind her, but it didn't seem that she was being followed. She told herself not to be so melodramatic. But then she remembered that Arnaud **had** followed them the previous day – he had admitted as much – so why shouldn't he be doing the same now? And as he knew where she was going, he didn't need to keep behind her: he could get ahead of her and wait for her to pass. The idea, however illogical, that she might be the object of some cat-and-mouse game unsettled her, and she set off again, quicker now.

She entered the echoing empty space of the food market and strode across it, out into a winding lane of little ancient houses. At the end of that, she recognised where she was: the shopping street with the closed café, the bridge over the river where Arnaud had left her the previous morning, the Brusselpoort, and the wide boulevard of Koningin Astridlaan. As she approached the British headquarters, she imagined herself to be a pilot at the end of a hazardous mission glimpsing his home airfield.

The officers' mess was already busy. The two lieutenants from the Survey Regiment – Sandy, the good-looking one, and the gloomy Yorkshireman (what was his name? Bill, that was it) – were already seated at the same table as before. Sandy waved to her as she came in. He said cheerfully, 'Did you hear we managed to get a couple of the blighters yesterday?'

'So I gather. Well done you.'

'And you too! My God, the speed of those things! Blink and you miss them.'

'Did we stick at two, or were there more in the afternoon?'

'No, that was it. They didn't launch again. Maybe they've decided to pack up and go home.' He glanced at her more closely. 'Are you all right?'

'Yes, I'm fine.'

'You're out of breath.'

'It's a long walk. I was worried about being late.'

'Fancy a drink later? The four of us maybe?' He nodded to the corner where Barbara was sitting smoking a cigarette.

'That would be nice. I'll ask her.' She smiled and moved away. 'Good morning, Barbara.'

'I was wondering where you'd got to.' Barbara squinted up at her through her smoke. 'Well?'

'Well what?'

'**Well?** You know what I mean.'

'Let me at least get a cup of tea.'

She went over to the table beneath the window. Tin trays of bacon, scrambled eggs and fried bread were laid out next to the tea urn. She hadn't realised how hungry she was. That was sex for you, she thought. She resolved at that moment not to say a word about what had happened. If Arnaud was avoiding her, it was probably best forgotten, at least until she found out where she stood. She piled food on her plate. When she returned, Barbara said, 'Come on, then. Something's happened, hasn't it? I can tell. You've got that look.'

'I don't know what you're talking about. My goodness, I'm famished.' She started to eat her breakfast. The eggs were too chewy to be anything other than powdered, but it didn't matter. The effect of the warm food in her stomach was instantaneous. She felt her spirits lift. 'Anyway, never mind about me. How was your walk home with Jens?'

'Highly satisfactory.'

Kay stared at her, a forkful of bacon suspended in

mid-air. Despite her own behaviour, she was slightly shocked. 'You didn't?'

'It's wartime, darling.' Barbara took a drag on her cigarette. 'One could be killed at any moment.'

'So you're going to see him again?'

'I might.'

'Where did you go? Not to your old lady's house, I assume.'

'No, we went back to his apartment.'

'My God!' Kay shook her head and laughed.

'I'm a tart, darling, what can I say?' Barbara waved her cigarette dismissively. 'And you? Tell me he made a pass, at least.'

'He was a perfect gentleman.'

Barbara gave a knowing look. 'Ah, so he tried to kiss you.' Kay held her gaze and sipped her tea. 'God, you're so discreet! Old Sitwell would be proud of you.'

'Now you're just being rude.' She was keen to change the subject. She looked at her watch. 'Speaking of Sitwell, we ought to get over there.'

She took her dirty crockery to the table and scraped off the leftovers. When she came back, Barbara was on her feet, talking to Sandy and Bill. 'We were just arranging to have a drink tonight at six. What do you think?'

'Fine.' Kay forced a smile. And you'll go off with Sandy, she thought, and I will be stuck with Bill.

The four of them once again walked across the street to the bank and showed their identity cards.

It was becoming a routine. The men went off to the radar vans with a cheerful 'Good luck, girls', and the women descended to the vault. The atmosphere was stale with cigarette smoke and the odour of too many bodies pressed into too small a space with no ventilation. The WAAF sergeants lolled, bored, behind their desks. Joan and Joyce had the pasty-faced, red-eyed look that always came with the graveyard shift. Kay recognised the symptoms. It was the same at Medmenham.

'Anything happened?' She shrugged off her coat.

'No,' said Joan, 'not a peep all night.' Her normally cheerful expression was crushed and sulky. 'I expect they're saving it all for you.'

Flight Officer Sitwell came down the stairs behind them, exuding a strong scent of carbolic soap, followed by the morning shift of WAAF sergeants. She strode to the front of the room and dropped a heavy file on the table. She cleaned the blackboard until it gleamed.

'So, ladies: a new day, a new start.'

Kay took her seat, sharpened her pencil, blew away the shavings and made a determined effort to put Arnaud out of her mind.

17

GRUPPENFÜHRER KAMMLER WAS AT THAT moment arriving in Scheveningen.

He had left Hellendoorn at four in the morning, travelling the entire distance of some 180 kilometres under cover of darkness to avoid the daylight Allied air patrols. He was never still. He seldom seemed to eat or sleep. 'The Dust Cloud', his staff called him. These days he spent half of his life on the road, sitting in the front passenger seat of his armoured Mercedes with his personalised machine gun stowed in the footwell, restlessly driving between the five V2 regiments – four Wehrmacht and one SS – that made up his command. Division zV, he had insisted on calling it. He felt it had a certain ring – zV. **Zur Vergeltung.** For Vengeance.

Kammler the builder – the man in charge of revenge!

Graf watched his big car swerve at speed around the corner and pull up with a gangsterish screech of rubber outside the Hotel Schmitt, saw him throw open the door and spring out bare-headed onto the pavement, followed from the rear seats by his two staff officers. **Slam, slam, slam** – the volley of closing doors ricocheted in the still morning. Kammler paused to pull on his cap and adjust it minutely – there was vanity in even his tiniest action, Graf noticed – then trotted smartly up the steps and into the headquarters. There was no sign of von Braun.

Graf turned up his collar and resumed his walk.

A weak dawn was breaking over the dilapidated guest houses, with their peeling wooden balconies and salt-streaked glassed-in verandas. And as the tide of darkness receded, it revealed the scars of the previous night. Some had had their front doors broken down. Damaged windows banged in the strong easterly wind. Broken glass lay in pools across the pavement. The men of the rocket battalions were going about their duties with their heads down, not talking much. Graf waited for a lorry to pass, then crossed the road towards the engine shed.

Inside, the three faulty V2s were being readied for their return on the next train to Nordhausen. It had not proved possible to repair them on site; each now required its own docket to explain its particular malfunction to the engineers in Germany. He moved from bay to bay like an automaton, studying the diagnostic reports, exchanging a few words with the technicians, signing off the reports. It was a relief to be able to focus his thoughts on the familiar dry details of fuel pump pressure and electrical resistance. His mind was numb. He had not quite finished when the door to the shed was rolled back by one of Huber's staff officers.

'Dr Graf, you are needed at headquarters straight away.'

'I'm busy here.'

'Gruppenführer Kammler wishes to speak with you.'

'What on earth does he want with me?'

The officer bridled at his tone. 'No doubt he will tell you that himself. It is an order. Come with me, please.'

Graf followed the lieutenant outside, back across the street towards the Hotel Schmitt. He had a premonition of something unpleasant, as was generally the case with Kammler. For more than a year he had watched him slowly take control of the rocket programme – studied him with a kind of resigned and detached horror, as a man who had been bitten by a venomous spider might observe his body succumbing to paralysis limb by limb. Kammler had not only built the factory at Nordhausen; he had also been given the task of constructing a new testing facility for the V2 on an SS proving ground in Poland – another thoughtful gift from Himmler following the bombing of Peenemünde that it had proved impossible to refuse.

'Whereabouts in Poland?' Graf had asked von Braun when the plan was first mooted.

'About two hundred and fifty kilometres south of Warsaw.'

'What? **Inland?**' Ever since Max and Moritz in 1934, they had always fired their rockets out to sea, so that they would fall harmlessly into the Baltic at the end of the test.

'Yes, I pointed out the risk of civilian casualties, but apparently it can't be helped.' He had held up his hand to forestall Graf's protests. 'It has to be situated somewhere out of the range of the RAF.'

Graf had started attending the tests in Poland a couple of months later, flying down from Peenemünde to stay for two or three days at a stretch. The engineers were accommodated in railway cars in a siding near the village of Blizna. The whole facility, which was called Heidelager, was guarded by the SS. It was hard not to feel a prisoner. General Dornberger was still nominally in charge, but soon Kammler was turning up to watch the launches. At first he was content merely to observe, 'on behalf of the Reichsführer-SS'. But as the winter went on, he began to take a more active part in the technical conferences, arriving sometimes unannounced when Dornberger wasn't present. It was yet another period when the missile repeatedly misfired. As rocket after rocket flew horizontally over their heads or exploded in mid-air, Kammler's tone became increasingly sarcastic. He even challenged von Braun. 'Your head is in the stars, Professor! This whole project needs to be gripped more ruthlessly!' Once, when Graf was passing his office, he overheard him on the telephone to Himmler, talking sufficiently loudly to make sure his voice carried. 'Yes, Reichsführer – another failure! . . . I agree . . . I agree . . . Utterly irresponsible. Now that we have had the opportunity to study them more closely, I am starting to think we should arrest the whole lot of the swine for treason!'

It was clear the poison was spreading from the limbs to the heart. Yet when it reached it four months later, the crudeness of the denouement still took him by surprise. Because of the bombing, he had been evacuated from his apartment in the Experimental Works compound and was living with the other senior engineers in a hotel in Zinnowitz, the Inselhof, that looked out over the reed beds to the sea. It was two o'clock in the morning when he was woken by a pounding on his door, and opened it to find two men in belted raincoats and black hats. 'We have orders to arrest you. Dress and come with us.'

'I demand to speak to Professor von Braun.'

'He's being detained as well.'

He could hear the Gestapo going from room to room. Four engineers were picked up that night, including von Braun, and driven in a night-time convoy from Peenemünde to Stettin. They weren't allowed to talk to one another – each prisoner in a separate car; each lodged in a separate cell; each interrogated separately.

Did you or did you not, on the evening of

Sunday 17 October 1943, at a beach party in Zinnowitz, in the company of Professor von Braun, Dr Helmut Gröttrup and Dr Klaus Riedel, state that the war was lost, the rocket would not save Germany, and your aim all along had been to build a spaceship?

'Gentlemen, I don't recall saying any such thing . . .'

Of course, he remembered it perfectly clearly, at least until the point when he became too drunk to stand up properly. It had been just after their second visit to Nordhausen, when he was still in a state of shock. Von Braun had put his head round Graf's door and said that Fraulein Butzlaff, the local dentist, was having a cocktail party further along the beach, and they were all invited. 'Come along, it will cheer you up.'

A warm, calm autumn evening. Chinese lanterns – pink, lemon, lime – strung along the dunes. Illegal American jazz music on the gramophone. Vodka cocktails, plenty of food – too many cocktails and too much food, in fact: he had thought at the time it was strange that a female dentist in a tiny seaside town should be able to lay her hands on such a spread in wartime. But what the hell? Perhaps it was the contrast with the slave labour factory that made them all get so drunk and loudly relive the good old days at the Rocket Aerodrome.

GRAF: I wanted to build a spacecraft, not an instrument of murder.

RIEDEL: On the bright side, it is not a very effective murder instrument.

VON BRAUN: When the war is lost, our task will be to ensure that what we have achieved is not destroyed.

GRÖTTRUP: Peenemünde will fall into the hands of the Soviets. It is only a question of time. The communist system is our best hope.

Every word had been written down, either by their hostess or by some other guest who was an informer for the Sicherheitsdienst. When Graf was shown it in black and white, he assumed they were all dead men. But as the questioning went on, for day after day, ranging back over the whole history of the rocket programme, he began to change his mind. After all, if the SS had known this much since October, why had they waited until March to arrest them?

After a week, they were driven back to Zinnowitz and released. The story was that Dornberger had spoken to Speer, and Speer had spoken to Hitler, and Himmler had magnanimously agreed to release them. Why shouldn't he? They were much more useful alive than dead. Their words were on file. He could snuff them out any time he wanted. Not long afterwards, Dornberger was shunted sideways and Himmler was formally given full control of the rocket programme. He appointed Kammler operational commander.

'In Germany now there are three choices,' Kammler told them. 'You are shot by the SS, you are imprisoned by the SS, or you work for the SS.'

He was seated now in Huber's office, leaning back in Huber's chair, with his polished boots on Huber's desk, as usual speaking loudly into the telephone. His two staff officers stood behind him, stiff as footmen in their immaculate uniforms. 'Yes . . . Yes . . . So I have your agreement to proceed?' He noticed Graf and beckoned him forward with a single crook of his finger. Huber, Drexler, Biwack, Klein and Seidel were standing at a respectful distance, watching him. 'Excellent!' He gave the receiver to one of his aides, who replaced it in its cradle. 'Dr Graf?' He frowned and cocked his head, waiting.

Graf extended his arm. 'Heil Hitler.'

'I shouldn't have to remind him, Huber. It is the law. Make sure your men give the correct salute at all times.'

'Yes, Gruppenführer.' Huber gave Graf a withering look.

Kammler swung his boots off the desk. He went over to the conference table, where a map was spread out.

'So, gentlemen. There has been a development overnight. It seems the enemy bombers may not have received their intelligence from the local population after all.' He bent over the map. Behind his back, the Wehrmacht officers risked a brief exchange of glances. Seidel caught Graf's eye. 'Our intelligence department still has a few sources operating in Belgium, and one of them made contact with his controller last night. It appears the British have brought in some advanced new radar units and installed them here, in Mechelen.' His finger tapped the town repeatedly. 'In addition to the survey troops, a group of **women**' – he pronounced the word derisively – 'are apparently being employed to make mathematical calculations based on the radar data.' He turned to Graf. 'A technical question for you, Doctor. Is it possible for the enemy to determine the location of our launch sites using radar?'

Graf's hands had balled into fists; his fingernails were digging into his palms. In his head he was hearing the rattle of the machine-gun fire in the woods. He stared at Kammler. 'I'm sorry, Gruppenführer. Could you repeat that?'

Kammler sighed. 'Is there any way the enemy could determine the location of our launch sites using radar and a team of female calculators?'

'May I see the location?' He indicated the map.

'Of course.'

Kammler stepped back. Graf took his place at the table. He hunted around for Mechelen and found it, glanced up at The Hague and then down again. The town was almost exactly due south of them – significant, given that the axis of the V2's flight path was roughly east to west. And it brought the radars much closer, too: they were less than half as far distant as the stations on the English coast.

He was aware of Kammler and the others waiting for his verdict. Well, that is clever, he thought. That is ingenious. Why did it never occur to us?

He straightened. 'Obviously I am not qualified to judge the sophistication of the enemy's radar. But that would certainly appear to place them within sufficient range to detect our rockets shortly after take-off – the terrain between us and them is entirely flat, so their view is unobstructed.'

'The distance is significant?'

'Yes – the distance, and more importantly the southerly position, which gives them a side-on view. If their radars can see high enough, it's possible they could collect sufficient data to track the flight path for a few seconds. Then they would have the point of impact in England three hundred and ten seconds later. Put these two pieces of information together and it should be possible to calculate the parabolic curve, which would provide a rough approximation of the launch site.'

Kammler said, 'And they could do this in sufficient time to direct their bombers to attack us within thirty minutes?'

'Theoretically, if they were quick enough to make the calculations.' He couldn't resist adding, 'It would seem we have been betrayed not by women in brothels, but by women employing the laws of mathematics.'

Kammler was frowning, preoccupied; he seemed not to hear. 'This is a serious flaw in the missile programme. Why were we not warned of it before now?'

'We never thought of it.'

'You never thought of it! All you clever fellows at Peenemünde, and you never thought of it!'

'I suppose we never expected the rocket to be fired from such an exposed position, with the enemy all around us.'

Kammler stared at the map and folded his arms. 'Well now, we must respond.'

Huber said, 'If I might make a proposal, Gruppenführer? The simplest solution would be for us to switch all our launches to night-time, and take care to vary our locations. That way, even if the enemy does get a fix on our positions and attacks them the following day, the intelligence will be too late to be operationally useful.'

Kammler shook his head. He was still brooding. 'Too passive. We need to meet aggression with aggression.'

'What alternative do we have? Are you suggesting we should ask the Luftwaffe to bomb Mechelen?'

'There is no Luftwaffe left to speak of; certainly not a force capable of bombing a town in Belgium.' He looked up, suddenly inspired. 'But who needs them? We have the weapon in our own hands, surely?' He glanced around the room. 'Isn't it obvious, gentlemen? We should strike them with a rocket!'

Seidel's eyes opened wide in surprise. Klein looked at the floor. Huber said, 'With respect, Gruppenführer, the V2 is not designed for use as a tactical weapon. It lacks the accuracy.'

'We're speaking of a **town,** Colonel, not a bridge!

Look at it!' He pointed at the map. 'Are you telling me you can't hit a target the size of a town?'

Huber hesitated. 'We may be able to hit the town, but the chances of us knocking out the radar units are tiny.'

'Then we will fire two missiles, and double our chances!' The Dust Cloud was whirling now, unstoppable. 'When are we next due to launch?'

'We were planning to wait until after the funeral ceremony.'

'Which is when?'

'Eleven.'

'But that's not for two and a half hours! I want this done immediately! What better way to honour our dead than to strike a blow against the enemy?'

Graf said quietly, 'It wasn't the enemy who killed them.'

Kammler turned on him. 'You people make me sick! You've bled the Reich dry to build your damned rockets, and now you tell us you can't even hit a town two hours' drive away! I want this done at once, is that understood?'

Huber came to attention. 'Yes, Gruppenführer!'

Kammler gave him a curt nod. 'The name of the target should be kept secret from the men. We need to protect our source. You may go.'

The three Wehrmacht officers trooped out of the office. Graf followed them. In the passage, Huber said wearily, 'Well, you have your orders. Seidel, get your platoon ready to launch. Graf, you had better oversee the re-targeting of the missile.' His shoulders slouched. He looked crushed. He will be sacked by nightfall, Graf thought.

They crossed the lobby and went out into the morning.

Graf hunched over a map in the technical troop tent, measuring the distance with a pair of dividers. He calculated the flight path from Scheveningen to Mechelen as 121 kilometres. The protractor showed him that instead of a compass bearing of 260 degrees, the rocket would need to fly on a southerly course of 183. The engine cut-off time would need to be reduced from 65 to 26 seconds to flatten the trajectory. That would mean bypassing the onboard accelerometer and instead turning off the motor by radio signal from the ground. The arithmetic was all very crude, but it was the best he could do. Beneath his breath, he cursed Kammler.

He pulled back the tent flap. The missile lay in its wheeled cradle beneath the trees, hooked up to a tractor. The number 3 control panel was open. He used a screwdriver and a pair of pliers to rewire the accelerometer, nodded to the corporal and stood aside as the panels were fixed back in place. The corporal banged his hand on the side of the tractor cab, the engine started and the rocket was slowly moved forward to the warhead mounting section, where the nose cone with its one-ton charge of amatol hung suspended, still housed in its metal shipping drum. It took five men to lower it by block and tackle and guide it into place. Once it was screwed to the end of the fuselage, the container was lifted away. Five minutes later, the fuses were installed and she was ready to go.

Graf walked beside the rocket at a steady pace, like an undertaker beside a hearse, as the missile was moved along the forest road. In the clearing ahead, beneath the wide gantry of the mobile crane, the Meillerwagen was already waiting. The transporter halted alongside it, the V2 was hoisted up and swung across, her nose cone nodding judiciously in the wind. Three men strained on ropes at the back to hold her steady. When she had been lowered onto the Meillerwagen and clamped in place, fore and aft, Graf walked up to the cab of the tow truck and opened the door.

'Any chance of a lift?'

'Sure. Get in.'

They moved off towards the launch site. Graf wound down the window and stuck his head out into the fresh air. He gazed at the passing trees. He wondered if his exchanges with Kammler would land him back in a Gestapo cell and he realised he did not care. He felt disturbingly detached. He was not even much bothered that he had just re-targeted a ballistic missile to hit a Belgian town. British or Belgians – what was the difference? How many civilians had he killed already? He passed his hand across his face. My God, he thought, what am I? Was he really any better than the SS? In a way he was worse. At least they had the stomach to kill their victims face to face.

The launch table was already in position. A dozen men stood around it waiting for them. The tow truck halted at a distance of fifteen metres; Graf jumped out of the cab and watched as the Meillerwagen was uncoupled from the tow truck. Steel cables were connected to the chassis and it was winched by hand until the base of the rocket was over the launch table. The supporting jacks were screwed down. The hydraulic rams began to raise the missile. Such simplicity! After a couple of minutes, the V2 reached the upright position, where it was held rigid by the arm of the Meillerwagen a few centimetres above the circular platform. The position was checked and then it was slowly lowered. Once the missile was standing upright, the Meillerwagen withdrew a couple of paces. The hydraulic arm was lowered, testing platforms were attached at various heights, it was raised again and hauled back to the rocket. Cables were run out for the electrical tests.

Graf went over to one of the surveyors, who was peering through his theodolite to make sure the V2 was perfectly vertical. 'For this launch, we have a different aiming point.'

The soldier blinked at him in surprise. Every missile launched from The Hague in the past six weeks had been set on the same course towards London. 'Is this a new order?'

'One hundred and eighty-three. Check with the lieutenant if you like. He'll confirm it.'

He could see Seidel making his way over from the firing control vehicle. He beckoned to him. 'I've calculated a bearing of one eight three.'

'Very good,' said Seidel. 'You heard Dr Graf, soldier. Re-orientate the rocket.'

'Yes, Lieutenant!'

A rumble of engines signalled the approach of the fuel tankers – two carrying methyl alcohol, one liquid oxygen and one hydrogen peroxide. Graf and Seidel walked away. Graf said, 'I've disabled the accelerometer. I calculate we need to cut off the engine by radio signal after twenty-three seconds.'

'What happens if the signal fails?'

'We'll hit Reims.'

Seidel stopped in mid-stride. 'You're joking?'

'No. I checked it twice. If she flies the full distance, that's exactly where she'll come down.'

'My God, this is insane – even for Kammler! Does he know this?'

'Why would he care? It's only the French.'

Seidel walked off, shaking his head, to supervise the fuelling and Graf took up his usual position, leaning his back against a tree, ready to step forward if his expertise was required. He watched as the men of the fuel and rocket troop took over the preparation of the V2. The protective cones were removed from the jet nozzles. The carbon vanes – too fragile to be fitted until the last minute – were attached beneath the fins. The batteries, which had been drained during the electrical tests, were lowered from the control compartment and replaced. The fuel tankers drew up around the rocket and hoses were run out.

Each one of these procedures had become routine. None of the soldiers would have the faintest notion of how many months and years of effort had gone into devising each one. My life's work, thought Graf, and it has come to this – a long shot at hitting an unsuspecting Belgian town. The 6,000 litres of alcohol were pumped in first – that took ten minutes – followed by 6,750 kilos of liquid oxygen, which took eight. The pipes gleamed beneath a layer of ice. Clouds of condensed water vapour billowed across the clearing. Hydrogen peroxide was pumped into the steam unit. The sodium permanganate, which reacted with the hydrogen peroxide to produce the steam to power the turbine, was removed from its heated container and tipped into an opening in the tail unit. The compartments were closed. The tankers withdrew. The arm of the Meillerwagen was lowered. The igniter was fitted. Finally the surveyors moved in to turn the rocket on the launch table so that the number one fin was precisely aligned on a bearing of 183 degrees.

Graf pulled his back away from the tree and made his way over to the firing control vehicle as the klaxon sounded. He pulled the heavy door of the armoured car shut behind him. Seidel was peering out of the hatch in the roof. He closed it and slid down into his seat. In his hand he held a stopwatch. 'Twenty-three seconds, right?'

'That's it.'

He picked up a telephone. The radar station in The Hague announced that they were clear to launch. He nodded to the sergeant. 'Begin the procedure.'

Graf braced himself as the countdown started. Through the thickened glass he saw the familiar spectacle – the shower of sparks, the spreading flame, the sudden rush of noise and heat as the rocket reached full power. Seidel pressed the stopwatch the instant the missile erupted out of sight.

He spoke into the telephone. 'Stand by to cut off engines. Twenty seconds . . . fifteen seconds . . .'

18

IN MECHELEN, A TELEPHONE RANG. It made them jump. In the confined silence of the bank vault the clang was as loud as a fire alarm.

Kay looked up hopefully. Waiting for something to happen had started to prey on her nerves. A dozen pairs of eyes went straight to the Signals Corps corporal as he lifted the receiver.

He listened, raised his hand. 'They've launched!'

The bell sounded briefly. Kay picked up her pencil.

The corporal began his incantation: 'Contact bearing one eight three; altitude thirty-one thousand; velocity three two two zero feet per second . . .'

'Hang on,' muttered Knowsley. He looked at the corporal, puzzled. 'One eight three? That can't be right.' He grabbed a protractor, propelled himself out of his seat and strode over to the map.

Kay kept her head down, writing.

'Contact bearing one eight three,' said the corporal, 'altitude forty-seven thousand, velocity—'

Knowsley interrupted him. 'Request confirmation of the bearing.'

'Can you confirm that bearing, please?' The corporal waited. 'Bearing confirmed.' He listened to the voice on the other end. Now he too looked bewildered. 'The missile's rising but they aren't picking up a track, sir.'

'No, that's because it's coming straight at us.' The wing commander's voice was calm. 'Sound the air raid warning. Everyone take cover.'

The V2, its engine cut off by radio signal, flashed over Rotterdam in free flight at twice the speed of sound.

All around the room everyone was ducking to find shelter, apart from Kay. She could not believe this was happening to her again.

Barbara said, 'Kay – get under the table!' She had to shout again to get her attention. 'Kay!'

Kay got down on her knees and crawled into the cramped space. The howl of the air raid siren carried from the street outside. Barbara said, 'Well, this is thrilling.' They lay on their stomachs, side by side. Kay turned her head to look at Barbara. Beneath her cheek the parquet floor smelled sickly sweet of beeswax polish. Barbara gave her an encouraging smile, took her hand and squeezed it. Kay placed her other hand over the crown of her head to protect it – as if that would do much good, she thought. She closed her eyes. **Holy Mary, Mother of God, pray for us sinners, now and at the hour of our death . . .**

The air raid siren stopped.

Time seemed to stretch and tauten, to elongate further and further: unbearably far.

Suddenly, a change in the air pressure – the same minute click in the ears, like the whisper of a premonition, that she had experienced in London – followed a beat later by a tremendous bang overhead. Then came the thump of a distant explosion, subsumed in its turn by the avalanche roar of the incoming rocket.

Kay lay still in the ensuing silence. I have heard that three-part sequence twice, she thought. Not many among the living can say that.

After half a minute, Barbara whispered, 'Is that it?'

'I think so.' She felt a surge of claustrophobia and used her elbows to wriggle out from under the table. The others were emerging from beneath their desks. She stood and brushed the dust from her skirt and tunic. The all-clear wailed from the street upstairs. Someone started to cry.

'Oh do shut up,' said Sitwell.

They filed up from the vault and gathered on the pavement outside. Across the road to their right, dark smoke was rising in the distance behind the spires of the Brusselpoort. People had stopped in the street to look at it, exactly as they did in London, thought Kay – shocked by what had happened, appalled to think who might have been under it, relieved it wasn't them.

Barbara said, 'I wonder what they hit?'

Kay peered at the tower of smoke. It was toppling slightly in the wind. 'It looks to be in the same direction as my billet.'

'God, let's hope Arnaud's all right.'

'Come on,' said Sitwell. 'Don't dawdle.'

As they followed the others towards the headquarters building, Kay kept her gaze fixed on the smoke.

Barbara said, 'Every time you kiss a man, the Germans drop a rocket on him – have you noticed that?'

Upstairs in the mess room, Knowsley asked for the doors to be closed, then clapped his hands to get their attention. He had an army major standing next to him, square-faced and thickset, like a boxer, who seemed to be examining each of them in turn. Kay could feel him looking at her. 'All right, listen, everyone. It's important we stay calm. The Mechelen area **has** been hit by a couple of V2s before, but they originated from launch sites in Germany and were almost certainly intended for Antwerp. That one came from The Hague where the batteries are only firing at London. So unless they've suddenly changed their targeting, we have to assume it was deliberate.'

He allowed the implications to sink in. A nervous murmur ran around the mess.

'I need to talk to Stanmore and to our head of security.' He turned slightly and nodded to the major. 'In the meantime, it's probably best if we suspend this shift. You can either wait at HQ or go back to your billets, and we'll reconvene here at fourteen hundred. And please remember – I cannot emphasise this enough – you are to tell no one about what I've just said. As far as the local population and our own service personnel are concerned, that was just another rocket meant for Antwerp that went off course. Is that understood? Right, stand down.'

The room broke up into separate conversations. Barbara turned to Kay. 'What are you going to do?'

'I think I ought to go back and see if the house is still standing.'

'Do you want me to come with you?'

'No, I'll be fine.'

The smoke from the V2 was like an optical illusion. The faster she hurried towards it, the further it seemed to recede, as if it were a malevolent spirit beckoning her on. Alarm bells sounded occasionally, but only faintly, and always far away. By the time she reached the Vermeulens' street, it was obvious the rocket must have landed well outside the centre; it might even have fallen short of the town altogether.

She opened the garden gate and walked up to the front door, rang the bell and waited, then tried the door. Locked, of course. She remembered how Arnaud had retrieved the key from the lintel the night before. She stood on tiptoe and felt along the smooth stone until her fingers touched metal.

Inside, the house was silent and empty; dim even in the daylight. Standing in the hall, with its shadowy religious decorations, she felt nervous, like a thief. She went into the kitchen. The dishes had all been cleaned and put away; everything was straight and tidy. She retreated back to the hall, considered taking a look inside Dr Vermeulen's study but decided against it: that would have been too much like trespassing. She climbed the stairs to her room.

The curtains had been drawn open. On the bed – her perfectly made WAAF bed – there was a slight depression, as if someone had sat on it. She looked in the wardrobe at her clothes, then sat at the desk and opened the drawer. Her slide rule was there, and her logarithm tables, and the sheets of calculations she had practised on her first night. However, the pages were not precisely as she had left them. They were slightly disordered. Most people would not have noticed, but she was trained to spot such things.

It was like using the stereoscope at Medmenham. You examined a single photograph and the picture was flat. You laid another beside it, taken a fraction of a second later, and the images leaped up at you in 3D. Gazing down now at the desk drawer, everything that had happened over the past two days acquired a new perspective. For almost a minute she sat calmly, remembering every tiny detail: incidents that had meant nothing by themselves but that together made up a different picture. The reluctance of the Vermeulens to take her in. The photograph of the dead son placed face down on the desk in the study. The Nazi salute in the waterfront bar.

Arnaud's nervous glances at the ceiling while they were making love. The empty food cupboard. The lingering smell of cigarette smoke outside the back door that morning.

She rose, left the bedroom and walked along the passage to the landing, then began to climb the stairs to the second floor. She guessed that the room directly above hers must be at the rear of the house, on the left. The door was half-open. Inside, the sheets on the single bed were tangled, as if someone had been tossing and turning in a fever. There was a strong male smell of sweat and stale cigarettes. Piles of books. A first-aid box, its lid open, containing rolled bandages, gauze, lint pads, a bottle of antiseptic. On the dressing table, a tin of the Fray Bentos corned beef she had presented to Madam Vermeulen, empty, with a spoon stuck in it that had been licked clean. She opened the dressing table drawer. A small grey identity card, like a passport, with **3. SS Panzer Division 'Wiking'** written on the outside, and on the inside a picture of a young man remarkably like Arnaud, made out in the name of Guillaume Vermeulen, with his blood group, the signature of his commanding officer, and a purple swastika stamp.

Although her heart was thumping, her mind was cool and sharp. Guillaume was not dead. He had fought for the Germans. He was in hiding – wounded, by the look of it. He would not dare show his face out of doors. Therefore, while the others might have gone out, he must still be in the house. He would almost certainly have heard her knocking at the front door, heard her come in, heard her go into the kitchen and come upstairs.

Slowly she turned around, half expecting to find him behind her. But the doorway was clear, so too the landing and the staircase. She descended to the first-floor landing and peered over the banister down into the hall. The black-and-white tiled floor was deserted. He was unlikely to be in any of the other bedrooms, so either he was in the parlour or – more likely, given how cold and unused the parlour seemed – he was in his father's study, probably listening. She calculated the distance to the front door. She could make a run for it, but that might bring him out to intercept her. Better, then, to walk normally. She looked around for anything she might be able to use as a weapon, but there was nothing she could see. Very well. She squared her shoulders. Go.

She descended the stairs, crossed to the front door, opened it and stepped outside. The key was still in the lock. She locked the door and replaced the key on the lintel. The study window looked out over the garden. The curtains were drawn. She could imagine him behind them, the heavy material parted slightly, watching her. She suppressed her instinct to hurry and walked carefully across the grass. She was half-way to the gate when it opened and Dr and Madam Vermeulen came in with Arnaud.

They stopped in surprise. She advanced towards them. 'You're all safe,' she said. 'Thank goodness for that.'

Dr Vermeulen said coldly, 'What are you doing here?'

'I came to see if you were all right.' Her voice sounded strangulated, high and false, so she added, rather too brightly, 'Where did the rocket land, do you know?'

Arnaud was looking at her intently. 'We went to see but we couldn't get close. It seems to have hit a field.'

'That's a bit of luck.' She managed to smile at him. 'Well, as long as you're safe. I'll see you all this evening.'

They were blocking the path. She made a move to leave, and for an instant she thought Arnaud would stop her. He seemed to be trying to weigh her up. 'Yes,' he said, 'that would be good.' He stood aside, and an instant later she was through the gate and out into the street.

In the square close to the cathedral, she flagged down a British army jeep – a corporal and two privates. It swerved across the cobbles and braked. The corporal said, 'Yes, ma'am. Is everything all right?'

'I believe there is a German soldier hiding in a house near here.'

19

AT THE HEART OF THE regiment's launch zone, midway between Scheveningen and Wassenaar, in the flat landscape of woods and dunes about two kilometres from the sea, lay the Duindigt racetrack – an eight-furlong oval course, with three stands, built before the Great War. It was here that the mass funeral ceremony for Lieutenant Stock's launch troop was to be held.

Graf had not wanted to go. Four days after the raid on Peenemünde, in a hastily dug cemetery next to the railway line, more than a hundred coffins had been lowered into a communal grave; he hadn't even known which of the plain wooden boxes was Karin's. But how could he use that as an excuse, especially to himself? The deaths of the men were his responsibility as much as anyone's. It was his duty to pay his respects. So once the V2 had been fired at Mechelen, and after the launch crew had packed up the site, he found himself slipping into the front seat of Seidel's Kübelwagen, with Sergeant Schenk and a corporal in the back, and setting off to the racetrack.

By the time they arrived, the dilapidated stands, with peeling paintwork and patches of rotted timber, were nearly full. A thousand men had been turned out, willingly or unwillingly: the headquarters troops, who administered the regiment; the technical troops, who unloaded the missiles from the trains and prepared them for flight; the fuel and rocket troops, the launching troops, and all the other ancillaries – drivers, maintenance men, signallers, cooks, flak men, firemen, radio operators – who had been consigned to this deserted stretch of coast in order to fire rockets at the English. They sat in sombre rows, listening as the regimental band played a selection of hymns.

The sky was high, grey, clear; no sign of the RAF. On the sandy track, overgrown with couch grass, half a dozen chairs and a microphone had been set out on a low platform. A Protestant pastor and a Catholic priest sat next to one another. Twelve coffins were lined up in front of it, each draped with a swastika flag and bearing the dead man's cap. An honour guard stood to attention beside them. The sight of those lonely caps in conjunction with the mournful music had a dismaying effect on Graf. It had been exactly the same at Peenemünde. He took off his hat and wiped his eyes on his sleeves.

Seidel looked at him with concern. 'Are you all right, Graf?'

'Yes, I'm fine.'

They climbed the steps of the stand and found the last few empty seats. The men rose to let them pass. Just as they sat, Kammler's Mercedes drove onto the racetrack. It made its way slowly in front of the stand and pulled up in front of the coffins. The front passenger door opened and Kammler stepped out. From the rear came Colonel Huber and another tall SS officer. The three arrivals lined up in front of the coffins with their backs to the spectators and extended their arms in the Nazi salute, then mounted the platform and took their seats. Respectful in the presence of the dead, they removed their caps. The easterly wind that had been blowing since before dawn lifted the edges of the swastika flags and ruffled the thick blond hair of the second SS officer. He raised his hand to smooth it back, and Graf would have recognised him by that familiar gesture alone, for he must have seen it a thousand times in the past – on the windswept derelict ground of the Rocket Aerodrome in Berlin, on the test ranges at Kummersdorf, on the North Sea beaches of Borkum, on the Baltic foreshore at Peenemünde, on the central Polish plain of Blizna . . .

There was a roll of drums. Everyone stood. The band struck up 'Ich hatt' einen Kameraden', the soldiers' lament. A thousand voices joined in the words:

I once had a comrade
You won't find a better one
The drum was rolling for battle
He was marching by my side
In the same pace and stride . . .

Von Braun sang with the rest, but all the while his restless gaze swept the stands – back and forth, up and down, back and forth – until at last it came to rest on Graf.

Graf looked away.

He barely noticed the ceremony after that – the hymns, the pious sermons from the two clergymen, Huber's eulogy ('They died in the service of the Fatherland, yielding up their lives for our sacred cause . . .'). His mind reviewed a parade of ghosts – Karin on the beach that final evening, the girl in the brothel standing over him with the knife, Wahmke holding the tin of kerosene in the instant before he died, the human remains strewn around the crater of the exploded rocket, the shadows of the slave workers passing through the tunnels of Nordhausen. Only when he heard Kammler's voice – that rasping, staccato delivery, made even more metallic by amplification – did he make a conscious effort to claw himself back into the present.

The SS general was standing at the microphone, holding a sheet of paper. Graf tried to focus, caught odd words – 'crusade for Western civilisation . . . historic destiny of the Führer . . . ultimate victory assured . . .'

He flourished the paper. 'Men of the Vengeance Division! I wish to share with you the following communiqué from the Reich Ministry of Public Enlightenment and Propaganda. "As of today, the V2 has destroyed three Thames bridges in London. The Houses of Parliament have been extensively damaged. There is not a building standing within five hundred metres of Leicester Square. Piccadilly Circus has also been devastated. The Tower of London has suffered considerable damage from blast." Let that be their epitaph.'

He folded the sheet and returned it to his inside pocket. 'Our comrades did not die in vain! You do not serve in vain! Each rocket you fire inflicts a smashing blow upon the enemy! We are the Vengeance Division! We will prevail! Heil Hitler!'

The silence that met his words seemed to disconcert him. He dropped his arm and stepped back from the microphone. He glanced at von Braun and then at Huber, who nodded to the commander of the honour guard.

'Prepare to fire!'

The men aimed their rifles at the sky.

'Fire!'

The shots rang round the racetrack. The soldiers reloaded.

'Fire!'

They reloaded again.

'Fire!'

As the echo of the final volley died away, Graf stood. He had made up his mind, and he wanted to get away before von Braun had a chance to speak to him.

Seidel caught his arm. 'What's the rush?'

'We have a missile to launch, remember?'

'Even so, I think you need to rest.'

'I'll prepare the rocket. Then I'll rest, I promise.'

The V2 was waiting for him on its cradle beneath the trees. He asked the corporal to open control compartment number 2.

The man looked confused. 'It was number three this morning.'

'And now it's number two.'

The soldier did as he was instructed. They all knew Dr Graf; they trusted him. The component was awkward to get at. Graf had to lie on his back under the rocket and reach into the interior, working blind. With both hands he felt around the plywood platform for the programme clockwork – a small device, no bigger than his hand – and pulled apart the wires.

He slid out from beneath the fuselage. 'That's fine. You can close the compartment.'

Once again he walked beside the rocket as it was towed over to the crane. He stood watching as it was transferred to the Meillerwagen. He did not ask for a lift to the launch site. He had plenty of time. He ambled along the road through the trees, found a decent spot, spread out his coat and sat down. He smoked a couple of cigarettes and listened to the sounds of the wood. For the first time in many weeks, he felt at peace. His mind was pleasantly empty. He lingered for the best part of an hour, then resumed his journey.

The rocket was on its launch table, fully fuelled. The electrical tests had been completed and the cables were disconnected. The men were preparing to unfasten the testing platforms from the vertical arm of the Meillerwagen. Standing watching them, his notebook open, was Sturmscharführer Biwack.

Graf said cheerfully, 'Still collecting information, I see.'

'I think it's noteworthy, don't you? A missile fired directly at a British army unit for only the second time in history?'

'Noteworthy – yes, I suppose that's one word for it.' And then he said, to no one in particular, 'I just want to check the transformer one last time.'

'No need, Doctor. Everything's been tested. It's working fine.'

'Even so – we've had so many faults. Remember what happened to Lieutenant Stock? Just give me five minutes.'

Before the soldier could object, he began to climb. How huge she was, he thought! How powerful!

He could sense the latent energy through the thin metal membrane. It was a mighty thing they had made, no question of it. She deserved a better purpose. He kept on climbing steadily until he reached the topmost platform. He fished in his pocket for his screwdriver and opened the door to control compartment number 3. Inside, next to the metal dome that housed the roll-and-yaw gyroscope, was a radio receiver. He reached in with his pliers and cut the electrical connection, closed the door and screwed it shut. He started his descent.

Back on the ground, he said, 'You were right. It's fine. Enjoy the launch, Biwack.'

He waved in the direction of the firing control vehicle and gave a thumbs-up. The hydraulic arm was uncoupled from the rocket. The Meillerwagen was pushed back.

Graf walked a couple of hundred metres up the road, stopped and turned. The klaxon sounded. He took out his binoculars. The rocket stood alone apart from the thin metal antenna and its umbilical cable. The familiar cloud of white vapour was issuing from the vents above the liquid oxygen tank. All was quiet. All was good. The fireflies began to dance around the base. The sparks became a solid roaring orange jet. The mast fell away, the cable snapped free, the noise and blast wave of the engine at full power made him stagger back, but he kept his binoculars trained on the V2 as she lifted off.

One second into the flight . . . two . . . three . . . four . . .

Now!

The rocket did not tilt. In the control compartment, the clockwork mechanism clicked in vain. Held steady on her course by her pair of gyroscopes, she hurtled upwards at an angle of ninety degrees – vertically, perfectly, gloriously – towards the heavens.

A warning blast on the klaxon. A voice over the loudspeaker: 'Tilt programme failed! Engine cut-off initiated!'

He could imagine the panic in the control wagon as they tried to send the radio signal.

'Engine cut-off failed!'

A few moments later, the men of the firing platoon, Biwack among them, emerged from the undergrowth and ran up the road towards him. They sprinted past, shouting at him in panic to get clear of the site. Biwack gave him a frowning sideways look as he went by. Graf stood unmoved.

He could see the flame of the exhaust quite clearly through his binoculars. At Peenemünde that summer, they had fired a test rocket in exactly this manner to observe re-entry. They had recorded a maximum altitude of 176 kilometres before gravity reclaimed her. She would continue to rise unstoppably through all the restraining layers of the atmosphere – troposphere, stratosphere, mesosphere – into the boiling heat of the thermosphere; then she would falter, begin to tumble, flip over, and fall with the precision of a feathered dart.

The red dot of the rocket dwindled and disappeared into the cloud base. He put away the binoculars and advanced purposefully towards the deserted clearing.

20

KAY SAT ALONE AT A corner table in the officers' mess. It was a little after half past four: sunset – not that she had glimpsed the sun all day. The lamps had been turned on. A couple of off-duty army captains were standing at the bar, drinking and telling dirty jokes. They had asked her if she wanted to join them.

'No, thanks all the same.'

Apart from them, the mess was empty. Every so often, one or the other would roar with laughter and bang his glass on the counter. Her suitcase stood beside her chair, her greatcoat laid across it. Somewhere in the building, her fate was being decided.

She had led the patrol to the Vermeulens' house. In the street outside, they had sat in the jeep while she explained the layout. They were plainly sceptical, suspected she was just a hysterical woman. The corporal said, 'So is he armed, this German?'

'He's not German, I told you – he's a Belgian who fought with the Germans. I don't know if he's armed.'

'Sounds a bit unlikely, if you don't mind me saying.'

'He fought with the third SS Panzer division, if that means anything to you.'

That changed their attitude at once. 'Fucking hell,' said one of the privates. 'Should we send for reinforcements?'

'Nah,' said the corporal. He reached for his rifle. 'We can take him.'

They went in through the gate. One of the privates took up position in the garden, with his rifle trained on the house. The other slipped quietly down the side path to the back door. The corporal stood on the front step with Kay. He gestured to her to ring the bell.

For half a minute, nothing happened. Then came the sound of the key turning, the bolts being drawn back. The door opened, and there was Dr Vermeulen in his dark green cardigan.

Kay said, 'I'm sorry, Dr Vermeulen. We need to search the house.'

His body sagged slightly. He rested his head against the door jamb, seemed on the point of saying something, and then gave up. 'Guillaume's in the kitchen. Follow me.'

Until that moment, Kay had half expected the whole thing to turn out to be a figment of her imagination, an embarrassing misunderstanding requiring an apology to all concerned. But there in the kitchen, seated at the table, was Arnaud and his mother and a young man, little older than a boy, with a dead-white pallor and long unkempt hair. He was wearing a scruffy blue pullover. His left hand was bandaged. They looked up, made no effort to move, as if this was a moment they had long expected.

The corporal said to Kay, 'Which one is it?'

'The one in blue.'

'Him?' the corporal said, as if he couldn't believe it. He pointed his rifle and gestured with the barrel. Guillaume swayed to his feet and raised his hands. 'Out.' He nodded to the door.

After they had gone, Kay stood awkwardly in the kitchen, alone with the family. She looked at Arnaud. She spread her hands. 'I'm so sorry.'

He stared back at her – a terrible expression, full of accusation and betrayal: she would never forget it – and then the back door opened and the soldier came in. He trained his rifle on the Vermeulens. He said to Kay, 'Tell them to get their coats and come with us.'

Dr Vermeulen said wearily, 'It's all right. We understand.'

'And then she said, "Don't worry – I'm not a virgin!" ' The captain laughed at his own joke. His companion drummed his glass on the bar.

'Section Officer Caton-Walsh?'

She looked up. A young lieutenant was standing in the doorway. 'Yes?'

'Come with me, please.'

She collected her coat and suitcase and followed him up the main staircase to the second floor. Behind a closed door, a telephone was ringing. A corporal crossed the corridor carrying a stack of files. The lieutenant knocked on a door at the end of the passage and opened it. He stood aside to let her enter.

The square-faced major was seated behind a desk with a file open in front of him. Wing Commander Knowsley was in a chair to one side. Kay saluted. The major said, 'Take a seat, Section Officer.' She did as she was told. She felt numb. He placed a pair of meaty fists on the table, one on either side of the file. She noticed the black hairs on the back of his hands and fingers; they were like paws, she thought. 'Well, that was quite a show you were involved in.'

'Yes, sir.'

'Anything you want to say about it?'

'Only that I'm sorry, sir.'

The two men exchanged glances.

Knowsley said, 'Sorry for what, exactly?'

'I should never have left evidence of our work in my room – that was an unforgivable lapse.' She hesitated. 'And I should never have allowed myself to have any kind of relationship with someone from the local population.'

Knowsley said, 'This was the other son, I take it?'

'Yes, sir.'

'You disclosed details of our mission?'

'No, sir. Absolutely not.'

'But he tried to find out what you were doing?'

'He asked a few questions. I didn't tell him anything. But I drew attention to myself.' She was squirming at the memory of her foolishness. 'In my defence, I wasn't to know the family were German sympathisers.'

The major said, 'In your defence, I don't think they **are** German sympathisers – the younger son was, obviously, but the other three were just trying to protect him, as far as we can tell.' He looked down at the file. 'He volunteered to join the Germans in 1941, soon after they invaded the Soviet Union. Thousands of young men in occupied Europe did the same. They fell for the line that they were joining a crusade for Christian civilisation. He was seventeen. His unit was cut up pretty badly this year on the Eastern Front and they were shipped out of the front line. He seems to have deserted and come running home to mummy and daddy just before we arrived in Belgium.'

She considered this information. It wasn't at all what she was expecting. 'May I ask a question, sir?'

'Go on.'

'If he was a deserter, in hiding, how did he manage to tell the Germans about what we were doing?'

'Well, obviously he didn't.'

Years afterwards, whenever she allowed her mind to go back to Arnaud – which was rarely – she was to remember this moment as the worst of all.

The major said, 'At about one o'clock this morning, the Radio Security Service intercepted a short-wave transmission from Mechelen to Berlin, which they were able to trace to a block of flats in town. The building was cordoned off, the residents detained and questioned, all the apartments were searched. A radio transmitter was found in the home of a local teacher. According to our friends in the resistance, he's long been suspected as a collaborator, but there was no proof and in the end they left him alone. I think you know what I'm going to tell you next.'

She bowed her head. 'Yes, sir.'

'Section Officer Colville spent part of the evening in this man's flat. She's insistent she never told him anything about her work, and he's refusing to talk, even though he's almost certain to be hanged as a spy. But . . .' He rolled his eyes in disbelief and opened one of his paw-like fists. 'Let's just say the text of the radio transmission suggests otherwise.'

Knowsley said, 'She is very indiscreet, unfortunately.'

'Oh God,' said Kay, 'poor Barbara.'

'Poor Barbara indeed.'

'What will happen to her?'

The major said, 'She's on her way back to England. Just between us, I doubt she'll be prosecuted – there's no proof we could offer in court.'

Knowsley said, 'I can, however, safely predict that she'll lose her commission and be transferred to other duties.'

'And the Vermeulens?'

The major shrugged. 'That's a matter for the Belgians. Jail, certainly, I would have thought. There isn't a lot of forgiveness in the air, as you've probably noticed.'

'No, sir.'

Knowsley said, 'Which brings us to you, Section Officer.' He leaned forward and studied her. 'Do you want to go back to Medmenham or stay on here? I can't guarantee the Germans won't lob another rocket in our direction, but they must know it's pretty pointless. And if they do – well, it's one less rocket on London, I suppose.'

She looked at him in surprise. She had come upstairs expecting dismissal, and now she was being offered a choice. She remembered the exhilaration of the previous day – the feeling that she was actually properly at war at last, striking a blow directly at the enemy. It wasn't really a choice at all. 'I'll stay, sir. Thank you.'

'Good. I'll tell Flight Officer Sitwell. You can have Colville's billet tonight, and I'll see you on duty tomorrow morning.'

She stood and saluted, picked up her case and coat. ‘Could I ask, sir, if the enemy has launched any more V2s today?’

‘Only one,’ said Knowsley, ‘but that seems to have been a misfire. It didn’t fly towards any target, as far as we could tell.’ He made a soaring motion with the flat of his hand. ‘It just went straight up into space.’

21

GRAF STOOD BESIDE THE LAUNCH table, his face raised to the sky, his arms thrown wide, willing his own destruction.

Come on, you bastard! Come home to Papa!

It was pure histrionics. He knew it. Either the easterly wind that had been blowing all day or the winds in the stratosphere, which could reach 200 kilometres per hour, would affect her descent. That was what was absurd about this British effort to calculate the launch positions by extrapolating the parabolic curve. The gyroscopes and the rudders would battle against nature to try to hold her on course. But without electronic guidance by radio signal, the rocket could never fly exactly true.

After five minutes of scanning the clouds, he dropped his arms. She must have been blown out to sea.

He turned and began to walk back through the

still-empty woods towards Scheveningen. He felt ready for whatever might come next.

When he reached his hotel an hour later, half a dozen soldiers of the artillery regiment were standing in the passage. They parted silently to let him pass. Upstairs, his door frame was shattered and a couple of Gestapo men were inside the room. They had upended his bed and mattress. Biwack had already opened the suitcase, and was standing at the window holding up one of the strips of microfilm to the fading light, frowning at it.

'What is this?'

'I don't know.'

'You expect us to believe that?'

'I don't care what you believe. I don't know what's on it.'

'Why do you have it in your room?'

'I was asked to look after it.'

'By whom?'

'Professor von Braun – you can ask him if you like.'

'Oh, we will, don't worry. And there is a lot more we intend to ask you.'

They marched him down to the street, where a car was waiting, and drove him through the darkening streets to the big modern house not far from the town centre that the Gestapo used as their headquarters – a curious, high-roofed, sinister place, much more brick than windows, shaped like a monk's cowl.

In the interrogation room on the ground floor, his file was already on the table. It was ten centimetres thick. They must have sent for it some time ago, Graf thought, either from the regional office in Stettin or, more likely, from the national headquarters in Prinz-Albrecht-Strasse in Berlin. No wonder Biwack had known so much about him from the start.

It was Biwack who took the chair opposite him.

'You are a saboteur.'

'No.'

'You sabotaged a missile three days ago, resulting in the deaths of twelve men, and you sabotaged another this afternoon.'

'No.' If it had been anyone other than the National Socialist Leadership Officer, he might have been tempted to tell the truth just to get it over with. But he would not give Biwack the satisfaction. 'The missile was faulty. Ten per cent of them are, you know. Or do you think I'm responsible for every launch that goes wrong?'

'A soldier in the technical troop says that you asked him to open control compartment number two rather than number three.'

'He is mistaken.'

'Shortly before the launch, you climbed up and disabled the radio receiver.'

'No. As I said at the time, I wanted to check the transformer. You've seen me do it before.'

'Why lie, Graf? If nothing else, your behaviour after the rocket misfired establishes your guilt.'

'If you're asking why didn't I run away with the rest of you – why should I? The chances of it landing at the precise point from which it took off are a million to one against.'

Biwack was starting to look irritated. He glanced at the two Gestapo men who were leaning against the wall, watching with their arms folded. 'Listen to his lies!'

One of them said, 'Do you want us to take over?'

'Yes, by all means. I can't bear to look at the swine. I'm going to find out what's on those microfilms.'

He stood and left the room. The two Gestapo men settled down opposite Graf. The second one opened his file. He sounded weary before he even started. 'You were first arrested on the twenty-second of March this year . . .'

Graf lay on a thin mattress in a windowless cell in the basement. The naked low-wattage light bulb cast a jaundiced glow. The cell was cold. His belt and shoelaces had been taken from him, but not his coat, which he had pulled over himself as a blanket. The place had a fearsome reputation. The old brownish specks of blood on the mattress seemed to confirm it. He preferred not to look at them, and stared at the concrete ceiling.

What would he miss? The truth was, not much. His parents, of course: he had not seen them for a year. Some of the fellows at Peenemünde. He would miss sunny days on the Baltic, the play of light on the water and the scent of the pine trees in the evening after a hot day. But Karin was dead, and he would not miss the rocket. He was done with it. And with it went the central purpose of his life.

After about an hour, he heard the scrape of footsteps in the passage. The door was unlocked. Two heavily muscled bullet-headed men, like nightclub bouncers, came in and pulled him to his feet. Now the unpleasant part starts, he thought. They bundled him into the corridor and told him to move fast. But it was hard without laces in his shoes. He shuffled along as best he could. One of the men gave him a shove in the back that sent him sprawling, then kicked his backside. He managed to scramble up the stairs, and fell again. They hauled him upright and marched him along the passage to a door, knocked and opened it.

The same two Gestapo officers but a different room. Biwack was seated at a desk winding a roll of 35 mm film onto a bulky microfilm reader. The words **Top Secret** briefly flashed across the screen, followed by a blur of mathematical calculations and various complicated diagrams. He stopped at one and adjusted the focus. He squinted at it.

'What is this?'

Graf bent to look. 'That's a vacuum reservoir . . . compensator . . . fixed diffuser . . . Laval nozzle . . . honeycomb . . .'

'Yes, but what is it?'

'I can't tell you that – it's classified.'

Biwack hit him in the face. Graf stumbled backwards. His head was ringing. He put his hand to his nose and felt blood.

'That was for impertinence. The next will be for refusing to cooperate. So I ask you again: what is this?'

Graf inspected his fingers. His nose was hurting more than he thought possible. And that was only the beginning. 'I am not authorised to share classified material with anyone without security clearance.'

Biwack drew back his fist. Graf closed his eyes and braced himself. When nothing happened, he opened them again. Biwack's fist was still raised, but his head was turned away, distracted. Through the buzzing in his ears, Graf could vaguely make out an argument going on outside the door. It was abruptly flung open and an SS officer strode in. On his collar were the four silver squares of a Sturmbannführer. Biwack and the two Gestapo men came instantly to attention.

'Heil Hitler!'

Von Braun returned their salute. 'What is going on here?' He glanced at the screen. 'Turn that off immediately!' Biwack hastily pressed a switch and the screen went dark. 'I shall need the names of every man in this room.'

Biwack said, 'If I might explain the situation, Professor von Braun. Dr Graf has been arrested for sabotage. In his room we discovered one hundred and seven reels of microfilm. I was asking him for an explanation.'

'Asking him? My God! Is this what you call asking?' Von Braun pulled a clean white handkerchief out of his pocket and gave it to Graf. 'Are you all right?'

'I think so.' He dabbed at his nose. It felt loose, spongy, painful to touch.

Von Braun turned back to Biwack. 'How dare you mistreat one of my senior staff in this manner? Has this arrest been authorised by Gruppenführer Kammler?'

Biwack looked uncomfortable. 'No. I tried to contact him, but he was already back on the road to Hellendoorn.'

'So,' said von Braun, **'unauthorised.'** He transferred his gaze to the two Gestapo men. He was magnificent in his authority. 'This is what is going to happen, Sturmscharführer.' He didn't even deign to look at him. 'You are going to take that microfilm off the machine – without switching on the screen, unless you wish to be prosecuted – and return it to me, along with all the other rolls I had entrusted to Dr Graf for safe keeping. He is then going to accompany me back to Peenemünde, where he will be available for questioning if you wish to pursue this absurd allegation of sabotage any further. Is that clear?'

'With respect, I have the authority of the National Socialist Leadership Office—'

Von Braun ignored him and spoke to the other two. 'Is that clear?'

The Gestapo men looked at one another, nodded.

Outside, von Braun handed the suitcase to his driver. Graf crouched down on the gravel to lace up his shoes. 'Do that in the car,' said von Braun. 'Let's not push our luck.'

Graf climbed into the back seat beside him. The Mercedes pulled out of the gate into the road and swung left. The driver looked in the mirror. 'Where to, Professor?'

'Peenemünde. We can stop for fuel in Bremen.'

The big car gathered speed.

Graf had his head tilted back, the handkerchief pressed to his nose. 'I don't want to go back to Peenemünde.'

'Don't be absurd. You can't stay here.'

'Even so. It's all finished for me.'

Von Braun sighed. He leaned forward. 'Get clear of the town,' he said to the driver, 'and then find a place to pull over.'

It was dark, beginning to rain. The windscreen wipers scudded back and forth. Graf had no idea where they were. They drove for another five minutes. Just beyond a crossroads, they left the road and bounced up onto a flat stretch of grass. The driver switched on the interior light.

'Come on,' said von Braun.

They walked away from the car. The rain was soft and soothing. Graf tilted his face towards it. He dabbed at his nose. He could hear the sea in the distance, the roll of the waves hitting the shore. They found shelter under a tree. Von Braun lit a cigarette and gave it to Graf, then took one for himself. In his black uniform, in the brief flame of the lighter, his face glowed, disembodied.

'It's not all finished,' he said, 'not for me, and not for you either. For Germany, yes, it's finished, certainly, but that's a different matter.'

'I don't want to hear it.'

'Listen to me. There's a plan. I've been discussing it for months with Dornberger and one or two others. We want you to join us. Every specification, design and test result has been microfilmed at least twice and dispersed for safe keeping: the rocket motor, the turbo system, the guidance mechanism – everything. That's why I gave you the blueprints of the wind tunnels. They can measure up to Mach 8 – there's nothing like them in the world. Over the next couple of months, we're going to start gathering it all together into a single priceless archive.'

'To do what?'

'To offer it to the Americans, along with ourselves, as soon as the war is over.'

Graf stared at him. In the shadow of the tree, he could barely make out his face, just the red dot of his cigarette bobbing in the darkness. 'You're crazy.'

'Not at all. We'll offer to continue the whole programme after the war, and it will be as if nothing has ever happened – you'll see.'

'So we'll build missiles for the Americans?'

'Missiles to start with' – the cigarette tip described an expansive arc in the damp gloom – 'and then we'll get back to what it's always been about: spacecraft!'

'Spacecraft!' Graf started to laugh. It made his nose hurt like the devil. He was sure it must be broken. Even so, he couldn't help himself.

'Do you think I'm joking?' Von Braun sounded offended. 'If I could convince Adolf Hitler to spend five billion marks building a rocket, do you think I couldn't convince an American president to go to the moon?'

Graf looked over his shoulder at the road and wondered if he should walk back to Scheveningen. But it was raining harder now and he felt very tired. He would drift with the current and see where it took him. 'Whatever you say.' He threw away his cigarette. 'Let's get back in the car.'

22

Tuesday 4 September 1945

'IT'S ALL A MATTER OF geography,' said the man from the Ministry of Supply. 'The Russians got Peenemünde, the Americans got Nordhausen, and I'm afraid we've ended up with not very much.'

'Apart from the craters,' said the air commodore. Everyone laughed. Kay stared at her hands. It was the first time she'd seen Mike since the previous November. They were back in the same panelled conference room in which the Mechelen operation had been approved, and he was in his element, surrounded by top brass from the army and the RAF.

'Quite,' said the Ministry of Supply man, whose name was Sir Marley Rook. 'We do have the four intact missiles at Cuxhaven, and a few captured technical troops. We're planning to fire the rockets next month. But it's all very much crumbs from the big boys' table. The Americans have got a hundred V2s. So we need to make the most of today.'

'What time did they get in?'

'They landed at Northolt from Munich yesterday evening. The War Office put them up overnight at a place they have in Wimbledon. The Americans want them back in Germany tomorrow.'

'What are they offering them, do we know?'

'A new life in the States for them and their wives and children – restricted movement at first, but full citizenship in due course.'

'It's hard to compete with that.'

'We know. And of course money will be no object over there.' Rook's expression was morose. 'On the other hand, they'll have to live in White Sands, New Mexico, at the atom bomb test site, God help them, whereas here at least they'd be closer to home. It's worth a try, anyway.'

'Who do we have coming?'

'Von Braun – he's the head man; Steinhoff, who was in charge of guidance and control systems; Schilling and Graf, who between them ran rocket propulsion. Von Braun and Graf speak English, apparently, but we've got a translator on hand in case it gets too technical.'

'All right,' said Mike. He looked at his watch. 'They'll be here in a bit. Why don't we talk to them in here? I've arranged for beer and sandwiches to be brought in at half-time. Flight Officer Caton-Walsh?' He somehow succeeded in looking her directly in the face without actually focusing on her.

'Yes, sir?'

'Why don't you wait with your stuff in an office

down the corridor, and we'll get you involved if we have enough time?'

'Yes, sir. Thank you, sir.' She stood and saluted. She had rather dreaded the prospect of meeting him again, but now it came to it, it had not been too bad. She felt nothing for him at all.

The four Germans were all in the same car, an Austin 12, the biggest the Air Ministry could provide. Von Braun was in the front seat next to the driver; the other three were squeezed in the back. A smaller car full of military police followed immediately behind.

The day was thundery, the car stuffy with the smell of warm leather and cigarette smoke. The south London suburbs seemed to drag on forever. Graf said, 'Does anyone mind if I open the window?' Nobody replied. They were all staring at the bomb-damaged street. He wound down the window. Where the houses in the middle of the terrace had been demolished, they had left ghostly images of their former selves imprinted on the neighbouring walls – patches of paintwork and fading wallpaper, sheared floors, the ragged saw teeth of vanished staircases.

Van Braun said in English to the driver, 'What district of London is this, please?'

'Wandsworth.'

'Was it hit by V2s?'

'Yes,' the man said grimly. 'Often.' They halted at a traffic light beside a sudden vista of rubble and weeds. Graf noticed a pram with no wheels lying on its side. 'That was done by a V2 last November, since you mention it. Nine houses gone. Thirty-four dead.'

November, thought Graf. I might have fired that.

Von Braun craned his head to look. 'It's all been cleared up.' He sounded disappointed. 'You can't see how the damage was caused.'

They passed over a bridge and drove beside the Thames. The wide river was grey and choppy, like the North Sea. The Houses of Parliament came into view ahead, with a big Union Jack flying above it, vivid against the yellowish-grey sky. Graf said, 'I thought Kammler told us that had been destroyed.' He leaned forward and spoke to the driver. His English had improved after three months of American interrogations. 'Is it true Piccadilly Circus has gone?'

'It was still there this morning.'

'Leicester Square? The Tower of London? Three bridges over the river? Weren't they all hit?'

The driver looked at him in the mirror. 'Someone's been having you on.'

Steinhoff looked professionally affronted by how intact the government district appeared to be. 'What is that he's saying?'

'He seems to be implying we mainly hit houses.'

'I don't believe it. We fired more than a thousand rockets at London, all aimed at the centre.'

'Relax, Steinhoff,' said von Braun. 'The war's over. It's all for the best. Do you think they'd be so friendly if we'd hit Buckingham Palace and killed the king?'

They pulled up outside a massive building on the

corner of a wide curved road. 'Here you are, gents,' announced the driver. 'The Air Ministry.' Under his breath he added, 'And now go fuck yourselves.'

Kay was in the corridor when they came up the stairs, escorted by Mike's aide – four men in slightly shabby civilian suits. Two of them carried their hats and were nervously twisting the brims, looking about them as if they couldn't quite believe where they were. The Peenemünde scientists had been so much at the centre of her life for the past couple of years, had assumed such an almost mythic status in her mind, that it was odd to see them now, so ordinary. The flight lieutenant knocked, opened the door to the conference room and they filed in. The last man, just before he entered, turned and looked at her – a flash of human connection in the dreary light – and then he was gone. She prowled up and down the corridor a couple of times, listening to the drone of male voices. Occasionally there was laughter. They seemed to be getting on tremendously. She went back into the office and laid out on the desk the photographs, maps and plans, and the stereoscopic viewfinder she had brought up from Medmenham that morning, then sat down to wait.

Von Braun commanded the room. He stood at the blackboard, his left hand hooked over his jacket pocket, his right holding a piece of chalk. He spoke without notes. Occasionally he would turn and write up a chemical formula or sketch a diagram, and the British technical experts would dutifully take notes. The room grew hot. So many perspiring male bodies clad in thick khaki and blue-grey serge, the civil servants in their own uniform of black suit jackets and pinstriped trousers. Towards the end of the morning the windows were opened, letting in the sound of traffic.

Graf studied von Braun dispassionately, without listening to the words. He owed him his life, almost certainly. At the end of February, von Braun had donned his SS uniform yet again and had led them out of Peenemünde in a convoy of cars and lorries, south to Nordhausen, and then south again to the Bavarian Alps, always keeping an eye on the position of the American front line. They had been in a ski hotel on the Austrian border when they learned first of Hitler's suicide and then of Kammler's: he had ordered his driver to pull over, walked up the road and shot himself. A week later, the engineers had surrendered to the Americans and von Braun had told their captors where to find the Peenemünde archive, which he had hidden in a mine. The negotiations had gone smoothly. The deal was done. More than a hundred scientists, Graf among them, had been offered a new life in the US. Soon the first contingent would board a ship from Le Havre to New York, en route to New Mexico. This presentation to the British was purely for show, although one would never have guessed it watching von Braun now. He seduced in the manner of a Don Giovanni. He always meant it at the time.

They stopped for lunch. Graf drank warm flat beer and stood in a corner answering technical questions. 'Speak freely,' von Braun had instructed them the previous evening, standing in the garden to avoid the British microphones. 'Tell them everything they want to know – except the fact that we will be going to America. We don't want to find ourselves detained here on some trumped-up charges of war crimes.'

Twenty thousand people had died at Nordhausen making the V2, four times as many as had been killed by it. The matter was being investigated by the Allied war crimes commission. All the more reason to get to the safety of America as soon as possible, before the facts became too well known.

In the middle of the afternoon, von Braun beckoned Graf over. He was talking to an air commodore, who shifted slightly as Graf approached, to try to block him from interrupting the conversation. 'It would give His Majesty's Government great pleasure,' the officer was saying quietly, 'if you and your colleagues would consider working with us to develop your technology further, as fellow Europeans.'

'That is a very appealing concept.' Von Braun nodded and looked over his shoulder. 'Ah, Graf. The air commodore would like one of us to answer a few questions about Peenemünde. Would you mind?'

*

Kay was standing by the window when he came in. She had begun to think her trip up to town was wasted. The flight lieutenant said, 'This is Dr Graf. Dr Graf, this is Flight Officer Caton-Walsh of our Central Interpretation Unit. Would you like me to stay?'

'I think we'll be fine,' said Kay. 'It shouldn't take long.' After the door was closed, she said, 'Do you speak English?' He was staring at the photographs of Peenemünde spread across the desk. 'I don't speak much German, I'm afraid.' He seemed not to have heard her. She gestured towards the door. 'I could fetch an interpreter . . .'

'Yes.' He looked at her for the first time. He had very clear blue eyes – she had noticed them in the corridor earlier – dark hair, chewed fingernails. 'I speak English.'

'As you can see, we have extensive photographic reconnaissance of the Peenemünde facility. But unfortunately the Russians won't allow us access to the site, and the Americans seem not to be able to lay their hands on the necessary plans. So we wondered if you could fill in some of the gaps in our knowledge.'

'Of course.'

'Please, do sit. Have you used a stereoscopic viewer before? It's perfectly simple.' She leaned over him. 'You place one image here. And then the other next to it here.'

'My God.' He drew his head back. 'It comes alive.'

'Everyone has that reaction.'

He peered into the viewfinder again. 'This is test stand seven.'

She sat opposite him, making notes. 'And those huge oval rings around it are blast walls, presumably, made of earth?'

'Sand mostly.'

'How long would it take to process a missile through the test stand?'

'At the beginning? Eight days, minimum.'

'And the large building next to it? How high is that?'

'Thirty metres. It had to be high. We stored the rockets upright.'

'In the centre of the test stand there's a channel of some sort . . .'

'The duct for the exhaust gases. Seven metres wide.'

After ten minutes, she slid another pair of images across the desk towards him. 'Perhaps we could move on to these.'

They worked for more than an hour, picture after picture. At first he was curious, then nostalgic, and finally haunted. His life was laid out before him as it had been at the point when he could last call himself truly happy. Everything was in perfect perspective. There was the propulsion laboratory, where he worked with Thiel. There was the wind tunnel. There was his apartment block. There was the launch site. There was the old hotel where Karin lived, and the beach where he swam that last evening.

He sat back and rubbed his eyes.

'Are you getting tired?' asked the young Englishwoman. 'Do you want to take a break?'

'When exactly were these taken?'

She picked up one of the photographs and turned it over. 'The twenty-first of June 1943. Two o'clock in the afternoon.'

She passed it across to him. He held it to the light. 'I remember seeing a plane that June – its contrail, anyway – flying very high. Maybe it was the one that took this picture.'

'It could have been. There were actually three reconnaissance sorties over Peenemünde that week.'

'This was so that you could bomb us?'

'It was. Were you there?'

He nodded. 'If you could magnify this photograph sufficiently, you would be able to find me just here.' He tapped it. 'On the road out of the Experimental Works compound, on the edge of the woods, looking up at the sky.' He returned the photograph, sat back and studied her. She was pretty, with her auburn hair and blue uniform. His recording angel. 'This was your job, was it? Watching us?'

'One of my jobs, yes. First in photographic analysis, then in radar.'

'Radar?' That caught his attention. 'Were you one of the women in Mechelen?'

She was not sure how to answer him, or even if she should answer him.

She said briskly, 'I think we've finished now, thank you. You've been a great help.'

She began gathering up the photographs. She was conscious of him watching her.

He said casually, 'I once fired a rocket at Mechelen.'

'Did you really? You missed me, I'm afraid.'

'And you missed me, when you bombed Peenemünde.'

'Well, that's good for both of us.' She laughed and shook her head. 'This is an absurd conversation.'

He helped her collect up the photographs. 'It was a very clever idea, to try to calculate the curve. We never thought of it. But of course it was quite pointless.'

'I think you'll find it wasn't. I was in Mechelen until the end of March. We destroyed a number of launch sites.'

'No. I'm sorry to have to tell you, but you never destroyed one.'

He gave her the photographs. She stared at him, searching his eyes to see if he was lying, but it was obvious he was telling the truth. The Germans had gone on firing V2s at London from the Dutch coast until six weeks before the end of the war. The last one had killed 140 people in Whitechapel. So of course she had known they had not hit all the launchers. But not one?

There was a knock and the flight lieutenant put his head around the door. 'The others are leaving now.'

'Thank you. I'm afraid we've run out of time, Dr Graf.' She was surprised by how sorry she felt suddenly to see him go. There was so much more she would have liked to ask him. She put out her hand. 'Well, then. Goodbye.'

He took it, smiled, looked at her, into her, through her. **'Auf Wiedersehen.'**

At the door, he turned. 'We were both misled,' he said.

He walked thoughtfully along the corridor and down the stairs. Von Braun was in front, talking with the air commodore, making a joke. His broad shoulders heaved with laughter at his own good humour. Steinhoff and Schilling trailed behind him.

In the lobby, the air commodore shook their hands.

'It's been a fascinating day,' he said. 'We have been curious to meet you for a long while. Have a safe flight back to Germany. And please remember our offer.'

Von Braun said, 'We shall be in contact next week. I hope very much we can work together.'

The air commodore walked away. A military policeman opened the door. Graf hung back. Von Braun stood in the doorway, his tall figure framed in the glare of the late-summer light. He held out his hand. 'Are you coming, Graf?'

He knew that if he followed him out into the street, he would end up in White Sands, New Mexico, building missiles for the Americans, and there would be no returning. That way the moon, this way the earth.

'Graf?'

He swung round and contemplated the marble lobby. He wondered if he could remember his way back to the Englishwoman's office. He thought he could. He was fairly sure he would be able to find her again.

ACKNOWLEDGEMENTS

THE BULK OF THIS NOVEL was written during the lockdown imposed by the COVID-19 pandemic. For four hours every morning, seven days a week, for fourteen weeks, I retreated to my study and closed the door – a lockdown within a lockdown – and I would like to express my love and gratitude to my wife, Gill Hornby, and our two youngest children and fellow isolators, Matilda and Sam, for their good company and cheerful forbearance during this surreal interlude.

My editor, Jocasta Hamilton of Hutchinson, read the manuscript in weekly instalments and made innumerable shrewd suggestions. Huge thanks to her for being such a pleasure to work with, not only on this book but on the five that preceded it.

I have been with the same UK publisher for over thirty years and would like to record my gratitude in particular to Gail Rebuck, chair of Penguin Random House, for her friendship and wisdom during all that time, and also to Susan Sandon, managing director of Cornerstone, for her constant encouragement. The launch troop who have worked on **V2** – Rebecca Ikin, Mathew Watterson, Glenn O'Neill, Sam Rees-Williams, Laura Brooke, Selina Walker and Joanna Taylor, to name only a few – have been brilliant.

Sonny Mehta, editor-in-chief of Alfred A. Knopf, who commissioned this novel in the United States, did not live to see it completed. Like many others who knew Sonny, I miss his judgement and friendship very much; with his widow Gita's permission, **V2** is dedicated to his memory. I am grateful to Edward Kastenmeier for stepping into the breach and overseeing publication in the US.

Nicki Kennedy and Sam Edenborough and their colleagues at ILA have also been part of my professional life since the beginning, and I thank them for all they have done for this book and many others. Patrick Niemeyer, Tilo Eckardt, Doris Schuck and my other friends at Heyne Verlag in Munich have been a great support, and so – as ever – has my German translator, Wolfgang Müller. Thanks to Donatella Minuto of Mondadori, and to Marjolein Schurink and Chris Kooi of my Dutch publishers, De Bezige Bij. One rainy Saturday morning in November 2019 – a day not dissimilar to the one that opens this novel – Chris and I were driven around the old launch sites in Scheveningen by Roel Janssen, who kindly shared his local knowledge.

Ralph Erskine, an expert on signals intelligence, generously answered my questions and put me in touch with Mike Dean, an expert on the history of radar. They are not, of course, responsible for my errors. Precisely what went on in Mechelen in the winter of 1944–5 is hard to establish, and I have had to rely on guesswork and some artistic licence.

The genesis of this novel was an obituary in **The Times** on 5 September 2016 of ninety-five-year-old Eileen Younghusband, which described her work as a WAAF officer in Mechelen. I subsequently read her two volumes of memoirs, **Not an Ordinary Life** (2009) and **One Woman's War** (2011). My fictional WAAF officer bears no resemblance to Mrs Younghusband, either in character or career, and nor do any of the other members of my (entirely invented) unit. In her memoirs, which provide a vivid insight into wartime life, she asserts that two launch sites were destroyed during her first shift. I assume this is what she and her colleagues were told. Unfortunately, it was not the case. Nevertheless, I would never have written **V2** were it not for her disclosure of the existence of the Mechelen operation. I will always be grateful for her inspiration.

A full list of published sources follows. I would like to acknowledge five works in particular. Michael J. Neufeld, of the Smithsonian's National Air and Space Museum, is the world's foremost expert on the history of the V2, and his two volumes – **The Rocket and the Reich** (1995) and **Von Braun: Dreamer of Space, Engineer of War** (2007) – were invaluable.

Also essential was **Hitler's Rocket Soldiers: The Men Who Fired the V2s Against England** (2011) by Murray R. Barber and Michael Keuer, which consists of the testimony of a dozen or so men who belonged to the artillery regiments stationed in The Hague. As far as I am aware, no other historians have gathered such valuable eyewitness material – and given that any surviving veterans must now be aged around a hundred, it is highly unlikely it will ever be surpassed.

Murray R. Barber also wrote **V2: The A4 Rocket from Peenemünde to Redstone** (2017), which sets out in admirable clarity, and with superb illustrations, how the V2 actually worked.

Women of Intelligence: Winning the Second World War with Air Photos by Christine Halsall (2012) helped bring the people and work of RAF Medmenham to life.

Other books that enabled me to write this novel include:

Evidence in Camera: The Story of Photographic Intelligence in World War II by Constance Babington Smith (1958)

A4/V2 Rocket Instruction Manual, English translation by John A. Bitzer and Ted A. Woerner (2012)

Operation Big Ben: The Anti-V2 Spitfire Missions 1944–5 by Craig Cabell and Gordon A. Thomas (2004)
V2 by Major-General Walter Dornberger (1954)
Spies in the Sky: The Secret Battle for Aerial Intelligence During World War II by Taylor Downing (2011)
V2: A Combat History of the First Ballistic Missile by T. D. Dungan (2005)
From Peenemünde to Canaveral by Dieter Huzel (1962)
The Peenemünde Raid by Martin Middlebrook (1982)
Hitler's Rockets: The Story of the V2s by Norman Longmate (1985)
Dora by Jean Michel (1979)
The Eye of Intelligence by Ursula Powys-Lybbe (1983)
The Hidden Nazi: The Untold Story of America's Deal with the Devil by Dean Reuter, Colm Lowery and Keith Chester (2019)
Spitfire Dive-Bombers Versus the V2 by Bill Simpson (2007)
Britain and Ballistic Missile Defence 1942–2002 by Jeremy Stocker (2004)
The Peenemünde Wind Tunnels by Peter P. Wegener (1996)
Operation Crossbow: The Untold Story of Photographic Intelligence and the Search for Hitler's V Weapons by Allan Williams (2013)

*

Some 20,000 slave labourers died building the V2. It killed approximately 2,700 people in London, and injured 6,500; it left 1,700 dead in Antwerp and wounded another 4,500. Approximately 20,000 houses in Greater London were destroyed and 580,000 damaged. In the words of the social historian Norman Longmate, the V2 'did a great deal to create the housing shortage that was to be the dominant social problem of the immediate post-war years'.

Daniel Todman, in **Britain's War** (2020), has described the V-weapons programme – which cost the German economy more, dollar for dollar, than the US spent on the Manhattan Project – as 'by a distance, the greatest waste of resources by any combatant country in a supremely wasteful war'.

ABOUT THE AUTHOR

ROBERT HARRIS is the bestselling author of thirteen previous novels: **Fatherland, Enigma, Archangel, Pompeii, Imperium, The Ghost Writer, Conspirata, The Fear Index, An Officer and a Spy, Dictator, Conclave, Munich,** and **The Second Sleep.** Several of his books have been made into films. His work has been translated into forty languages. He lives in England.

Twitter: @Robert_Harris
Facebook: @RobertHarrisAuthor

GRAY'S INN
GRAY'S INN
Gray's Inn Gardens
11·548
GRAY'S INN SQUARE
B.M.70·5
L.B
Sch.
BROOKES
TRAMWAY
FIELD COURT
Hall
SOUTH SQUARE
GRAY'S INN PL.
FULWOOD PLACE
Fairfax House
WARWICK COURT
F.W.
P.H.
Station (Elec. Sy)
D.Fn
Gray's Inn P.H.
Gate
+ 73
B.M.39·0
68
Bank
Bank Chambers
SOUTHAMPTON BUILDINGS
STAPLE INN BUILDINGS
B.M. 71·2
STONE BUILDINGS
Patent Office
Staple House

'My God, the speed of her . . .'

Sitwell said, 'Has anyone got the positions for the y-axis yet?'

One of the WAAF sergeants was writing rapidly. 'Yes, ma'am.'

The corporal announced, 'Contact lost.'

'She's already out of range,' said Knowsley. 'Well!' He shook his head and let out his breath. 'Now we wait.'

One of the sergeants sat with the phone tucked under her chin, on an open line to Stanmore, a pencil in her hand. Another stood by the large-scale map of London and south-east England holding a tin of pins.

The room fell silent again. Minutes passed. It was sinister to contemplate the rocket soaring towards space, Kay thought, the curve of its flight path flattening, the gradual turn, the speed of its descent. **There will be someone on the ground in London just like I was, someone going about their life on a normal Tuesday morning, full of plans and trivial concerns, entirely unaware that the mathematics of the parabolic curve have already condemned them.** She looked down at her sheet of paper – at the pencilled figures representing the values of bearing, height, speed and position. The integers of death. She remembered how she had just pulled her dress over her head in Warwick Court when something changed in the atmosphere, as if the air had been sucked away, and then came the crack of the sonic boom, the express-train roar of the incoming rocket, all of it swallowed by the rumble of the collapsing building.

'Report of impact,' called the WAAF sergeant with the phone. Her voice pulled Kay back to the present. Another pause, while the radar operators in Home Defence in England made their calculations. 'Latitude bearing fifty-one point thirty, three one point six one four six. Longitude zero, zero, thirty-seven point eight seven nine two.'

The sergeant put a red pin in the map. Kay picked up her slide rule. All thoughts of what was happening in London evaporated. She was surprised at her own calmness. Her mind bifurcated, one part concentrating on the procedure that had to be followed, the other making sure her calculations were accurate. The window on the slide rule moved back and forth, comforting in its precision. The world reduced to numbers. After exactly six minutes, she raised her hand and passed her notebook across the table to Barbara. Knowsley and Sitwell gathered at Barbara's shoulder to watch her check Kay's calculations against her own. Kay studied their faces. Now she was nervous. She would have liked a cigarette. After a minute, Sitwell took the notebook over to the map that showed London and the North Sea all the way to the Dutch coast. She measured off the distance.

'Latitude bearing fifty-two point seven, four point two seven zero two. Longitude four point one seven, fifty-two point three zero nine eight.'

'Latitude bearing fifty-two point seven . . .' One

of the WAAF sergeants, in the polished accent of a BBC announcer, repeated the coordinates clearly and calmly down the line to Fighter Command.

Barbara smiled across the table at Kay. 'Don't worry, sweetie, you got it bang right.'

At RAF Coltishall, nine miles north of Norwich, four Spitfire pilots – members of 602 (City of Glasgow) Squadron – who had been sitting in their cockpits for several hours, were ordered to scramble. Their warplanes were brand-new Type XVIs, only received from the factory that month, specially modified to serve as bombers. For several days the squadron had been studying high-altitude reconnaissance photographs of The Hague, familiarising themselves with the Type XVIs and practising dive-bombing. Straining under the weight of two 250-pound bombs, one under either wing, they roared down the runway and took off into low cloud. Flying in tight formation, they turned east, crossed the long sandy beach between Waxham and Winterton-on-Sea and headed over the North Sea towards the Dutch coast, 120 miles away. The attack coordinates were radioed to them by the control tower. At a maximum speed of just over 300 mph, they would reach their target in twenty-five minutes.

Sitwell moved to the large-scale map of The Hague, carefully rechecked the bearings, and pressed a pin into the corkboard. Kay rose from her seat and went around the desk to examine it. The red bead – like a drop of blood, she thought – was positioned precisely in the centre of the Scheveningen Wood.

On the corporal's desk, the telephone rang. All eyes turned to watch him as he reached to answer it. He listened, nodded, covered the mouthpiece.

'They've launched again.'